The Reinhold Chronicles
The Fiery Arrow

The Reinhold Chronicles
The Fiery Arrow

Bo Burnette

The Reinhold Chronicles: The Fiery Arrow
Copyright © 2016 Bo Burnette
Published by Tabbystone Press

Tabbystone Press

All rights reserved. No part of this book may be reproduced or transmitted in any way—electronic or mechanical—without the written permission of the publisher, except where permitted by law.

Scripture quotations are from The Holy Bible, English Standard Version® (ESV®), copyright © 2001 by Crossway, a publishing ministry of Good News Publishers. Used by permission. All rights reserved.

Cover design by Damonza.
Arrow design by Kendall Schlender.
Map by Kelsey Halverson.

ISBN-13: 978-0985061265
ISBN-10: 098506126X

First Edition
Printed and bound in the United States
Also available in eBook editions

To Kit—my brother, who understands the power of stories.

A princess on a carven throne
Clothed in simple raiment
A queenly look is in her eye
And grace is on her forehead

Bo Burnette/2

Chapter One:
The Fire Begins

Arliss blinked twice, wondering if the fire and flame outside her window were fragments of her dreams. Clearly they were not. She was not sleeping. Everything felt too real for that. Yet something wasn't right. The sounds and sights that billowed outside the house sounded like a dream—confusing and unnatural.

Outside the empty window's wooden frame, the panicked shouts of islanders swirled with a faint rumbling as of an earthquake.

A deep fear grasped her heart and squeezed her pulse into a rapid shudder. This wasn't right. This island—her home—had always been a safe place. Screaming and flames seemed as out of place as a flower growing in the midst of the ocean.

"Mother?" She squinted into the dark. Neither of her parents were in their bed. Gripping the edge of her own bedcover, Arliss scoured the darkness of the small house for an answer. The ground trembled again. Two of her wooden dolls toppled onto the dirt floor.

She wanted get up from her bed and run outside, but her legs felt like water. She'd never felt such terror before, not even when she'd nearly drowned once when the ocean's tide had come in. Father had been there, then, with his strong arms and steady voice. But now—where were her parents?

The tall, slender form of her mother—Elowyn—pushed the door open, spilling flaming light into the house.

A surge of joy filled her pounding heart. She leapt from the bed and ran to her mother.

Mother gave Arliss's hair a swift stroke, then began striding through the house.

"What is it?" Arliss asked, snatching the folds of her mother's dark woolen dress.

Her mother stooped to retrieve a large leather satchel from the sandy, hard-packed floor. "It's an earthquake. The volcano is erupting. We must leave quickly."

"But, Mother..." The confusion knotted up in her chest again. She had to trot now to keep up with her mother's long stride as she glided through the house, grabbing various items and stuffing them into the satchel.

"Arliss, this is serious. We have to go—now." With the satchel strapped around her back, she lifted Arliss onto her hip and walked out of the dim shack and into the orange light.

Kenton breathed in the salt air and found it tainted with smoke and sulfur. He tore across the beach, trying to reach his house. Elowyn and Arliss had to escape this isle alive. Yet they were not his only duty. A king had a duty to everyone he ruled.

As he neared the cluster of a dozen houses, he found the entire island had erupted into pandemonium. Elowyn emerged from their house, firm and deliberate. Yet besides her, few had retained the sense to act methodically, and instead had yielded to fear. A few village men were dashing about, trying to get their families and friends into the small boats which lay anchored on the shore of the bay.

Through the crowd, Kenton saw Arliss's clear blue eyes shining with fear. He gritted his teeth. They hadn't come so far for nothing. If anything, their children would survive this earthquake. *So help me God, the line of Reinhold will not be broken.*

He vaulted onto a boulder to elevate himself above the crowd. Perhaps he was only twenty-five, but he was still their king.

"Quiet!" he shouted, trying to hold his voice steady. The crowd's noisy hubbub shuddered its way into silence. "We will not have disorder! We must act swiftly and carefully! Get everyone to the boats—women and children first—and make for the mainland!"

"The mainland?" one man questioned. "It's wild—and dangerous."

"It's our only hope. Save what belongings you must, but leave the rest behind! Go!"

He watched as his words took instant effect. Order threaded its way through the crowd of people as they righted themselves and acted upon their leader's words. He stepped off the rock as Elowyn, her flowing brown hair spreading in the wind, fought her way toward him. She carried their golden-haired daughter and a satchel.

He gripped her shoulder. "You need to get to the boats."

"I'm not leaving you." Her dark eyes pierced his.

"Very well," Kenton grunted. "But we must make haste. Save as many supplies from the house as you can, and whatever else you think necessary. You always know these things better than I, anywise."

Elowyn's mouth spread into a smile as she set Arliss down on the sand and ran back into the house.

He almost smiled, too. Any other time, he would have held her close and kissed her. Now, there was no time for anything but haste.

He glanced upward. Lava streamed from the volcano's pinnacle, streaking down its mountainous sides. The lava would collect in the lake which lay at the island's center. But once the true eruption began…

They were running out of time.

Arliss did not want to remain standing by the house. She wanted to follow her father and help him, but she felt too afraid to disobey her mother's orders. A four-year-old girl underfoot would not be much use to the other villagers, after all. They would ignore her—or worse, trample her in the darkness.

A sharp, shimmering noise sliced through the air just behind her.

She whirled around, her golden hair swishing into her eyes, and gasped. Ten paces in front of her stood a tall, dark-haired man with a sword that gleamed in the moonlight. She recognized him—and she did not like him at all. Often, she had heard this man and her father arguing late at night with angry voices.

"Where are your parents, little one?" The man stepped closer.

Her voice wouldn't come. She glanced around, but once again her parents were nowhere to be found. She looked at the door of her own house—about as far away from her as she was from the man. Maybe she should run.

"Are you afraid?"

At the sound of his smooth voice, she turned back to him. What was his name? She couldn't remember.

"Come with me." He beckoned to her with his sword. In his other hand, he held a wooden chest with a rusty lock. He had tucked it under his arm, and now readjusted it on his hip.

Thane—that was his name. Father always said it with great disgust. Should she go with him? Had her father sent him to fetch her?

He smiled without showing any teeth. "You don't have to be afraid like the rest of them."

She took a step back. "I'm waiting for Mother."

His lips pursed as he stepped toward her, his sword pointed. "No, you're not!"

Arliss screamed.

Kenton's blood pounded with rage as he rushed in between Thane and Arliss from out of the shadows, his own sword flashing up. What insolence had the treasurer reached, to threaten his own daughter?

Thane could barely use his own sword due to the chest he carried under his left arm. His lip curled as he shouted at Kenton. "Let me be, you fool!"

Kenton slammed his sword down on Thane's. "What are you doing?"

"Trying to rescue the treasures."

"And you would threaten my daughter?"

"I'm trying to help her! And you, and the rest of these fools." Thane parried Kenton's blow and swung his own sword around his head, just missing Kenton's blade.

"Thane, stop! There isn't time. You must help—help the others get to the boats!"

"This is my duty. The treasures are my assignment. Your father was foolish not to hide these last few. You'd be even more a fool to lose them!"

"Thane, please! The volcano could erupt at any moment. This island will be nothing but ash and smoke!" The ground quaked beneath Kenton as he fought on. He didn't want to kill Thane, but the treasurer seemed closed to reason.

The two blades tore into each other.

"You must save lives, not gold! What good will it be anyway, if we are all dead?"

"This is more than just gold." Thane spun about. "You know that. It would be worth many lives, I think."

Kenton roared and channeled all his strength into his raging muscles.

Thane couldn't deflect the powerful blow. He staggered backwards as the tip of Kenton's sword grazed his jaw.

Spitting curses, he tottered back and strained at the wooden chest. He sheathed his sword and began an ambling run.

"You don't need me, my Lord Kenton," he shouted in mock respect as he hurried toward a lone rowboat stored at the far edge of the beach. "So I take my leave of you."

"Thane, I forbid it!" Kenton bellowed.

Thane stopped running. "You are not my lord and king! You never were. And you shall never be!" He spat the words out as blood began streaming from his jaw.

"You cannot leave your clan of Reinhold in this dark hour!"

"I want no part of this clan. Always you belittle me, but no more. The clan of Reinhold shall henceforth be nothing but an enemy to me. And, by my life or death, I swear I will have the blood of your house!"

Defiance and hatred engraved on his bloodied visage, Thane turned away and looked at Kenton no more.

Arliss watched the entire fight, speechless as she stood frozen upon the sand. Her father had protected her once again.

Her mother rejoined her just as her father reached them, his boots treading ruts into the gravelly sand. Mother struggled under the load of a massive metal chest, worn and rusted in places. She dropped the chest to the ground and extended her hands toward Arliss. Arliss leapt into her mother's arms.

"Let's go quickly. I saw Nathanael waiting for us with the last boat." Mother squeezed Arliss close.

Father's arms rippled as he hoisted the heavy box. "What's this, darling?"

"The most important thing I could think of saving," she answered, jostling Arliss as they walked toward the boats. "Books. And a few other necessary items."

"You are a fine woman." He gripped the box handles as he strode along the moonlit beach. "Though books are not the first thing I would have saved."

Mother's voice vibrated through Arliss's head as she pulled her close to her chest. "I am certain you will thank me later."

A tall, gangly teenage lad—Mother's brother—was awaiting them with a boat ready to cast off. Arliss smiled in spite of the strange rumblings. Uncle Nathanael was here, and they were all together. Surely they would be safe.

Mother set her down and started shaking sand out of her own thin leather shoes. Arliss's bare feet crunched against sand.

"Elowyn! Kenton!" Uncle Nathanael called. "We have to hurry—there's no time at all. A few more moments and the mountain will explode over our heads. Come on, come on!"

"Thank you for waiting for us, Nathanael." Mother tucked the satchel into the boat, next to the chest of books. She climbed in and held Arliss on her lap, close to the pounding of her own heart.

Arliss, tired as she was, kept her eyes open. She observed many things: the rippling of the dark water beneath the boat, the creaking of the boat as they rowed, the subtle trembling of her mother's fingers which gripped her so carefully. The other villagers' boats were already far beyond. Thane's boat hurried off opposite the others, into the dim shadows of the western sea.

Her father's voice pierced the eerie smoothness. "Is it coming?"

Arliss gazed at the looming volcano. Streams of fire seemed to flow like rivers from it, but she felt the worst was yet to come. The terror started to crawl up her skin again.

Mother shook her head, but at the same instant the ground trembled with a violent shudder. The ocean's waves shook the small rowboat.

"Oh—" Her voice caught. "Oh, it's coming, it's coming." She gripped Arliss's body closer.

Father's muscles strained as he fought to row his family from the impending doom.

The dark, trembling sea clashed with the raging, fiery mountain. For a long moment, everything was as tense as a bowstring.

Then the string snapped, and the arrow was let loose in a rage of fire.

The most horrible sound Arliss had ever heard, like the crackling of a giant's burning firewood, erupted on the island. Flaming rocks pelted all over the almost-distant island. Many fell into the water and were extinguished. Some the size of boulders plunged into the ocean, disturbing the already-quaking sea.

Without warning, one of the massive boulders came hurtling toward the rowboat as if aiming for a target. Arliss screamed as the rock streaked towards the boat. Father and Uncle Nathanael poured themselves into the oars, casting frightened looks over their shoulders at the stones hurling toward them.

As the stone shot towards them, Arliss could hear her mother's whispered prayer: "God, save us...save my daughter."

With a deafening splash, the boulder crashed through the sea just behind the boat. It flung a wave which rose high over the stern, dousing everyone in seawater. The waves shoved the boat on, farther and farther from the eruption.

Arliss blinked back the saline spray and the tears that sped into her eyes. Her mother's tense back relaxed. They would be safe.

The night's hours passed away as swiftly as the island did, its flaming peak still shining in the far distance. Even now, Elowyn could not bear to watch the inferno on her home. Her island. Tears worked their way down her cheeks as she looked away.

Kenton's brow furrowed with sympathy. "It's all right, Elowyn. We're safe. All of us." He nodded toward the rest of the boats that glided far ahead of them, then to Arliss's yawning form on her lap.

"Thane?" she whispered.

"He escaped as well, I believe." His voice was grim. "Though I doubt he will survive on his own."

"It's all over. Everything we hoped for. For us. For Arliss." She stroked her sleeping daughter's yellow hair.

"It's not over. We have survived this terrible thing, so I think God has some use for us yet." Kenton offered a smile. "The line of Reinhold will not be broken. Not now, not ever."

She blinked back another set of tears. Kenton was right. Their clan had escaped the evil of tyranny once before, seeking shelter on the island, far from home. Even farther back, their clan and two others had staged a secret exodus from a land of constant invasion and oppression. Now, the flames of destruction had ousted them from their home once more. But they would survive. They would endure. The line of Reinhold always endured.

Nathanael's hoarse voice was no more than a whisper. "Sister, look." He pointed east. "The mainland."

She took in her breath. A dark mass rose from the ocean, barely lit by the rising of the sun. This was to be her new home, Arliss's new home. She gently shook her daughter's shoulders. Arliss stirred and sat up. Her young blue eyes searched the land revealed by the new day's crimson sun.

Elowyn drew in a deep breath.

"This is your land."

Bo Burnette/12

Chapter Two: Arliss

The breeze that rustled the pages of Arliss's book smelled like adventure. The wind's invisible arms wrapped themselves around her, ruffling her clothes and tossing her hair.

She drank in a breath of forest air for what seemed like the hundredth time, letting the wildness of it fill her lungs. That special pureness of undefiled nature, of tall trees and strong limbs, of colorful leaves and slippery moss, had reached its yearly pinnacle. It was autumn, and autumn in the land of Reinhold was the time when creation's seasonal changes revealed themselves most majestically. She sighed. Sometimes she had debated with herself which season was the best. Yet now that autumn was here, the choice became plain.

She let her bare feet dangle from the enormous limb, and the breeze tickled her toes. How could she concentrate on such a day as this? Even the book's illustrations of a brave queen and her life-saving flaming arrows couldn't compare with the urge in Arliss's heart to jump from the tree and shoot her own arrows. She'd never had such an adventure as the legend's queen, of course. Yet whenever she shot her own bow, she was most like that heroic queen in the story.

She shook her head and tried to refocus on the story. But the fiery arrow on the page reminded her of the great fire from twelve years ago—the burning volcano that had driven her people to this land. But more, it reminded her again of her own bow and arrows which lay in a wooden box at the base of the tree.

The book could wait. She slapped it shut and slid nimbly down the aged trunk. At the bottom she exchanged book for bow. Her fingers tingled as she strung the weapon and strapped the leather quiver around her chest.

Thick, ancient trees, with gnarled branches and nearly impenetrable bark, surrounded a wide clearing in the woods. The trees made for fine archery targets. They had always willingly accepted her arrows in their wooden pillars as she released whatever tension was pounding in her head at the time. Here, in the forest, she could get away from every anxiety, and trouble became but a vague shadow in her mind.

She always shot alone. Always. If only she'd had a brother, perhaps they could have shot together. Even a sister would have been better than nothing. As it was, she had to make do with nothing.

Arliss worked her fingers around the groove of the smooth bow, her hand finding the familiar worn place in the wood. She nocked the first arrow and let the wealth of memory flood her muscles. Life seemed to flow into the wooden shaft itself as it streamed towards a crude target drawn on the tree trunk.

THUNK! It pierced the bark near the darkened circle at the target's center.

Not close enough—she could do much better. She had shot far too hastily. Readying a second arrow, she raised the bow and bent it, judging the wind as it cast her hair. The arrow seemed to release itself and hurry to the target.

She followed with several more shots, until all the trees but one held arrows. She smiled. This was the last shot. It had to be perfect.

The years of training with her father flowed through her body and fueled her every move. She held the bow level, tilted just slightly; placed the arrow on the right, threading three fingers around the nock; drew the shaft back, pushing the bow away. Then she released her fingers. Time itself seemed to slow as the arrow sailed—rushing—into the perfect bull's eye.

Time…time. Arliss gasped as the arrow hit its mark. The ceremony! How could she have forgotten? She'd promised herself only a few moments in the woods. Now she'd be late—and everyone would know it.

She threw her bow back into its box and snapped the lid shut. "How could I have forgotten?"

The trees made no answer.

She panted like an animal as she rushed out of the forest, the wide plain opening around her.

Arliss hurried through the vast field of amber grasses dotted with haphazard outcroppings of rock. These stones were merely roots of the mountains—magnificent structures that grew out of the forest and spread their foothills out into the flat plains. Those mountains seemed to form an impenetrable wall which hid the heart of the realm from the rest of land.

On any other day, she would have made her way slowly, savoring each sight and scent. But this was not just any old day.

She could have slapped herself for her forgetfulness. How had she managed to forget? Of all the days to lose track of time in the forest, why did it have to be the day of the knighting ceremony?

Her feet pounded on a slab of stone which interrupted the grass. She would be within sight of the castle just over the subtle hill that rose under her feet.

She wanted to stop for rest, but there was no time. Her lungs heaved as she darted on. Her bright red dress flapped about her heels like a flame streaking across the fields.

Her father would be furious. Positively fuming. And didn't he have every right to be? She was the princess of Reinhold. That made every offense—every slip-up, every late arrival—a hundred times more dreadful.

When she reached the top of the hill, the silver stone of the castle tower became visible, jutting out of the horizon. Beneath it lay the village, its homes and buildings wreathing the lower tiers of the hill. The castle seemed to be a crown to the town that lay on the mountain which was its foundation.

Today marked a great day in Reinholdian history. Today, her uncle Nathanael would become the first officially dubbed knight of her father's court, and the new Sir Nathanael would also become Lord Nathanael, as he would take over the governance of the city guard.

Her role in the ceremony was rather small. Still, her father's inevitable anger hurried her on. She almost stumbled on the uneven ground. In truth, all she had to do was kiss her uncle. A little kiss. Apparently, tradition in the clan of Reinhold dictated that the ladies of the immediate royal court would kiss the new officer on the head—a formal gesture for which she saw no purpose.

Now she was here! The hill sloped above her as she entered the iron gates of the city.

Arliss drew out the lone arrow that remained in her quiver and flung it aside into the dust beside the gates. It certainly would not do to show up to the ceremony wearing *that*. She unfastened the strap of her quiver as she maintained her pace up the hill.

The road wound its way through the three-tiered city: the first level contained most of the common houses; the second sported inns, shops, and wealthier homes; and the crowning tier held the castle itself. An eerie quiet reigned in the typically bustling marketplace. The entire village must have crowded into the great hall for the ceremony.

Arliss dared not enter by the main door and announce her lack of punctuality to the entire kingdom. Instead, she crept around the vast, lone tower and entered the lush castle gardens—her mother's personal project—where there was another entrance.

When she reached the back door, her best friend Ilayda's high, mellow voice rang out from inside the overhanging stone doorway that shadowed the wooden door.

"You're very late," Ilayda said. "Your father's delaying with one of his grand speeches. But I can tell you, he's not going to be happy if you show up looking like that. Look at your hair! It's all—"

"Hush, Ilayda." Arliss stepped closer to the door and set her quiver down in the grass. "You're loud enough to alert the entire city guard."

Ilayda lowered her voice to a whispering hiss. "Where have you been? The knighting ceremony began thirty minutes ago!"

"I was out...just doing things." She still hadn't told Ilayda about her sanctuary yet. Not just yet.

"Well, if you have secrets, keep them to yourself. Hurry up! Get inside!" Ilayda commanded. "Here's your cape. I figured you'd forget."

Arliss donned the cape and touched Ilayda's shoulder. "Thank you. I don't know what I would do without you to pester me, scold me, and get me out of all my scrapes."

Ilayda grinned, and Arliss nudged open the door with her bare foot, wincing at the soft squeak.

Wide windows, their curtains removed as during all daylight hours, caught the sunlight and threw it across the many people standing in the room. Arliss seated herself in the wooden throne beside her mother, trying to act as if nothing was ado. She put on a blank face, tilted up her chin, and fixed her gaze on a spot in the ceiling.

The king, pausing his speech, turned and met her eye. His brow found its habitual furrow.

"Well," he continued, turning to the mass of citizens gathered in the hall, "it seems the time has *finally* come for the knighting itself!" The subtle rebuke stung Arliss. "Nathanael, come forward!"

Nathanael bowed his acknowledgement to Arliss and her mother, then knelt before her father.

Kenton's ceremonious voice boomed throughout the hall. "In these twelve years since we settled this land, we have seen peace and plenty. Despite hardship, we have persevered, endured, and prospered. Today we come to see a great man of this city rise to command the army of Reinhold. From this day, Nathanael will be a wise and forthright lord of Reinhold."

Kenton turned to look at his wife and Arliss. This was her cue. She rose, following her mother, and came to stand in front of Nathanael.

Elowyn bent and brushed a kiss against her brother's forehead. Her own forehead knotted with emotion before she relented to a tenuous smile.

Arliss's own turn now came. She paused. If there had been a prince of Reinhold—if she hadn't grown up the only child—how would it have felt to do this honor for *him*?

She bent awkwardly toward her uncle's head and gave him a quick peck, but he grabbed her face and smooched her cheek. The entire hall erupted in laughter.

Nathanael grinned. Arliss's lips pursed playfully.

Kenton cleared his throat, and Arliss found her seat again, careful to move slowly so as to not reveal her bare feet. Even her mother would be aghast at that.

Kenton drew his sword and tapped both Nathanael's shoulders. "I knight you, Sir Nathanael the first-sword; and I also dub you Lord Nathanael, head of the guard of Reinhold. All hail Lord Nathanael!"

The crowd shouted in unison, "All hail Lord Nathanael!"

Arliss observed the subtle boundary which cut through the crowd. The first few rows of people were the other lords and their families, as well as the more well-to-do craftsman types, all of whom lived in the upper tier of the village. Behind these stood the rest of the populace: the farmers and the craftsmen of meaner work, all of whom lived on the lowest tier of the village. How curious—how uncomfortable—that the people had been thus partitioned.

The distraction lasted but for a moment. She smiled and joined in the applause for her uncle.

Then Kenton turned, sheathing his sword. His eyes pierced hers. She braced herself for the talk that was coming.

"You're a bit rash sometimes, you know," Kenton remarked.

Arliss almost stopped walking. She was not shocked at his words, but at the sudden breaking of the silence that had reigned for what seemed an age. She said nothing in reply, hoping her father would take the initiative in continuing this reproachful conversation.

They were walking along the edge of the forest. The trees waved their limbs gently in a breeze that spread down from a sky which had sprouted clouds sometime in the last few minutes.

Kenton's chest heaved. "Responsibility, Arliss—that is what you must learn. As princess, you have to demonstrate a sense of true responsibility. Your levity about court matters affects more than just me. Everyone in the village sees it—and it reflects poorly on me."

"I'm sorry, Father." Her words rushed out like a river. "I didn't mean to be late. I just lose time in the forest. I always do. Forgive me."

His brow relaxed, and he shifted his head to look her in the eye. "I forgive you. But you cannot keep making these mistakes. You know, the young knight Brallaghan was supposed to escort you in the ceremony. You let him down."

He sighed, paused, and sighed again, as if preparing to impart an important piece of information.

Arliss slowed her pace on the wide, grassy plain between the castle and the woods. Green in summer, the plain's grasses had now turned to a dusty yellow.

At last her father spoke. "You are almost sixteen years old, Arliss. That means it is time for you to take part in matters of the court—time to show the people your purpose and power." He slyly tilted his head toward her. "Time to begin thinking about a young man to carry on my line."

Her breath snapped. She stood still, and Kenton also ceased his steps.

"You are opposed to the idea of marriage?" he prodded.

"No!" She said, more forcefully than she intended. "No, I—I simply hadn't thought of it."

"Then you would, indeed, desire a young man to love?"

She closed her eyes. "Not like that."

He turned to stand opposite her. "My darling, you know your mother and I wanted more children as well. All these years since… All these years have been more than hard. But it was not God's will to give us any more gifts than just you."

The years of built-up emotion flooded out of Arliss in a moment. "But you don't understand! I don't want a young man to kiss and hold and be held by. I want a brother—a true friend. But I've never had that—and I shall never have it. I will never be able to hold his hand to help him walk, never be able to teach him to read, never be able to show him how to shoot a bow, or to go on adventures with him. I can never have that!"

He placed a strong hand on her shoulder. "I am sorry for your grief. I understand your pain, truly."

She kept her eyes closed as they filled with fresh tears.

He hesitated. "I take my leave. Please, do think about what I have said."

She looked up and watched her father walk toward the castle. Then, when he was nearly out of sight, she ran, ran as fast as she could, towards the foothills of the mountains which crept into the northern plains.

She stood upon one of the rocky hills, her hair flying, the sleeves of the red dress streaming out in the wind. There she wept, the bottled-up tears coming freely as a stream. How could he possibly understand her? She didn't want romance. She wanted *friendship*, wanted it so badly her chest throbbed.

Something cracked in the woods behind her. She turned to gaze into the near-distant forest. The sound repeated itself twice—a sound like something or someone treading on a limb or twig.

Then the noise vanished, and left her alone with only the sound of the wind in her ears.

Chapter Three: Roots and Seeds

As the sun sank in the afternoon sky, the castle tower cast a long shadow across the east side of the village. Arliss hesitated at the open gates. She could not return home just yet. Something held her back. A deep uneasiness settled in the pit of her stomach.

She would pass every building in the village—the market, the church, the inn, the homes—and would see the divisions that hid there. She would see the strife, the boundaries, the separation between the three tiers. After having the division of lords and peasants so blatantly displayed to her at the ceremony that morning, she couldn't bear to glance upon those invisible lines once again.

Her legs started to move, carrying her almost involuntarily around the west side of the city. She strode alongside the moat, whose waters were fed by a river flowing down from the mountains. She was nearing the fields outside the city, where many citizens still had well nigh an hour of work to go.

She entered a field of bean plants, their green streamers at the waning of the harvest. A dozen or so poorer folk were working the field, some yanking out the thorny tares, but most gathering handfuls of emerald bean pods.

She hesitated. The flaming red dress would identify her immediately. But did it matter? She picked up a stray basket that lay upturned at her feet and walked into the field. Her face flushed as she began harvesting, and she tried not to look up at the eyes she knew were staring back at her.

It felt so strange, working the field. When the people of Reinhold had first settled here and begun to build the village, everyone had to take a turn in the farming. Everyone had to provide food for his own family. But as the twelve years had worn on, the king and his men finished work on the city, and many men were no longer farmers, but lords, bakers, and smiths. Arliss had not worked for five harvests.

Hunger began to encircle her stomach like a slithering serpent, but she ignored it and continued working: plant after plant, bean after bean. The vines' spiky velvet scratched her wrists into an uncontrollable itch.

She soon lost count of how many beans she had yanked and dropped into the basket. The monotony of the job surprised her, but it had always been so. Pluck a handful of bean pods, cast them into the basket, pluck another handful, and so on until it seemed that one had never been doing anything but harvesting beans.

Her father had once partitioned these fields by families. Now, with many of the villagers no longer farming, the merchants and craftsmen rented their fields to the peasants—in return for a share of the crops. Kenton had praised this development, saying it was good for all.

Arliss wrinkled her brow. No matter what her father said, the renting benefited the higher classes more. After all, the peasants had no way to buy the fields outright. Land was money, and they couldn't buy land with land.

She stepped backward to reach a new plant. Someone bumped her from behind.

She snapped her thoughts shut and swiveled around. A young girl, no more than eight, clutched a basket of beans that dragged her arms nearly to the ground. She beamed up at Arliss, her eyes shining.

Then Arliss noticed the dropped doll lying on her feet. She bent to pick it up.

A young man—perhaps a bit younger than Arliss—came dashing over to grab the little girl.

"Oh, pardon me, my lady, I...Keelin didn't mean to..." His dark eyes darted to Arliss's face as he apologized.

Arliss laughed. "It's all right. No harm has been done." She lifted the doll and replaced it in its owner's outstretched arms.

Keelin offered a shy smile in return.

"Thank you, my lady," the young man said. He stood well taller than her, though his face was perhaps more youthful.

She peeked over his shoulder at another young man, older-looking than the first but not so tall. He rose from his picking to observe the kerfuffle with the princess and the doll. Sweaty brown hair clung to his forehead, and his hands were turned green from the beans.

Just then, the evening bell clanged from inside the village. It was five o'clock. Time to cease all work for the day.

The fellow took Arliss's basket from her, and she looked into his remarkable eyes. They were deep, full of joy and sorrow mixed together; so many colors wove together in them that it was impossible to say which shone most clearly: blue, green, and hazel. He nodded at her.

She turned and hurried back to the village, haunted by the look in his eyes.

As Arliss trekked through the bustling village that evening, the sun had already descended into the west, its light sinking towards the plain which stretched out for miles. At the end of the plain were the great Cliffs of Aíll; beyond the cliffs, the sea; and beyond the sea, who knew.

She paused outside the inn, The Bronze Lion. Lights and laughter flickered inside, beckoning to her. She hesitated. Her father would be in there, and probably the whole royal council after the day's festivities. She didn't want to have another useless conversation about her romantic life.

But the smell of fresh bread was too strong. She inhaled and pushed the wooden door open.

The Bronze Lion was the only inn in the entirety of the village, and thus the entire country. It welcomed dozens of Reinholdians into its wooden walls every evening—farmers and craftsmen ready for refreshment after a long day of work.

Fireplace and candlelight illuminated the entire building as she sat at one of the wide, wooden benches, gripping a hunk of bread in one hand and a book in the other. She tore through the warm, buttered bread. Exhaustion pulled at her from all angles. Both her father's urgent talk and the hour of work in the field had drained her more than she had been in many a day.

She finished the story and the bread at the same time. It was the story she had begun in the tree that morning—the tale of the brave queen and her flaming arrow. At the end of the tale, it had a poem which she knew well. Her mother had read this same story to her many times when she was a tiny lass.

> A princess on a carven throne
> Clothed in simple raiment
> A queenly look is in her eye
> And grace is on her forehead
>
> A princess on a smooth-hewn throne
> Clothed in linen raiment
> A queenly look is in her eye
> And grace is on her forehead
>
> A princess on a gilded throne
> Clothed in silken raiment
> A queenly look is in her eye
> And grace is on her forehead

The poem did not fit the story; after all, the poem told of a princess and the story of a queen. Perhaps the poem had another meaning. She would ask her mother about it later. Elowyn had saved dozens of books from the island and knew each one in the castle library inside and out.

As she started to devour the thick slice of cheese on her plate, Ilayda slid onto the bench beside her. Arliss continued eating and staring at the poem without acknowledging her friend.

"What're you doing?" Ilayda twisted to stretch her back.

Arliss thought it was rather obvious what she was doing. "Eating cheese."

The noise of dancing and music filled the large hall with a sort of clamor that made it difficult to hear anything—but easy to notice everything. Lines of young people skipped around to the informal scratchings of a single fiddle.

As Arliss turned to face Ilayda, she caught sight of her father in the adjacent hall, along with the three lords of the city. His brow was knitted together and he looked tired, almost old. What had caused his concern?

Kenton clamped his mug down on the table. "It's a dangerous idea, Nathanael."

"I know," Nathanael replied. "But I believe it's a good one. We must expand. There can be no more of this stagnant waiting."

Lord Adam lifted his hand. "We are not stagnant. The people are fruitful in everything they do. The crops have doubled from a few years ago. That, I believe, is anything other than stagnation." He stroked his short beard. "Though I daresay the leadership of this city could be more structured."

Kenton frowned. He disliked what Adam was hinting at. His words stank of disgruntlement and resentment. "And what is your meaning?"

Adam shrugged. "I'm curious why your daughter was so late for this morning's ceremony."

Kenton half-glared at him. "That was her own doing. I am not responsible for her lateness."

"Clearly she doesn't think herself to be responsible either," Adam pointed towards nothing, but Kenton knew very well to whom he was pointing fingers. "This is not the first such incident."

"Arliss is only fifteen." Nathanael's eyes sparked.

"Nearly sixteen, though, is she not? Aren't we celebrating her birthday at the ball tomorrow? Nearly a woman, by my standards! If she cannot—"

Kenton held up a hand. "Peace, gentlemen. I have spoken with my daughter about her tardiness. I trust it will not happen again. Now, to the business at hand. We must decide on this issue of villages: whether to remain here, or to branch out."

Lord Brédan cleared his throat as his mug met the wooden table. "There seem to be many opinions among us. I call for a counsel as soon as possible. I would like to hear what the queen has to say on this matter." His eyes twinkled beneath dark, bushy eyebrows. "P'raps even the princess could join."

"No!" Kenton said, a bit more forcefully than he had intended. He lowered his voice. "No, she is not of age to be on the royal council."

"You should not doubt her," Nathanael murmured. "She has more wisdom than you think."

To this Kenton could make no reply.

"Look!" Ilayda tapped Arliss's arm, pointing across the room. "It's your peasant friends from the field earlier."

Arliss noticed the two young men sitting in the corner, but she spun to face Ilayda. "I met them not more than an hour ago. How do you know about them?"

"I see more things than you know."

So she must have been spying from the library window again. Arliss narrowed her eyes. "Why did you call them peasants?"

"Because they are. Just like you're a princess, and I'm a lord's daughter."

"But, Ilayda, have you never considered why? Why we are treated like...well, like we're better than they are?"

"Aren't we, in a way?"

Arliss opened her mouth but found she couldn't say anything. These divisions between the people of Reinhold, they spread through everything and everyone—even to her best friend! Since when had the royalty become so much better than the commoners?

She fixed her gaze on the duo in the corner.

The one with the curious eyes turned to meet hers, and she dropped her head in haste.

Philip leaned his head onto his fist, still watching the princess. She had turned away—almost bashfully—and now was avoiding his gaze, her eyes darting everywhere but at him.

Why had she been working in the field today? She had been alone. She had spoken to no one but his cousins Erik and Keelin. And she had left without a word of explanation.

As he studied her, he recognized something in her demeanor. A look of longing, of regret and hope intermingled, and a desire for something else. It was a feeling he understood all too well.

"I'm going to dance with her," he said aloud.

"What?" Erik followed his gaze. His eyebrows shot up. "Princess Arliss? Now?"

Philip swung to face Erik. "No, of course not! At her birthday ball tomorrow. I'm going to dance with the princess."

Erik smirked, his face skeptical. He held up a coin. "One copper says you won't."

Philip slapped down another. "Two coppers say I will."

Chapter Four: Anarchy

"The poem does, indeed, have another meaning," Elowyn said. She rose from her chair and strode over to one of the few shelves that decked the wall of the castle library. Flickering candlelight trickled about her gliding form.

Arliss leapt up from her own seat, striding over to the queen. "What is the other meaning, then? And how do you know it?"

Her father frowned up from his Bible, his blue eyes narrowed and focused. "I believe your mother is going to answer you in due time, Arliss. Do not nag with incessant questions."

She narrowed her eyes, refusing to face him. His conversation from earlier still burned in her mind. "I was asking Mother."

"Arliss!" Elowyn stopped scanning the shelves. "Peace!" She continued to search for the desired volume. Finding it, she gave a triumphant "aha!" and pulled it out.

Arliss beheld the ancient book. Its thick leather cover smelled old and sweet, as if with a perfume. She loved old things such as this book, but they proved rare in a country barely twelve years old.

The title was emblazoned in a language she did not comprehend, but the sound of the letters felt magical when she read them aloud: *Finscéal agus Stair na Trí Clans*.

"It is an ancient language of our people, now lost in the depths of time," Elowyn said. "It means 'Legend and History of the Three Clans.' This book contains many treasures from our history—both comprehensible and incomprehensible. You see, before our flight to the Isle of Light and the wrath of its fiery volcano, the clan of Reinhold dwelt on the other side of the ocean. Our people were oppressed by the great clan of Anmór and desired freedom."

"I know the stories, Mother." Arliss smiled, idly fingering the thick pages of the volume.

"And it was just before that flight when this book was written. It relates many mysterious events of the past, present, and even the future."

"And the poem?"

"It also appears in this book, but here it comes with a prophecy. These accounts were written by a wise man of old—one who, it is said, advised kings and governed cities. With many of his poems he included a foretelling or a wise adage."

"But aren't they just legends? Surely they aren't actually true."

Elowyn shuffled through the pages of the book. "And why would they not be?"

Arliss kept silent. Her mother, too, was quiet as she found the poem and laid the book out on the reading stand nestled between the shelf and a window framing a starlit night.

"Here is the poem and the prophecy." Elowyn read aloud, "'In a time of great need, such a one will arise. Fire shall arm her, and water shall guard all. War, hate, and greed shall come with their lies. Yet from such a great harm she shall save her people from fall.'"

"Well, I suppose it makes for decent poetry," Kenton chimed in from the corner.

Arliss pressed her hand into the reading desk to restrain herself from speaking.

"Kenton!" Elowyn scolded, her tone hard but her eyes playful. "It may yet hold true. The prophecies of the very wise rarely fail."

He shrugged. "Stories are stories. They hold neither power nor sway in real life."

Arliss couldn't contain the fierce fire in her heart any longer. "That's simply not true!" She turned from bending over the desk and stood tall. "Stories are powerful. Stories have life—truth!"

He sighed and closed his Bible. "Arliss, have you ever seen a story save a man's life? Or feed someone?" He cocked his head. "Of course not. There is no profit in fleeting myths and daydreams."

She took two steps forward, her feet padding on the woven carpet which draped the stone floor. "But there is! These stories don't just flee away. They endure. This tale has lived on for many generations, and it is not forgotten. You're wrong, just wrong, terribly wrong! And I will certainly not—"

"That is quite enough, Arliss!" Kenton's sudden outburst stopped her words short. "It is not your place to lecture me." He frowned. "You would give me orders? And you would carry yourself carelessly—associating with commoners? I saw you in the fields this afternoon, Arliss. And I am not alone. The lords have noticed your behavior as well. If you do not know your place, then perhaps you ought to adjourn until you can find it."

Heat rose to her cheeks, and she hurried out of the room. Once in her own bedchamber down the hall, she leaned against the wall. She tilted her head back against the stone and closed her eyes. How could he say these things? How could he…

What had he said? *Associating with commoners*, was it? Her eyes snapped open. The monster of division was rearing its head in a new way. The schism was widening.

In her dreams that night, she wandered up the tiers of an endless hill, on which every layer felt more foreign and more opulent than the last. She walked ever on, looking for someone whose name she could not remember.

Ilayda walked ahead of Arliss, her brown hair bobbing and flashing in the morning sun as she hurried through the crowd. She was a true friend, but was as unpredictable as Reinholdian weather—one moment perfectly sunny, the next pouring down a storm from its cloudy expanse. The storms were always brief, though, and so were Ilayda's inconsistencies.

"Il-*LIE*-da!" Arliss sidestepped a man with a wheelbarrow full of potatoes and shooed aside an angry hen that flapped its wings indignantly. "Wait!"

She had determined not to be distracted. Her mother's orders had been simple: half a dozen apples and a length of blue ribbon, then home again as swiftly as possible.

This morning, the market bustled far more than on an ordinary day. Today was the day of a ball—*her* birthday celebration—and that meant feasting and dancing for all. The baker had to bake dozens of loaves, the farmers would have to have their freshest crops displayed, and the tailor—Mrs. Fidelma—would be up to her chin in orders for alterations and hems and ribbons and capes. Elowyn had sent Arliss with a length of fine green ribbon to trade for the beautifully embroidered blue one Mrs. Fidelma had displayed in her shop.

Ilayda pulled Arliss into Mrs. Fidelma's shop. "Let's at least look around for a minute."

"No, no, and no. We haven't time to shop for dresses." Arliss would rather have spent the morning shooting arrows. She held up the green ribbon she needed to exchange. "One blue ribbon, that's all." She found the ribbon and laid her exchange on the counter as Ilayda waltzed about the shop.

"I wonder where Mrs. Fidelma is?" Ilayda strode into the adjoining room. "Not here."

Arliss stepped through the doorway and grabbed Ilayda's shoulder. "Come on, let's go. I really don't think we—"

Male voices sounded just outside the front of the store. Ilayda grabbed Arliss and pushed her against the wall, shushing with her finger. Arliss rolled her eyes and complied, sidestepping to avoid the spinning wheel next to the wall.

The voices paused, then the men entered the shop.

"There's not a one in here." The voice belonged to Lord Brédan.

"Good." It was Lord Adam, Ilayda's father. "As I was saying, I believe this council will be a decisive one."

"And a divisive one, if last night's conversation was any indication," Brédan noted.

"Indeed. Kenton will want to turn the seaside outpost into a second village. He will want to split up our people. We must make him see what is best for us."

"I would remind you, he is *King* Kenton, and his opinion holds no small sway. He may be brash at times, but he is no fool."

"The way his daughter acts, you would think they are both fools."

Arliss avoided Ilayda's eye.

Ilayda's father continued. "In all honesty, I hold no inseverable allegiance to Kenton. He has led our people well, and for that I am grateful. But should he choose to pursue this frivolous expansion, I will neither serve him nor pay him homage."

"Would you turn to anarchy and rebellion to achieve your purpose?"

"It is not anarchy I propose. Only freedom."

"But are we not free enough?"

"I disagree enough with Kenton. I doubt I could ever serve his daughter," Adam growled. "If she's this careless at nearly sixteen, what will she be like at his age? A careless, bumbling idiot."

"Would *you* wish to be king, then?" Brédan asked.

"Perhaps we do not need a king. A careful governor might suffice. Consider the current situation. The merchants and craftsmen rent their fields to the peasants for a portion of the crops. By the same way, we royalty outfit guards from among the craftsmen in return for some of their work: bread, swords, furniture."

"So y'think this system could remain without a monarch atop it, eh?"

"Indeed. It would flourish. But, do promise me this: that you will speak nothing of what I have told you."

"Aye," Brédan said. "I shall not say a word of it. P'raps you are right. Come, let's get on."

Arliss didn't realize she had been holding her breath until it burst out in a stream.

Ilayda's mouth had fallen open. She stepped back into the shop's main atrium just as Mrs. Fidelma reentered from outside, blissfully unaware of the conversation that had just occurred.

"What can I fetch for you two girls, hm?" she asked.

Arliss could barely move.

Bo Burnette / 34

Chapter Five: Peasant and Princess

Arliss almost felt sick as she walked back to the castle. So this was what the lords thought of her? Perhaps what everyone else in the village thought as well? She didn't want to know.

Ilayda had been silent the entire walk home. Now, she must have noticed Arliss's troubled visage, because she broke the silence that reigned in the evacuated homes of second tier, whose inhabitants were mostly all at market down below. "I don't think my father means it. I mean, he cannot really hate you that much. You aren't all that awful."

Arliss shut her eyes. "You are extremely comforting."

"Thank you, my dearest," Ilayda tittered. "I do try."

"Ilayda," Arliss said presently, "your father spoke nothing but what is in his heart. People may put on a show for someone else. But what someone says in private can be nothing short of the truth."

"But what if it is not the truth?"

"Well, it is what is in their heart, true or not."

"I know, but—well, what if they've convinced themselves of a lie? Lied to themselves so many times they do not know the difference."

Arliss gawked at her. "You think your father is lying?"

Ilayda stared straight ahead, her stride stiff. "I think he is wrong."

"You mean, wrong about my father? And about the expansion?"

Ilayda stopped, turning to look her in the eyes. "No, about you."

The sheer amount of light in the room dazzled Philip the moment he entered the open doorway. The entire great hall of the castle beamed with candle and torchlight, and the white-painted stone walls shone like ivory. Across the wide hall, the king and queen sat on carven thrones of wood. The three lords—Adam, Brédan, and Nathanael—sat in adjoining chairs.

Philip's uncle, aunt, and cousins shuffled in around him, leaving him standing alone near the doorway. Although a few already thronged the hall, many townsfolk still trickled into the warmth of the festive occasion from the deepening chill of the October evening.

A glimpse of Queen Elowyn's rich purple brocade and King Kenton's sumptuous furs caused Philip to glance at his mean attire in shame. It wasn't too shabby—a long-sleeved blue tunic, midnight cape, tan breeches and leather boots—but each piece of clothing had seen more than its share of wear. His father had worn the tunic and breeches many years ago, and now they fit snugly on Philip's broad shoulders and lengthening legs. His father had been a smaller man, so he'd been told.

When all the guests had arrived, a hush crept over the room, and two guards stood at attention by the curtain which hid the staircase to the second level.

King Kenton rose to speak. "I would thank every one of you for coming to this merry celebration. Today, we celebrate the sixteenth year of my daughter, and we welcome her into the new heights of womanhood. We come for joy and cheer and food and dancing. Please welcome her grace, Princess Arliss of Reinhold."

The two young guards drew the curtain aside, revealing the princess poised at the top of the stairs. She descended the steps with a steady grace. Emerging fully from the shadows, she joined the golden light of the room in a flash of color.

Philip became entranced, his attention fixed and immovable.

She looked like a vision, a picture of some legendary queen of immortal beauty. The light blue satin of her dress streamed down about her heels like waves of the ocean. Her often unkempt hair was now smoothed and gathered to the side, resting over her shoulder like strands of pure gold.

He'd seen her so many times before this week. He doubted she'd ever so much as noticed him. Still, what was she *really* like beneath the royal exterior? Wager or no wager, he would find out who the princess really was.

Arliss fought to maintain her composure all the way down the steps. The flaming wash of light, the clapping crowd of people, the dresses and capes and furs and rings, all met together and overwhelmed her senses. Her mother had commanded her to stay calm and collected, to which her father had added, "And no unexpected antics, either. You must emanate the grace of the royal family." This was rather a lot of posh.

She reached the base of the stair and glided onto the smooth, polished stone floor. Brallaghan, the Lord Brédan's son, stood at attention by the base of the stairs. He had been one of the ones to pull back the curtain. With a steady gaze ahead, she avoided both his eyes and those of her father. She dipped in a deep curtsy to the room at large. The clapping subsided as a trio of fiddlers began to play rousing tunes.

"To the dancing!" Kenton roared, and a few dozen younger people lined up for the first dance. They spun around each other, the two lines crossing and linking arms.

Striding around the room, Arliss collected everyone's wishes for a happy birthday. Some complemented her dress, some her crown—a thin silver circlet which had been one of the few treasures rescued from the island. Some had saved rings, necklaces, and even coins from the inferno. Others were not so fortunate, and had saved little more than the clothes on their own bodies.

She watched the dance, smiling as she followed the intricate winding of bodies, the skipping of feet, the clasping of hands. All seemed happy with their partners. Yet the classes didn't blend. Peasants danced with peasants, craftsmen with craftsmen, and nobility with nobility. Ilayda and Brallaghan had joined hands with another couple—which included Ilayda's brother Arden—and now slipped around in a circle.

Arliss folded her arms across her chest. How she envied Ilayda of having a brother! If she had a brother, he'd have whisked her onto the dance floor already. She wouldn't be a watcher, an outsider.

The dance ended.

Ilayda poked her in the back. "Happy birthday."

Arliss grabbed her friend in a hug.

"Thank you." Arliss's embrace spoke every word she couldn't express. She paused a moment and leaned close. "I want to tell you something. Look around the room."

Ilayda scanned the hall.

"Look—do you not see it?"

She tilted her head. "I see people dancing and laughing."

"What I see is this: the king, lords, and other royalty sitting on one side of the room, but the main bulk of the people standing on this side of the room. I see an invisible line."

"But look." Ilayda motioned. "All are mingling as one in the dance."

Following Ilayda's eyes, Arliss glanced about.

Her pulse quickened, and her heart thrummed beneath her silken bodice. From across the room, Brallaghan had begun striding towards them. She whirled to face Ilayda, her back toward the approaching guard.

"Oh look, it's—" Ilayda chimed.

"Hush! Act like we're deep in conversation."

"See, it's Brallaghan! He's coming to dance with you."

"I know. And no, he is not dancing with me."

"Arliss!"

"Ilayda, stop."

Ilayda smirked. "Oh, look the dancers are lining up. Off you go!"

With that, she gave Arliss a shove. Arliss tripped backwards, sputtering, and almost fell before a steady arm slipped around her.

"Happy birthday, Arliss." Brallaghan offered his hand. "May I have this next dance?"

She forced out a breath. "I suppose you shall."

He dragged her into the line of dancers just as the music began. She couldn't collect herself before they launched into it all—casting off around one couple, spinning around her partner, and feeling generally flustered.

She huffed as he spun her beneath his arm. It is one thing to do something when you have had a drink and a few deep breaths; being thrown straight into it, on the other hand, is quite another. This fact, combined with Brallaghan and Ilayda's combined impudence, left her breathless and hot-faced.

Did he really think *she* fancied *him*? And, for that matter, that she could fall for him this easily? They'd always been friends, but this step seemed a pace too far.

Brallaghan maintained his dashing nonchalance throughout the dance, spinning her around with ease. He seemed to be having the time of his life. She deemed it the most uncomfortable experience of her entire day—which was saying quite a lot, given the incident at the tailor's that morning.

When the dance—which seemed to last forever—concluded, she honored her partner by curtsying to him, then stiffly allowed him to escort her back to the edge of the room. Once he was gone, she turned on Ilayda.

"You are the most outrageous—"

"Oh, hush. You needed to do that."

Arliss rolled her eyes. "And I suppose you needed to push me into it. Aye?"

"Calm down. I had to or your father would…or…you needed to dance."

"My father?" Arliss stared at her. "What about my father?"

Ilayda cast a furtive glance about the room, focusing on the king, who had risen from his wooden throne. "You mustn't speak a word of my telling you this. Your father asked me to do it. You know, to get you to dance with Brallaghan. He said you would listen better to me. I'm sorry. Please, don't tell him I said anything."

Ilayda seemed to be expecting Arliss to explode.

Arliss walked away. That was enough! She couldn't bear to hear another word. Ilayda had simply been doing as she was told—but her father? How dare he!

She wanted nothing more than to walk up to him and shout at him until he recognized the darkness that was growing in the land of Reinhold. If only he'd listen to her! These wrongs needed to be mended before they became irrepressible. Could he not see that?

But of course he wouldn't listen to her. Why should he? In his eyes, she was the one who had disgraced him before the entire village with her lateness.

Yet she had to try. All these twelve years, he had never once chosen to explore the land, never once named Reinhold's rivers and mountains, and never once given thought to his daughter's adventurous spirit.

She would never change his mind. Maybe her mother could do it, or perhaps the divisions would grow to the point where her father could not possibly ignore them, but she—Arliss, the sixteen-year-old princess of Reinhold—had no such power.

Someone behind her cleared his throat—that young man from the fields. His eyes were as curiously colored as ever. Perhaps it was the light of the room, but he looked a fair sight nicer when not in field-work clothes. His tunic had seen better days, but she could sympathize. Her fine dress had been worn by her mother years ago.

He bowed deeply, then offered his hand. "Might I have this dance, my lady?"

Arliss caught her breath. "Of course."

She felt like she was floating as they walked into the center of the hall. Was this what it felt like, to be danced with by one's brother? Did it really feel so like magic?

The fiddlers played a soft, unobtrusive melody as other dancers began to glide towards the center of the room. Her parents had seated themselves again to observe the dancing.

Despite his simple charm, the young man seemed to be unaware of how to dance with a partner.

"No," Arliss touched his hand. "Your right hand goes...here, and your left hand holds mine...here."

He smiled, almost laughing as his hands found their proper place.

"Then," Arliss continued. "Your foot steps forward—"

"I know how the steps go."

She said no more and allowed him to prove himself.

Then the dance began in earnest. In this dance, couples stood not in lines but in simple pairs, weaving in and out and around each other throughout. The fiddles quickened their pace as Arliss and her partner floated through the steps.

They separated once, each spinning to the outer edge of the group of dancers. She felt uncomfortable dancing on her own. Alone, she felt exposed to the judgment of every eye in the room. They all watched her: Ilayda would be giddy, Brallaghan jealous, her mother curious, her father critical.

Her partner met her again and clasped her hand. The music swelled until it filled the entire hall. The hands that held hers were strong, rough and callused, yet tender and subtle. A new feeling spread through Arliss's crisscrossing legs and whirling torso, a feeling so strange and wild she could not give it a name. They spun faster and faster, wider and wider, longer and longer. Then the fiddles ceased their building reel. Arliss found herself spun backwards into the young man's arms.

She was panting as she stepped out of the dance, her arm extended but her hand still gripped by his.

His words were so quiet Arliss had to lean closer to hear them. "I'm Philip, from the village."

"I'm Arliss, the princess."

Philip released her hand and stepped away.

Bo Burnette / 42

CHAPTER SIX: FORBIDDEN

When the noise of the ball had ceased and the lights dimmed, Arliss's father half-guided, half-dragged her up the stairs and into her bedchamber. She pushed back from him and stepped away, facing him as he closed the wooden door. When he turned, his face seemed marred by sorrow and disgrace. Her breath came in short, rushed intervals.

"Arliss, why must you do this to me? Why? Why must you disgrace me in such a brazen manner?"

"I don't understand. What in the world are you talking about?"

"I think you know quite well what I am talking about. That dance with the peasant! I said no fooling around, no unexpected acts. Nothing! And yet you proceed to dance with a peasant in front of the entire village. Did you not think the lords would notice? Or Brallaghan?" He paused while the force of his words sank into Arliss's realization. "Did you not think that *I* would notice?"

Her blood chilled. So this was where he stood. He was responsible for all of this. He was the one who drew the invisible lines. And now his pride was severing her from her newfound friend.

"I danced with no peasant at the ball." She held her head high.

He scoffed. "Lies are not befitting one of so royal a bloodline. I saw you, Arliss."

She shook her head, and her hair swished free from her mother's meticulous arrangement. "I danced with only two young men, both free, honest, noble citizens of Reinhold. I danced with no others."

He stepped over to pull the curtain over the window. "There are certain rules which we royalty must follow, rules which help us maintain our standing over the people. Without rules, no country can last long."

"Without *good* rules, no country will last at all."

His head snapped toward her. "Your disrespect has grown too great. You seem to think you can lecture and command me. No more." He stepped toward her.

She backed away, nearing the door.

"I will be blunt with you, daughter, since subtlety seems to have failed me. You are the heir to the throne of Reinhold, the only true heir of my bloodline. You are a daughter of kings, and I would have you marry as such. A queen needs a king at her side, not a commoner."

Arliss licked her lips. "So you would have me marry Brallaghan. That is your plan, isn't it?"

"No, don't be ridiculous. I would not push you to love one who did not have your heart. However, I do deem Brallaghan to be a noble young man."

"And what about the other young man I danced with, Philip? Was he not noble?"

"Arliss, he is a peasant."

"Yes, because you call him one. But your words have no power over me!"

He growled, his broad shoulders silhouetted by the lone candle at her bedside. "I think you might find that statement false had you tested it before it flowed from your mouth."

Arliss backed away from him. Who was this man who so criticized her every action and word? She feared even to think, lest he discover that as well. "Do you not care for any of my wishes? I want adventure, excitement. I want to know more about this world I live in."

"Many men have said that very thing at the wrong time and for the wrong reasons, and have paid for it deeply. A man must first plant his feet before he can stretch out his hand!"

"Well, I consider myself fortunate not to be a man." The volume of her own voice surprised her. "I have wounds, wounds that you continue to ignore. Do you really think I have forgotten the hurt, after all these years?"

He stared at the stone wall behind her. "Those are my wounds as well, but we must bear them with dignity."

"You mean forget." Arliss wept. "Forget everything, and pretend like nothing ever happened, pretend that I never wanted a brother."

"I do not ask you to forget. I only ask you to move on. You have come to a new stage in your life."

"I can see that! A stage in which all my friends are chosen and rejected for me, and my husband is handed to me on a platter." Anger burned in her lungs, her arms clenched. "If I want friendship with a peasant, why should you forbid it?"

"Peace!" he commanded. "You are speaking like a child. And I see now that one who acts like a child has no place thinking of marriage. You may not see that peasant boy again. I forbid it."

Her face flushed, her head shook in defiance and terror at the harshness of his words. She yanked the door open and flew through the hallway, down the stairs, and out the front doorway.

Even there she did not stop, but kept running at a great pace. It was nigh unto midnight as she ran down the lower tiers of the village, fumbled with the iron gates, and slipped through them. Crossing the small drawbridge that spanned the moat, she fled into the forbidding blackness of night.

Blinded by hot tears, Arliss stumbled across the fields, her feet guiding her to the place she knew all too well. The sky was dark, the moon veiled by menacing clouds that promised to bring one of the brief showers which were familiar to the land of Reinhold.

She stared heavenward. Let the shower come. Nothing could dampen her spirits any further.

She did not slow down until already inside the forest clearing. Panting, she leaned against the ancient, gnarled tree which had been her companion for so many years. There she wept, the tears stinging her eyes. She wept until the tears refused to come.

What right did her father have to choose whom she could and couldn't dance with? That was her choice. If she wanted to dance with a lord's son, she would. If she chose a peasant farmer, who was he to stop her?

A droplet of water settled on her head. Then another wetted her forehead, trickling down her nose. In a moment, the rain was pattering through the dim canopy all about her head. Thousands of liquid beads flooded the shivering darkness.

As she stood to leave, a vague noise pierced through the rain to her left. A stealthy wheeze or hiss, perhaps. She froze. But the sound did not return. Probably just a phantom of her imagination.

She walked slowly all the way back to the castle, letting the rain bathe her troubled body.

She arrived at the castle soaked. Instead of scolding her, her mother eased her into a warm tub, filled with water which had been heating in a basin over the fire. After this, Arliss slipped into a fresh nightgown and crawled into her bed.

Once her parents were asleep, she crept into the library with a lone candle, thankful for the thick carpets which drank the noise of her footsteps. She lay on the floor for hours, poring over books of legend and lore and history and maps. The ancient tales, written in other realms, spoke often of "a wild land in the east, intimidating and deadly, yet plentiful and majestic." Reinhold.

But what—where—in Reinhold were the legends talking about? The landscape she knew was harsh and bleak, intimidating and deadly. Hardly plentiful and majestic. Yet those very words repeated themselves throughout the book.

The words reached into her mind and spun a labyrinth of ideas and plans which, perhaps, could reverse Reinhold's problems. And, it seemed to her, the best way to conquer those difficulties would be to reveal the faults of the king and his ways. She had to overstep his customs and violate his laws—which really weren't worth following, anywise.

Perhaps her father was right to expand the seaside outpost. Yet how could they ignore the treasures that might lie just a few days' journey into the forest? How could he not explore the heart of Reinhold?

By the time the sun dawned and she retreated into bed, she had created a solid, daring plan. The troubles of the night were over. Now, the day had come, and it was time for action.

CHAPTER SEVEN:
A COUNCIL OF DISSENSION

Armed with a leather satchel filled with books, clothes, and arrows, Arliss hurried downstairs to Ilayda's room. Lord Adam and Lady Elisabeth—and their children Ilayda and Arden—dwelt in the lower floor of the immense tower, which sat adjacent to the great hall.

Within the dim bedchamber, Arliss found the exact sight she had expected: Ilayda slumbering upon the bed, her dark velvet hair hiding half her face.

She chuckled to herself and yanked the covers off the bed.

Ilayda squinted at her, groaned, and buried her face in the pillow.

"Get up, you lazy goose!" Arliss said. "We have important things to do."

Ilayda turned her head from its place inside the pillow. "Sleep is an important thing to do, silly princess who dances with peasants."

"If anyone is silly, it's you, muttonhead. Now get up, or I will be rather inclined to leave you behind!"

At this, Ilayda tottered out of bed. She stumbled over to her dresser and began dragging a comb through her hair.

"I'll meet you in the garden in ten minutes." Arliss turned toward the door. "You'd better pack some things."

"Pack? Why?"

"You shall see." Arliss slipped through the door, around the corner, and back down the hall the way she'd come.

The footsteps shocked her so much she nearly fled back to Ilayda's room. She scanned the hallway, frantically searching for a place to hide as the steps drew nearer—steps which were neither her father's heavy trod nor her mother's gliding pace. These particular steps belonged to Lord Adam.

He would have no reason to be angry at finding her here—she frequented Ilayda's rooms—but after yesterday's eavesdropped conversation, she didn't desire a confrontation. At the last moment, she slipped through a doorway to her left, pulling the door to just enough so that she could see yet not be seen.

Lord Adam rounded the corner in the hall and paused a moment, heaving a sigh. A few paces behind him strode Lord Brédan. Both wore courtly attire.

"And your wife?" Brédan was saying.

"Elisabeth is unwell this morning," Adam responded. "Last night's festivities did not agree with her, I think." The two lords shared a knowing glance.

Arliss squinted at them through the crack in the door.

"Come." Adam motioned Brédan. "Let us enter and find our seats."

Arliss's heart thumped. If they found her hiding in here, they would almost certainly be suspicious—even angry.

But they did not enter her hiding spot. Instead they opened the double doors across the hall and slipped inside with the covertness of two wily cats.

Of course—the royal council was on this day. Her father had spoken to her mother about it. How could she have forgotten? Then again, in all the excitements and miseries of the previous evening, how could she have remembered?

After a few moments, she ventured to open the door a bit wider. She slipped back when she looked into the hallway.

Her parents and Nathanael were entering the council chamber.

Once the doors swung together, nearly clicking shut, she slipped across the hall and peeked inside.

When he entered the small room, Kenton found the lords Adam and Brédan already seated about the round table. How long had they been conversing together?

Elowyn, too, regarded the two men suspiciously, her dark eyes remaining steady and sure. "I see the council has begun prematurely, my lords."

Adam lowered an arm to the table. "We were merely waiting upon your highnesses to arrive and begin the council."

"Then it would seem your patience has failed you," she replied.

Adam glowered at her as she lowered herself into a chair in between Kenton and Nathanael.

Kenton regarded those around the table. "I declare this council begun. Let us establish such things that will build our country and honor our God. For Reinhold." He hesitated. "I think we all know what we must discuss this day."

"Indeed," Adam butted in. "We have clearly assembled to put into practice your plans for a new village."

Kenton clenched his brow. "What are you implying, my lord?"

Brédan spoke. "He means only that he knows you have a definitive plan for Reinhold's growth. A plan which, p'raps, you are quite determined to put into practice."

"You have long known my mind, O lords and lady of the court." Kenton nodded. "This village has grown great over this past decade. We must not all remain and fester until we are packed like too many arrows in a small quiver. The building of a new village is inevitable."

"Or is it?" Adam asked in a crisp, certain voice. "Is it truly wise to venture back towards the sea? Ought we not instead venture inward?"

"You know why that is forbidden." Nathanael spoke. "It is forbidden to cross the river which cuts through the forest. Have you forgotten the darkness so quickly? Would you be so hasty?"

"Enough foolish questions." Adam chuckled. "No, I have forgotten nothing. Still I maintain my position. I think an inward expansion would ultimately prove more fruitful than an outward one. That is my honest opinion. You may make of it what you will."

Elowyn spoke deeply. "Mayhaps that means you will be silent for a moment, for your wisdom has fled with your patience."

Adam appeared so surprised that he silenced altogether.

Kenton restrained his smile.

"With all due respect, my queen," Brédan said, "there may be more wisdom in Adam's plan than at first meets one's eye. I'll wager he may be right, though there is undoubtedly wisdom in the king's plan as well."

"So you are of a like mind with Adam, then," Kenton said grimly. "And what of the Lord Nathanael?"

Nathanael regarded him with serious eyes. "I am with you to the death, whatever path you may take, or service I may offer you."

"Then I suppose we shall look further into my plan, at least at present." Kenton pressed his chin into his palm. "I will not move forward in haste. It is in my heart to take a party of men and journey to the seaside outpost, examine the land, and see if there is suitable ground and water supply for a village. Then I will return and share what I have found."

Adam's fist clenched. "I thought this was a council, not a list of edicts."

Brédan looked uncertain. "The king simply wants what's best for his family."

"What about what is best for *my* family? Furthermore, for this entire clan of Reinhold?" Adam rose to his feet. His face reddened as he pressed his palms against the edge of the table. "You cannot even control your own daughter, Kenton. Ever she scuttles about, causing mishap and disturbance. How can we expect you to control an entire country?"

Kenton stared, unable to respond. What could one say to such impudence? He glanced toward his wife.

Her lips drew into a subtle smile. "If I am not mistaken, Adam, it is your daughter who accompanies her in many such escapades."

To that, Adam could make no reply.

Nathanael glared at Adam. "They are both young. Young *women*, but very young ones at that. Were you never a young man, Adam?"

"Do not speak to me of youth. You, one who is not yet thirty years of age. Your nerve surprises me."

Nathanael stood and set his fists on the table. "I seem to recall reading in the Holy Scriptures that it is not age, but the Spirit of the Lord which makes someone truly wise."

"Silence!" Adam shouted. "Kenton, I beg you to bring order to this council."

Kenton also stood, trying to restrain the rush of his pulse. "If I am not mistaken, it was you who destroyed its order in the first place."

Brédan looked uncomfortable as he also stood. "Let's resolve this, fellows. No sense in squabbling when we have already come to a decision."

Adam spread his arms wide. "And what decision is that? The king's command! It's as I believed—the king will march on with his plans and leave our counsel in the dust."

Kenton's muscles tightened. "I am not ignoring your counsel. I am merely choosing to explore the option of a new seaside town. No clear decision has been made. I am going so we may have a clearer council on this matter."

Adam took a deep breath. "Kenton, you listen to me—"

"Peace!" Elowyn's powerful voice left all four men silent. She too had risen from her seat. "You will listen to *me*. The king's plan is solid, and leaves room for much counsel and wisdom. He will journey to the sea, and will take one of you with him. As for the princess, I will speak with her about her behavior."

Kenton nodded gratefully to her. She always was the peacemaker, the arbiter.

"Then it is decided," Kenton affirmed. "I will take with me Brédan and a dozen other men. Elowyn and Nathanael will be left in charge of ruling the city. And Adam, try to see that no trouble comes to me on your, or anyone else's, account."

Something flickered in the crack between the double doors. He squinted, but saw nothing. Had someone been eavesdropping?

The council would tarry and discuss dozens of other more trivial things—laws regarding selling and bartering in the village, most likely—but Arliss needed to hurry. She arrived in the garden only moments before Ilayda burst out of the wooden back door. She was panting and had a canvas knapsack strapped about her.

"Arliss, I'm sorry. I know you said ten minutes, but there were so many things to do."

She held up her hand. "No, it's fine. I made good use of the extra minutes you provided."

"Doing what? You really must tell me what you're up to or I shan't even come with you."

"No, I cannot tell you just yet. We have to find a more secret place." She leaned closer to Ilayda. "I happened to overhear much of the royal council. My father plans to build a new village by the sea. Your father disagrees."

"And how do you feel?"

"As few kind feelings as I have toward your father at present, I still disagree with my own father's refusal to explore the heart of this land. And...well, that is part of the secret."

Ilayda's eyes widened. "You'd better tell me soon."

"Come, silly goose, let's go."

The sound of clanging metal reached Arliss's ears long before they reached their destination. She and Ilayda scurried across the street of the city's lower tier, trying to avoid suspicion as much as possible. It seemed the entire city guard had been summoned to the castle in light of the council's decision. And, as it was Diathamon—a working day—many folks were toiling in the fields, even though the bean harvest was waning. The sun had hardly reached its mid-morning point.

As Arliss reached the door of the carpenter's workshop, she shuddered. Clanging metal within chimed an omen of both adventure and danger. She'd heard such sounds from within before and never given them a second thought. Now, she put a hand to the sword which she'd stowed beneath her cloak.

Glancing back at Ilayda, she gave a nod and stepped over the threshold. It wasn't strange for someone to enter the carpenter's shop uninvited. But today, she wasn't a customer for woodwork. Her heart fluttering, she gazed into the open room adjacent to the workshop.

Arliss stared at the intriguing fight within.

Bo Burnette / 56

Chapter Eight:
A Collision of Swords

Philip ducked as Erik's blade arced towards his head. It was a foolish move on his cousin's part—easily blocked or diverted by anyone who had any real sense. As the blade swept past him, Philip brought down a quick cut, which Erik barely countered.

Erik slammed his entire strength into the blade and spun Philip's sword off his own. He stepped backwards.

"Given up yet?" Philip teased.

"Not yet."

His blade and footing made sure, Philip let his cousin make the next move. Erik slashed his blade down with a sort of collected anger. Philip lifted his eyebrows and took a swift step backwards. He barely parried the blade before his cousin cut down upon him again.

The two swords met with a clash, scintillating in the morning sun which streamed through the open windows. Philip blocked the blow and saw his chance. He countered and slashed his blade into Erik's. Erik's blade nearly flew from his grip. Philip brought his sword down again, and Erik tried in vain to raise his blade from under the force.

Philip's strength won out, and he disarmed Erik with a twist of his wrist. He pointed his sword across the space between them, expecting Erik to pull out his usual trick—challenge Philip to a round of archery, at which Philip would surely fail.

Instead, a new blade swung up to meet Philip's. Startled and unprepared, he held the sword fast to keep it from arcing back into his face. He turned to behold the amateur swordsman who had challenged him this way.

It was no swordsman.

There, her eyes fierce and joyous, stood Princess Arliss. She wobbled her sword back and forth. The blade was larger even than Philip's, and took both of her hands to support and swing.

She swung again, and Philip half-parried. He hesitated. Ought he fight the princess? Clearly she had no idea what she was doing. He himself hadn't the slightest idea why she was here.

The princess stood poised for another move. "Are you tired so soon?"

He almost laughed. "No, my lady, though I feared you were."

Her eyes narrowed—whether in anger or amusement, Philip knew not—and she swung again. Obviously, she knew only a few strokes, and hadn't the faintest knowledge of real blocking and parrying. However, she at least knew what to make of her feet. Must have come from knowing how to dance.

She continued to thrash at him. In the midst of an easily blocked stroke, she began to speak. "I've come to you for a reason."

He grinned as he sliced into her sword. "Does this have something to do with last night?"

"No…and very much yes."

Waiting for an explanation, he pivoted and continued fighting.

"I need your help," Arliss panted.

"For what?"

"For an adventure."

The answer distracted him just long enough for him to relax his grip on his sword. She swung with all her might, and his blade clattered to the floor.

With a sly smile tugging at her lips, she pointed the sword near his chest. "I am leaving the city on a quest to uncover the secrets of the land of Reinhold."

He narrowed his eyes. He had never been held at sword's point by a woman before, let alone the princess herself. "Why does that concern me?"

"Because"—she tapped the tip of the sword against his chest—"I want you to accompany me."

"And why would the princess of Reinhold choose a carpenter's apprentice for this quest?"

"Because," she said in a soft voice, "you understand."

Their eyes met. Her eyes revealed a knowing acknowledgement of shared experience and emotion—of something he understood far too deeply for words. She spoke the truth.

But she did not quite understand.

In a swift, agile motion, he ducked under her blade, reaching for his fallen sword. He grabbed it from where it lay by her feet, flipped himself onto his back—his legs bent beneath him—and raised his sword to meet hers above. Then, leaping upwards, he snapped her sword from her grasp. The blade flipped upwards, and he snatched it out of midair.

With both weapons in hand, he faced her. "Tell me about this quest of yours."

Arliss hesitated, feeling about in her mind for the right words. Finally she spoke in a hushed voice. "As I said, I am leaving the city this very day on a mission of justice and adventure. I would ask you to accompany me and the Lady Ilayda in our quest."

"Where are you going?" Philip held her gaze.

"Into the forest, through the woods, and…across the river."

Behind her, Ilayda gasped.

"What on earth are you talking about!" Ilayda advanced to confront her. "Crossing the river? Are you such a fool? That is forbidden by order of the king himself. To cross the river is to break the law, not to mention to throw one's life away. Arliss, I really—"

"Enough!" Arliss snapped.

Ilayda huffed but silenced.

Arliss turned back to Philip. "It is my intention to discover what lies in the heart of our country. The books of legend drop hints regarding a beautiful and mysterious place far inland in this very realm. If I were to find it, I could change things."

"What do you want to change, my lady?" he asked.

"Everything," she whispered. "The way my father sees me. The way my father sees you. The way my father sees adventure."

Philip's companion spoke for the first time since she had arrived, stepping towards them. "So this is about your father."

"No. This is about Reinhold."

"And you will disobey the law of Reinhold by crossing the river?"

"Yes."

His eyebrows curved like longbows, he turned to Ilayda. "And what do you think about this, Ilayda?" He pronounced it rather like "ill-LAY-da."

"Il*ay*da!" she insisted. "Like 'lie.' Not like 'lay.' How is that so hard for everyone?"

"Pardon me." The tall fellow bowed slightly. "My name's Erik, with a 'k,' so it's a touch unusual, too, I suppose. But what do you think about the princess's plan?"

"I have always wondered why it is forbidden. Arliss?"

"No reason at all, I am sure." She shrugged, trying to stomach her secret. "Will you join me?"

A thick silence hung over them for several long moments. Philip's eyes darted about, as if calculating his answer.

Finally, he stepped closer to her and held out the pommel of her sword. "I will join you. If you are going to do this, you're going to need a bodyguard, as well as a guide." He motioned to Erik.

Erik nodded slowly.

Arliss smiled. "Let us make ready, then." She glanced around. In the center of the room sat a contraption of wood and rope, with a drawn longbow strapped to it. "Is this—"

"A tillering contraption? Yes." Philip strode over to it. "I make longbows from longer scraps of wood in my spare time, once the rest of the carpentry work is done. Usually I end up using a more common wood, but this—" he ran his hand over the smooth, bent wood "—is fine yew. Highest quality. It'll make a better bow for Erik once I've finished it. It is almost done."

She ran her hand down the bow. Such craftsmanship! She'd never seen the like. What a strange peasant—one who could both farm and work with wood and dance!

"We will need to bring weapons on this quest, for safety. Each of you must gather your things," she said. "I will see to the other provisions."

Elowyn paced the far end of the council chamber, her hands intertwined behind her back. So much division and conflict had passed this morn. A decision had been made—yes—but other things had been created. Spite. Jealousy.

She sighed and pressed her hands on the table. Brédan was loyal and always had been. What was more, he was a little afraid of her. Adam, however, was not. While Kenton was gone…

She swallowed a gasp, letting the breath tighten her lungs all the way up her windpipe.

Kenton glanced up from his map at the opposite end of the table. "Are you all right, El?"

She nodded. "I am well in body. The council…it did not go as I wished."

"You brought order to it well enough."

"Order and peace are not the same."

He stood. "Do you think they're right about Arliss?"

Now *there* was the sensitive spot—the point when Adam had started boiling her blood with his words. Attacks on herself, her plans, she could handle. But when he began to malign her daughter and her husband, she could be quiet no more.

She stepped around the table corner. "No, I think he is wrong. Arliss is not a fool."

"She's irresponsible. For a normal girl, it would be fine. But Arliss is a princess."

"She's more than that." Elowyn closed her eyes. "She was born to be more."

"What do you mean?"

"I mean she won't be princess forever. One day, she will be queen." Elowyn stared at the backs of her eyelids as a vision overtook her sight.

There was fire—an ocean of fire, spreading on and on and consuming many stories.

Arliss stood at the front of it all, bow in hand. A dragon rose up out of the fire and hurled itself at her.

Then the fire turned into a river of blood, gushing out into an ocean.

A splash of ocean became pure and clear before it took flight, rising above the land like a bird.

Then the whole vision crystallized until it reflected like a great silver ball, like the moon. It was the moon. It whirled around, flashing futures too fast for Elowyn to comprehend.

She staggered forward and into Kenton's arms.

He stroked her shoulder. "A vision? What did you see?"

"I don't know. But Arliss is at the front of it all."

The blue woolen gown tickled Arliss's skin as she lingered in the hall. She peeked down the long corridor which wound through the castle tower's lower floor and into the adjacent great hall. Not a soul was in sight, though voices still murmured in the council chamber.

As if treading upon water, she made her way down the hall, past Lord Adam and Lady Elisabeth's chamber, past the council door, past Ilayda's room, and finally to the wide-open kitchen, its sunny windows beaming with light. In this scullery, she and Ilayda had been taught the art of cooking by their mothers. Elowyn had asked Kenton and his men to place the cooking room on this side of the castle—a room which overlooked the gardens and had windows facing both east and west; sunrise and sunset streamed in unfettered.

Arliss worked quickly, opening her satchel with one hand and the storeroom door with the other. A brief glance about the deep closet showed her just what she would need to pack: a few loaves of bread, some salted pork, and several flasks of water. An orange or two, imported from the seaside outpost, would also be rather nice to have.

The bag already contained an extra dress, as well as her hunting knife, but she crammed in as many stores as she could. This adventure could take many days.

Not enough water flasks would fit in her bag, but she could swing them over her shoulder and let the other three carry their own once she returned to them.

She reached for another orange. The council's decision would get rid of her father for a few days or even weeks, but it would make her mother even more vigilant than usual. They couldn't take too much time. Ilayda had insisted that they leave right away, but Erik said that they ought to wait for cover of night, and Philip had responded that the princess would decide.

She smiled to herself. He already seemed so kind, so obliging—just the sort of person to have on this sort of adventure. Perhaps, even, the sort of person to have as one's brother.

She closed her eyes and could almost hear the music from the ball, feel the swirl of the steps. She leaned against the shelf and closed her eyes.

"A bit hungry, perhaps?"

She jumped. The orange in her hand slipped to the floor and rolled, coming to a stop at her mother's feet. With a smile pulling at the edge of her lips and eyes, Elowyn bent down and retrieved it.

For a long moment, Arliss gaped. She couldn't lie to her mother—she did not deserve that. However, she could not tell her mother the truth. Elowyn was far too close to Kenton to defy his authority in this matter. She would end the expedition before it began.

"What's all this?" Elowyn prodded the satchel.

"Ah, provisions," Arliss managed. A twisted truth entered her head like a wriggling worm, small yet deadly. "Ilayda and I wanted to go camping." That shouldn't surprise her mother. They had done such things ever since Arliss became a teenager—short trips at the edge of the forest.

Elowyn smiled. "You're escaping, are you not?"

Arliss's heart stopped. Had she guessed?

"You're trying to get away from it all."

"What do you mean?" Arliss ventured.

"I mean that you need not worry about trying to get away. Your father is leaving to explore the seashore lands. He will be gone for a fortnight at least, for it is more than a day's journey on foot." Elowyn tilted her head. "I suppose you want some time to yourself after what happened between you two."

"I do," Arliss said simply.

"You may go. I only ask that you stay within your father's boundaries, and that you come back within two days."

Arliss stared at her mother, her heart racing. "I will return by then."

Her mother kissed her on the forehead and glided out of the room.

She stood frozen a moment. She'd never lied to her mother like this before. It really wasn't right.

But once she completed her quest—once she discovered the heart of the land—would it even matter? When she returned, having explored the undiscovered with the help of two peasants, everyone would honor her. No one would doubt her anymore. What was more, Philip and Erik would get equal honor as the royalty.

If they succeeded. Ilayda had panicked over the idea of crossing her father's boundaries. Was she right to be so worried?

Satchel in hand, Arliss strapped four water flasks about her shoulders. She closed the satchel and exhaled heavily. She would not be staying within her father's borders. Her quest denied that.

And, despite her mother's instructions and her own endeavors, she would not return in two days' time.

Chapter Nine: Two Leavings

The dark cloak fluttered in the autumn breeze, as if trying to take flight with the other birds which flocked through the midday sky. Arliss pulled it down, making sure it covered the water skins and her bulging satchel.

Noises began to collect and multiply in the tiered village below. Usually she could hear little from the flat hilltop. Now, the familiar clink of the blacksmith's hammer intertwined with a rising hubbub of voices.

She stepped back towards the castle, only to hear a murmuring and clanking from the great hall. Her father, perhaps?

She couldn't risk seeing *him* right now. She fled around the bend of the dirt road and wedged herself in a rocky indentation which marked the pass between the third and second tiers.

She leaned out of the cleft and peered down on the street below. The marketplace seemed lively. Something had stirred the people together. She hoped it did not have anything to do with her visit to the carpenter's apprentice.

She did not hear the footsteps until they were almost upon her. She flattened herself into the alcove of silvery stone, straining to listen. The soft footfalls drew nearer, smudged into each other, then disappeared altogether. Then the person spoke.

"Oh, blimey idiot, where could she be?"

Ilayda. Arliss exhaled in relief and stepped from her hiding spot.

For a moment, Ilayda looked as if she was going to scream. Instead, she grabbed Arliss's hand and yanked her down the road toward the second level. "Hurry, if you care anything about your little quest."

Arliss wrinkled her brow. What did she mean? Usually she wouldn't give time to Ilayda's nonsense, but something urgent underlay her sharp words.

Rough marching pounded the ground above them. As they neared the fringe of the market area, Ilayda jerked her into a narrow opening between the hill's rocky outcroppings and the first of the village buildings. Her shoulders scraped the sides of the alleyway.

"What in Reinhold is going on?" Arliss demanded between breaths.

Ilayda's head bobbed. "A lot of things. Let me catch my breath."

"Catch it faster."

Ilayda snorted. "Your father is leaving the city, and taking two thirds of the city guard with him." So *that* was the marching sound which drew ever nearer. Ilayda continued, "Philip's uncle returned from making a delivery, so he and his sullen cousin are rather stuck."

"We need a distraction for them. Something that will give them time to pack and get away."

"You're rather slow, are you not, silly dear?" Ilayda motioned upwards.

The guards had now marched down around the bend almost to the second tier. Perhaps that was all the distraction they would need.

The two dozen guards marched past, their mail glittering, their bows protruding from long quivers. Such a glorious assemblage of arms! Very few carried swords besides her father and Lord Brédan—swords were a rarity in Reinhold. Iron had proven scarce. And in a land of farmers and builders, the bow was much more useful than the blade.

As the soldiers marched by, Arliss hid her face, hoping her father would not glance at the thin slit which served as their hiding spot. Such a discovery would bring disaster.

But he did not even glance their way; his gaze remained fixed ahead, as if in a trance. The company passed, and she felt free to breathe openly again.

"All right, come on," she said. "What's your plan?"

"I have no plan," Ilayda said. "If I had one, I wouldn't have come to get you."

Arliss stared into the knotted wood of the alley's side for a minute. They had to get to Philip and Erik. But how could they, with the king's company in the way? The entire town would be gathered to see the procession.

They needed to send a message. In many books of adventure, there were keen birds that could carry messages to others. Yet she knew of no such flying couriers in Reinhold.

Flying…flying, that was it. She needed to send a flying message to Philip.

The carpentry shop lay just visible on the bottom tier of the village. She drew her bow, strung it, and nocked an arrow.

Ilayda's eyes opened wide as mushroom caps. "What on earth—"

"Hush," she said as she knelt to the ground. She tried to steady her arm, but it still shook with what she was about to do. The entire village had gathered just below her. So many familiar faces—Lord Adam, Lady Elisabeth, Mrs. Fidelma, and even Philip's uncle—and this only made her nerves shake worse. She could not miss her mark. She could not be made known.

"Ilayda, where is that notebook you carry with you?" she tried to keep her voice steady.

"Right here." Ilayda pulled the small notebook out.

"Write upon it these words: 'I will grow in the west' and poke it over the arrow's tip."

Ilayda did as asked. "Are you sure about this?"

Arliss did not answer. With another glance at the arrow's flight and the many obstacles in its way, she closed her eyes and released the shaft.

As the citizens cheered and waved at the passing procession, Kenton tried to force a smile, but his mouth felt stiff and numb. Was this really the best thing for Reinhold? For himself, even?

Of course it was. What obstinate ideas. Absurd, they were. Nothing else could be better for his country than developing the outpost which had already proved more than prosperous. More than once he had thanked God for giving him the foresight to create the outpost, even when the clan was flourishing on the Isle of Light. Now, what had first been their life preserver might become their next step. The fish, the stone, the things that could be made with shells. Just what this land needed.

He searched the crowds. Everyone had gathered. Most were smiling. Not all condoned his quest, though; he could spot Lord Adam lingering with a livid expression still burning on his face.

Kenton frowned, his heart sinking. He needed all the lords on his side. Yet something else was amiss, and he hesitated in his steps as he realized what nagged at his mind.

Arliss. She had not come. Nowhere in the march through the city had he seen her, and he knew she did not stand with her mother. Elowyn watched alone from the top of the tower. She waved at the procession as he turned his head to acknowledge her. She was his greatest treasure, standing like a watchful guardian over the entire kingdom. He could trust her to manage the realm in his stead. To manage Arliss. Arliss loved her mother more than anyone.

Sometimes he questioned her love for *him*, though. If she truly loved him, she would have been here. She would be cheering, waving, celebrating with the others.

He heaved a sigh as the company approached the gates of the city. Two guards creaked opened the massive wooden doors which swept inward to reveal the wide drawbridge. As much as Kenton loved Arliss, he still yearned to leave. Nothing disturbed him more than the thought of another fierce argument with her.

Nothing, perhaps, except the dragging feeling he felt as he stepped through the gates and departed from the city.

Arliss eased downward, plodding her way through the descending alleyway. Ilayda tumbled behind her. They were on the western side of the village, cutting through the narrow corridor which crossed down through the two levels of the town. Sidestepping a dusty old pot, Arliss felt her way along the wooden walls of Lord Brédan's home. The hesitant lord's family lived here, though Lord Adam and the rest of Ilayda's family dwelt in the lowest floor of the castle.

Turning her head in an uncomfortably crooked position, Arliss could just see the castle tower at the top of the hill. Her mother still stood upon its heights, watching something in the far distance.

So the troops had left, then. People would be gathering back to their homes soon. She needed to make haste.

"Ilayda, come on!" She motioned and picked up her pace as the alley ground leveled out into an opening. She paused with her breath caught in her lungs. No one seemed to be coming. She eased forward and prepared to step out into the street.

Ilayda slammed into her back, pushing her forward. No sooner had she exited the alleyway than another body collided with hers. Flailing, she tried to brace herself for the fall to the stone pavement.

A strong arm wrapped around her back, steadying her. She smiled into what she expected to be Philip's face.

Brallaghan's befuddled expression greeted her instead.

She bit her lip, recalling their similar encounter from the previous evening.

He slipped his arm from around her back, and she took a few steps away and thanked him briskly.

With a puzzled slitting of his eyes, he examined her traveling cloak and satchel. "What are you doing, may I ask?"

She said nothing for a long moment. She glared at Ilayda, signaling her to stay in the shadows. "Just going for a little walk—to shoot some arrows, you know." She fingered the quiver which strapped across her torso.

"With a leather satchel?"

"I get hungry. Wouldn't you?"

"Of course, my lady."

She didn't like him calling her "my lady," as if they hadn't been friends all their lives.

He dug his boot into a chink in the road. "Perhaps you would like company? It's dangerous, you know. The fellows have reported hearing noises in the forest. They've seen strange things."

"Those who stay behind the king's border have no harm to fear." She stifled a feeling of guilt at her haughty words. "Now, if you will excuse me, my company and I must go."

As Brallaghan stared, she yanked Ilayda out of the alley by the arm and dragged her down toward the lowest tier.

With cloaks hiding their faces, they got through the peasant district easily enough. Arliss exhaled in satisfaction as they exited the city gate via a small door. They had made it. Ilayda hesitated before the eight-foot wide moat, but after Arliss hurled herself to the opposite bank, she complied and leapt with her eyes shut. The water did nothing but dampen her left foot.

They scrambled to their feet and strode toward the fields. Leaving the city portended to be the most dangerous thing they had ever done.

And Arliss loved that.

Chapter Ten:
The Dark Tree

"What if Philip doesn't come?" Ilayda asked.

They had been waiting for well nigh ten minutes. The ripples in the moat from Ilayda's tumble had long dissipated, and Arliss had even taken off her dark cloak as the October day grew warmer. Her skin tingled in the sunlight.

She inhaled slowly. "He will come. I know he will come."

"I doubt it. His sullen cousin has probably convinced him not to."

"Why would you malign the poor fellow? He's hardly said a word, good or bad."

"I'm not maligning him, silly. I'm agreeing with him."

Arliss scoffed. "Rather, agreeing with your imagination of him."

Ilayda bounded to her feet. "Arliss, you're ridiculous. Really. Who in their right mind would join you on such a quest? This Philip seems like a sensible fellow. His cousin…"

"Erik," Arliss put in.

"Yes, Erik. His tongue may not work, but his head is likely screwed on well enough. This is absurd—leaving the city, crossing the river. Why do it?"

"You know bloody well why," Arliss hissed. "Now hush up and do as you're told."

Ilayda instantly quieted.

Arliss winced. Had she spoken too sharply? Ilayda was only a year younger. Perhaps she didn't deserve that.

She didn't have time to amend her words. Just around the corner of the village, Philip and Erik strode toward them. Both carried satchels and had swords strapped on their belts, and each wore a long traveling tunic and cloak.

"Ho, princess!" Philip called. "We got your message." He fingered the arrow as he handed her the shaft.

She tucked it away in her quiver. "Thank you. Are we all ready?"

He opened his mouth to reply, but Erik cut him off. "Wait a moment, my lady. I have a question for you."

"Speak it freely."

"Does the king know of this expedition?"

She stiffened. "I have the permission of the queen. It is all right."

Erik nodded, but Arliss guessed he was less than satisfied with her answer. Philip seemed utterly satiated with the answer. Ilayda looked like she wanted to begin a speech. Arliss began one first.

"Well, my friends, we must set off. It is my purpose to spend two full days searching for the glories that lie at the heart of Reinhold. If I have not discovered anything in those two days, we will return to the castle in haste and secrecy. In either case, you will tell no one of our quest. It is…a matter of secrecy for the royalty. If we succeed, I will reward you all handsomely." Her eyes lingered on Philip and his sheathed sword. "And I will have you two fellows knighted."

She turned and faced the distant green woods. She could practically smell the wild forest wind from here. "Now, on to our adventure—for Reinhold!"

And with that, they marched toward the eaves of the forest. In the opposite direction, feet stamped away toward the sea.

"What is this place?" Philip asked as he surveyed the open clearing at the edge of the forest. The light of midday squeezed through the canopy of leaves and lit up the space with shafts of glorious sunshine.

"My little sanctuary." Arliss leapt up to the immense branch of the tree which had so often been her seat among the leaves. "When court life gets a little stiff, I come out here for a while."

"Stiff? It can't be all that bad, can it?" His eyebrow curved. "I've never found the court to be too awful."

She pressed her palm onto the rugged bark. "Well, you're not a princess. And be thankful for that."

He flourished deeply. "I can assure you, my lady, I thank God every day that he did not make me to be a princess."

Ilayda sniggered from behind him. "Yes—a princess who escapes to talk to trees and goes on outlandish quests! Thank heaven indeed."

Arliss glared in her direction.

Erik stopped circling the clearing and added, "A princess who wastes time talking when we ought to be moving on."

Arliss shot him a sharp look as well.

He amended, "All of you, I mean. We ought to be on the march if we are in earnest about this whole thing."

Arliss lifted her chin and, after a moment, slid down the tree. She stepped closer to the others. "I need you three to promise me this: that you will do as I say and follow my command."

Everyone agreed. But Erik's response bore a caveat, "As long as it is right to do so."

Then something caught his eye and enraptured his attention.

Arliss followed his line of sight. She saw nothing at first.

Then she noticed it.

Among dozens of other spindly birches there stood a strange tree. Whether sickened with decay or covered in moss, she could not say, but it was black and gnarled. The mere sight of it reeked of death and decay. They approached the tree.

With no small hesitation, Erik reached out and touched the darkened bark. "Something has poisoned this tree. I've never seen anything like it."

"An animal? Or some deadly blight?"

Erik turned to her, his eyes dark and serious. "Or some deadly person."

They walked in silence for some time. Arliss despised the silence. She longed to speak, to laugh, and to make it feel like a real adventure. However, her three partners were as mute as stones, and stones do not make very good companions.

Just as she was about to lengthen her stride to flank Philip, Erik sidled over to her and seemed to be preparing to speak. She waited, glancing askance at where he stood by her right hand.

"I hope you have not taken any of my words to be disrespectful, in any manner," he said at last.

"Disrespectful enough to make me angry." She stared straight ahead. "But not enough for me to have you executed."

He was solemn until she, unable to contain herself, let out burst of laughter. A minuscule grin flickered on his face as he realized the joke.

She glanced at the longbow strung about his torso. Unlike her own, Erik's quiver hung at his side, for which reason she had not noticed it before.

"You can draw a good bow?" she asked.

"Perhaps, but there stands a vast difference between one who can draw a good bow and one who can shoot a good shot." Erik smiled. "I've trained with it my whole life, to be honest."

"So have I!"

"Really? I love to shoot. It's the only useful form of weaponry in this country. Still, Philip insists on practicing with that blimey sword of his day after day. I spar with him—mostly to amuse his fancy."

"Swords aren't so useless. The king trained me a little bit, 'just in case, as a last resort for your life,' he told me."

Erik shrugged. "Swords are weapons of war, not the equipment of farmers and hunters."

She tilted her head back and forth, feigning indifference. She didn't want an argument. A debate could clearly go on for hours between them once it started. She reached out and fingered the edge of the longbow. "What a beautiful bow. Elm, just like mine, correct?"

He nodded. "Here, hold it." He removed it from his back and handed it to her.

She fingered the empty string and pulled it back, feeling the weight and tension. "This is the best bow in all of Reinhold."

"Keep it, then."

She shoved it back into his hand. "No, I cannot take this. It is yours."

"Philip made it, you know."

Of course—the tillering contraption had been in the carpentry shop. She glanced over at Philip where he walked in the lead, his boots stamping leaf and twig underfoot yet still gliding smoothly across the forest floor. The bow's craftsmanship seemed yet another confirmation that he could be the friend—the brother—she desired.

She hesitated a moment before crunching over to him.

Bo Burnette/76

Chapter Eleven: Crossing the River

At first, Arliss thought that perhaps Philip had not noticed her. He continued walking onward, crumpling autumn leaves beneath his feet and glancing about the woods every few paces. This went on for some time, and Arliss realized she would have to initiate any conversation which might occur.

She threw a glance in his direction. "Who taught you to use a sword?"

He maintained his brisk pace, but his steps seemed to stutter. "Myself, mostly. I mean, my uncle taught me some, but he never really learned much."

"Then why did he have two swords for you and Erik to practice with?"

"They're not his."

"You mean he stole them?"

"No, of course not! They were my father's. One of the few things I have left from him."

"Then…"

"Yes, my parents are dead."

"I'm sorry, Philip," she whispered. She liked the way his name glided off her lips.

"It's all right. They died back on the isle. I never knew them, really."

"How did they die?"

"My father was always rather sickly. Once he got very ill, far worse than anything the isle apothecary had seen before. Then, after he seemed to be taking a turn for the better, he died in his sleep one night. It was the strangest thing. Grief drove my mother to her grave, so they say. My aunt and uncle raised me, and Erik is quite like a brother to me in every way, as are the rest of my cousins."

"And your family is…decently well off?"

"We're not rich, if that's what you mean." He ran his hand through his hair. "I do sometimes worry that I am burdensome to my aunt and uncle. They have more mouths to feed and bodies to house than most others in the village."

"And you are happy? Even as a peasant? Maybe my new friendship with you could bring you some good."

He did not answer for a long time. Then he spoke quietly, and she stepped closer to hear his voice. "You don't understand."

"I don't understand what?"

"Anything. Can you not see that?"

"Excuse me, but do you remember who you're speaking to?"

"I can speak my mind as well as you can, Arliss."

"It's *Princess* Arliss, thank you."

"No, it isn't, according to you. You say we are equals, that princess and peasant ought not be so divided. So I shall speak to you as an equal. And—I'm not finished, so save your breath—it's true that you do not understand. You cannot even comprehend your own quest!"

Words failed her for a moment.

"You are in the woods with two people you hardly know on a fantastical quest to find a place that may or may not exist. In fact, I would wager you don't even quite know what it is we're looking for. You've no real sense of direction—so it's a good thing I'm in front—and you don't seem to believe your own ideas, at least not all the way. That sounds to me like you don't understand."

"What do you know? A peasant farmer who has hardly even been out of his own house!"

"I thought there was no such thing as a peasant."

He had brought her to the end of her rope. "I believe in equality between us, but I do not believe in honoring disrespectful subjects."

"I'm just explaining my thoughts, princess. You asked me to, remember?"

She looked away. She wanted to hit him. Every muscle in her body seemed to scream for revenge. She would do it—she would—she had to. He deserved it. No, no, that was a foolish idea; he was far too strong for her to do any real harm to him. She would get her revenge some other way.

She frowned at herself. Revenge? Absurd. He had insulted her, that was all. She needed to show him he was wrong about her. This quest was about more than just finding the heart of Reinhold.

If she was successful, she could prove herself, prove that she was indeed the princess on a carven throne which the poem spoke of. She would truly be that princess with a queenly look in her eye and grace on her forehead.

And perhaps—Arliss disliked herself for consciously entertaining the idea—perhaps she could turn that carpenter's apprentice into a surrogate brother. Perhaps.

Philip could hear the sound of running water long before they reached it. He knew every step toward that sound brought him closer to breaking the law of the realm. To cross the river was to dance with death.

Of course, the blame would lie on the princess. It was her quest, anyway. He glanced at her over his shoulder, noticing her thick golden hair streaming in the breeze. She refused to look at him or acknowledge him. Had he spoken too harshly?

No, of course not. She needed to hear every word he had spoken to her, and maybe more. If she chose to play the insulted child, then that was her choice.

He knew what she really wanted; her face gave it away all too plainly. Above anything, she desired a friendship with him. That desire lay under everything she said—of course, until he had knocked her thoughts around a bit. Why had she chosen him for this quest? Why did she want such a friendship? And why was she really doing all this?

Philip stopped short in his thoughts. They had reached the banks of the river, and greenish-blue water gurgled just beneath his feet.

Nowhere in sight was there a crossing.

The river appeared before Arliss so suddenly she had to steady herself on a nearby tree to keep from plunging in. She could have reached out for Philip's strong form for support. But she did not, would not, could not.

He paced the riverbank, searching for a crossing that simply wasn't there. He stopped pacing and strode away to the left. "I'll look for a crossing this way. You look in the other direction."

She nodded, then turned to call Erik over. She flinched when she saw he was already standing right beside her. His steps were noiseless.

He stared, transfixed, at the tree which had prevented her from drowning.

The moment she glanced at it, she jerked her hand from the bark and wiped it fiercely on the back of her cloak. But nothing could remove the feeling of having touched something so horrible.

Darkness seemed to have consumed the tree like a tangible shadow. It was like the first dark tree, and yet far more massive and deathly in appearance. She could not have wrapped her arms all the way around it.

Ilayda caught up to them and tilted her head, her brow wrinkled with curiosity. "What are you staring at?"

Erik ignored her and addressed his statement to Arliss. "I know it without a doubt now. Someone—evil beast, evil person, or otherwise—has intentionally poisoned these trees. Things like this do not just happen."

Arliss raised an eyebrow. "Maybe it's something of a disease among the trees, and it's just a matter of happenstance that we have come across two such trees in the same afternoon."

"Happenstance? Do you really believe there is any such thing?"

"Of course," she said, but felt inside that she did not know how to reply at all.

Philip came bounding back to them. "Nothing. There's not a crossing in sight."

Arliss glanced at him, then back at the dark tree. Then she squared her shoulders and faced him. "We're going to make a crossing."

The forest reverberated with the sound of clanging metal as the sword bit into the tree once more, slashing through the murky bark. With a sigh, Arliss folded her arms. How long did it have to take, really? Philip must have been hacking away with that sword for five whole minutes, but with little progress to show for it. She glowered at his bent back as he cut again, swinging the blade from over his shoulder.

A distant noise distracted her, and she gazed at the other side of the riverbank. It seemed darker over there, though the trees were all lit in a strange manner. Some stood clear as daylight, but whole groups of trees crowded in blots of shadow.

Those were dark trees, poisoned in a like manner as this one. Even now, she saw such a tree standing at the very edge of the river, just across from where she stood.

Philip stood. "It's weakening."

"One would hope," Arliss said.

He glared beneath lowered brows, then addressed Erik. "Come, help me push. I think it will go down now."

They shoved against the trunk, and the base of the tree crackled and swayed. Philip's sword had carved through a massive swath of wood. And, as they pushed and strained, Arliss saw that her plan just might work.

"Arliss, help. Now."

Philip's breathless, curt demand left her with no response but to obey. She squeezed into the gap between them and braced her hands against the tree trunk, shoving with every scrap of her strength. After many long, excruciating moments, wood crackled as if in a roaring fire.

His face blood red and his neck tense as a bowstring, Philip struggled with the massive log as he tried to slow its fall. It came slamming down on the opposite bank, right at the base of the other dark tree which she had seen.

Erik mounted the newly felled bridge with a catlike agility. "If your mind is set upon this foolishness, then let us do it quickly."

Arliss swallowed and knelt down, securing all her belongings.

"This is ridiculous," Ilayda huffed as Philip offered his hand to help her onto the log. "I don't think any discoveries or whatnot are worth this foolishness."

"You can stop talking about me behind my back," Arliss said. "I can hear you."

"We're not behind your back," Ilayda quipped. "We're in front of you."

Arliss pursed her lips and tightened the strap of her quiver about her waist, mimicking Erik's methods. Her bow she strung and slipped over her head, letting the string tighten across her chest. Making sure the leather satchel was latched tightly, she walked over to the makeshift bridge and took a deep breath.

Philip hesitated before offering a hand dingy with scrapings of tree bark and moss. She stared at it for several long moments. The temptation to refuse him was strong. Utter dislike and resentment for his harsh words rose up inside her chest and demanded that she rebuff him.

Yet, for all her misanthropic feelings at that moment, she remembered the inexplicable connection she had felt the moment she first saw him. She turned her gaze from his dirty hand to his pure, colorful eyes.

She grasped his hand and allowed him to pull her onto the log.

Philip stepped up onto the narrow bridge, placing one foot in front of the other, in an exaggerated swordsman's stance. Ahead, Erik led the way, glancing over his shoulder at them every few moments. Ilayda treaded a few paces behind him.

Moss and black debris glazed the entire tree, and Philip nearly slipped more than once. He had to stay focused. Step, step, one foot, another foot. Beneath the log, the river roared angrily on its course south. One misstep and any member of the company could be washed away.

He stared at the log beneath his boots. If they made it across, what then? What really lay deep in the woods in the heart of the country—the heart that Arliss so wanted to find?

Ilayda gasped sharply, startling Philip's focused movements. Erik reached back to steady her, his movements slow and stiff.

"Do you need help?"

Ilayda snorted. "I can walk across a log by myself, thank you."

Erik called back. "Why, again, is this forbidden, Arliss?"

"Because my father is a fearful fool. That's all I wish to say," Arliss snapped.

Philip narrowed an eye at her. What secret was she hiding beneath all these brusque answers?

"Look." She pointed at something, her sapphire eyes focused and fearful.

Philip followed her motion to the opposite bank and the dark tree which lay directly at the end of their log bridge. The felled log had smashed into the base of the other tree, and now the upright tree wobbled precariously. If it fell, it would surely break their bridge, if not crush them all into the river.

They had only made it halfway across.

"Hurry, Erik, please," Arliss commanded.

Erik stretched his steps.

Ilayda's breaths sounded short and halting, and Arliss knew she was terrified. With her hands stretched out on either side, she focused on her own balance. Ilayda could fend for herself.

Philip's voice jutted in behind her. "We're not going to make it in time."

"Shut up, and just try!" Arliss snapped.

Philip tottered closer to her, sidestepping clots of feathery moss and brown lichen. "Princess, I know you're still angry with me, and I know why. But you have to stop. If we are going to succeed at this thing, we need to be together."

"It seems like we are going to be together, so to speak, whether I want to be or not."

"I thought it was you who sought me out—wanted me as your guide?"

"Well, that was my mistake!"

"You really wanted someone to tell you that everything you do is right? Someone who obeys your every command?" He stepped closer, grabbing her arms.

Were he not holding her, she could fall at any moment, yet she shouted, "Let me go!"

"I don't feel inclined to obey your every whim at the moment, Arliss." He smirked, then whispered, "I am not Ilayda."

Unable to contain herself any longer, she burst into laughter.

Erik whirled around—as much as he could on the slippery log. "Arliss, Philip—focus! Please!" He and Ilayda had doubled the distance between themselves and the other two and had almost reached the other side.

"We can make it!" Arliss stepped away from Philip.

A massive crackling interrupted her words, thoughts, and steps. On the other bank, the tree had been slowly weakening, and now the blackened trunk began to fall, its base popping and snapping. Erik and Ilayda made a last attempt to cross, running and leaping towards the opposite shore.

"Arliss, quick. Tie that rope in your satchel to an arrow," Philip ordered.

Arliss wanted to argue, to defy his command. Instead, she did as he demanded, tying a knot around the arrow with trembling fingers. Ahead of them, Erik pulled Ilayda onto the shore just before the tree tilted several more feet.

"Arliss…" Philip's voice jolted.

"I'm trying!" She jerked the knot tight and nocked the arrow with shaking hands. "What now?"

"Shoot that huge tree near the shore."

"The one on the left?" She took aim.

"That one—hurry! Now!"

She pulled the arrow back as far as she could. It flew into the tree, embedding the shaft halfway into the bark. Suddenly, she felt his arms around her waist. He cinched the loop he had made with the other end of the rope, and steadied her now as the log bridge buckled under the bending tree.

"Philip!" Erik called.

"The rope, Erik!" Philip yelled back.

Erik ran to the arrow.

In an instant, the dark tree's base snapped and toppled over into the river. Arliss winced, preparing to be crushed.

Philip pulled her back several feet, just before the tree slammed into the bridge and split it in two.

"Jump!" he shouted, and they hurled themselves onto the split half of the log.

The strike of the wood and the chill of the river knocked out her breath for a moment.

Philip held onto the rope with both hands. Yet nothing was holding him to the log. The rope started to skid his body off the trunk.

Gasping for air, Arliss reached over and grabbed his ankle with one hand, wrapping her other arm around the log. The bark dug into her side as she hooked her arm tighter.

On the shore, Erik tugged at the rope, pulling against the flow of the river. The log which held Arliss and Philip wavered in the coursing waters, drifting back and forth, closer and closer to the shore.

Philip took the chance. He wrapped his arm around Arliss and tumbled off the log. They landed half on the shore and half in the water. Their legs were drenched, but they had made it.

Arliss lay there gasping for a while with Philip's arm still draped about her back. She dragged herself onto the shore and stood.

Philip sat up in the muddy sand and hid his hands behind his back. "Aren't you missing something?"

She tossed her soaked hair. "What could I possibly be missing?"

"Check your quiver."

Her arrows—gone. No. It couldn't be. She fumbled at her side, stuffed her hand into the stiff leather. Empty. "No—no! But…"

He brandished three arrows for her to see. "I managed to save a few."

Chapter Twelve: Lasairblath

Arliss wrung out her dripping golden hair. The bottom of her blue woolen dress stuck to her skin, so she strode around for several paces, trying to dry out. It helped nothing.

She leaned against a gnarled trunk, one of the only trees in the vicinity that showed no signs of poison—of darkness. The darkness permeated this side of the river, stretching as far into the woods as she could see. Had her father been right to forbid this passage?

No. No matter what had happened here in the past, it had gone. Surely no evil of consequence lurked here.

Something crunched beneath her feet. She looked down and saw what she had stepped on: a thin, translucent piece of papery material. It seemed to be a fragment torn from something larger, something strange and unfamiliar.

"What are we to do now?" Erik's question drew her attention away from the crackling item.

"Continue on the quest, of course."

"Arliss, are you mad?"

"Why do you ask?"

He huffed. "You cannot be serious. All this, and you're still insisting we go on?"

"I wouldn't call a bumpy trip across the river 'all this.' Just a mere interruption."

"Are you so blind?" He pointed into the depths of the woods. "To go into there?"

"Are you so afraid?"

"I am not a fool." Erik's lower lip pursed.

"Good," she snapped. "Then you will do as you are told."

Ilayda moved towards her. "You have to quit talking to all of us like we're children! We're your companions, not your students."

"You're my subjects, are you not?"

Philip shook his head. "You sound just like your father."

"Silence!" She turned on him, his brave rescue quickly slipping from her mind. "I sound nothing like that fool."

Ilayda gasped. Philip, for once, looked almost wounded by her outburst.

Arliss hesitated. Had she truly hurt him in what she had said? But no, she had neither time nor patience to care. He would learn not to be so brash in his words. "We move on until sundown."

So she turned into the darkness and walked on, not caring whether they followed her, and forgetting all about the strange item upon which she had stepped.

The day was growing old, nearing dinnertime. They would need to stop soon. Arliss's legs were beginning to complain about the many long miles of walking.

"We need to stop and get some victuals soon," she commented to Erik.

"A very perspicacious thought, princess." He stared straight ahead. "But not here. I don't like the look of this place."

His uneasiness was not unfounded. All around them, the dark trees towered, and the ground lay streaked with brownish moss. The woods permitted no view of an end anywhere in sight.

"It's not going to get much better, though." She sighed and continued dragging her feet along. What if the forest went on forever? Or at least for many days and weeks? How would she ever know, and how could they be certain of their way home?

What if they walked right past the heart of Reinhold and never knew?

Philip began singing in a soft, clear voice like a mountain stream, quieting her fears:

A princess on a carven throne
Clothed in simple raiment
A queenly look is in her eye
And grace is on her forehead

A princess on a smooth-hewn throne
Clothed in linen raiment
A queenly look is in her eye
And grace is on her forehead

A princess on a gilded throne
Clothed in silken raiment
A queenly look is in her eye
And grace is on her forehead.

Arliss stared at him. "That song! Where did you learn it?"

"My mother had a book of songs passed down through the ages by our people and others. I learned many of them. Eventually I gave the book to the castle's library, like so many others."

"Then you can read music?"

"I can follow along decently well."

She smiled. "I play the fiddle—my mother taught me."

"Really?" His eyes brightened. "I've always been curious about instruments. Do you think—"

Erik stopped them in their tracks with a downward wave of his hand. His voice dropped low as he spoke. "We have to leave now, by whatever means possible."

"What's wrong?" Arliss's pulse quickened.

"We're in grave danger," Erik whispered. "I found something on the ground over there."

He held something thin and papery, like the thing Arliss had stepped on, yet this one had not been torn. The entire ugly thing lay one and whole in Erik's hands. Philip peered at it in confusion, but Arliss recognized it with a sickening knowledge. This was the one thing which plagued her when she read books of forests and creatures, and the one thing which the first explorers of this land had feared, according to the book which was even now in her satchel.

Now, right in front of her face, Erik held the long, papery sloughing.

A snakeskin.

Her heart throbbed with unusual, almost frantic, intensity. A sick feeling of collywobbles rose up in her stomach, and she gripped Philip's arm for support.

He glanced at her distress, his brow knit with concern. "Are you well?"

She nodded. "Just fine. We must get back across the river…find another way in."

"There are no other ways, not unless you want to go all the way north and around the mountains. They're as sheer as sheets and well nigh impassable," Erik said. "Even here in the forest you'll eventually come to their rocky roots, and who knows if those, too, cannot be crossed?"

"Then we must—"

Behind her, Ilayda released a high shriek of terror.

"Don't move!" Arliss nocked an arrow as she hurried into the forest, toward her friend's voice. "I'm coming!"

Behind her, Erik and Philip unsheathed their swords and followed her, their feet crunching leaves and twigs. She clambered out into a clearing which seemed to materialize around her. Dark trees were clustered in edges round the clearing's border.

Ilayda trembled on the forest floor, her deep hair tangled, her purple dress quivering on her shaking shoulders.

Inches away from her, an incredibly long serpent undulated its girth toward Ilayda, its forked tongue flickering like a flame. The striped spirals oozed their way across fallen leaves.

The snake coiled up for a strike. Ilayda screamed again.

Arliss's arrow pierced through the coils, stabbing through the vile creature's head and pinning its corkscrewed body to the ground. It writhed and wriggled for many moments after the killing.

Wasting no time, Arliss gripped Ilayda's shaking hand with her own unsteady one and hoisted her to her feet. Erik and Philip burst into the clearing at that very moment.

"Arliss!" Philip shouted. He must have been shouting for her as he ran. His face was written in letters of worry and apprehension—but no fear. How did he even have the nerve to keep his sword upright?

The sun—or what she could see of it—had begun to set. The light in the forest dimmed and reddened. Soon it would be too dark to go on.

"Now we *must* go back." Erik nodded at the dead snake on the ground.

As if at his words, a dozen more snakes slithered from behind trees and blocked their path back to the river.

Arliss held her tongue and willed Ilayda to do the same. This wasn't a time for jabbering.

The four companions backed nearer to each other as the snakes slithered around the edge of the clearing as if it were a bordered realm or a walled fortress. Arliss could sense the tension emanating from Philip's taut body. The knuckles around his sword seemed white as…

…as the white patch of light which shone deep in the forest almost beyond her sight. She had not noticed it until now. What could it be? It was too white for a torch or campfire. Whatever it was, it was light and not darkness. They had to make it to the whiteness if possible.

It certainly did not appear to be a possibility at the present. The serpents neared every moment. Even now Arliss could see the intricate stripes on their backs, the hideously dark eyes. Never had she seen such unnaturally dark and evil creatures attack and move with such order.

Philip's whisper was hoarse. "What is your plan, princess?"

He'd been using her given name earlier. Why had he suddenly turned cold and formal? She hissed, "Surely you or Erik one must have a splendid idea."

"Please, princess," Philip said. "Think."

"All right. I see a light over there, in the opposite direction of the river."

"You mean go deeper in?" Erik put in with an angry whisper.

"Bloody yes, I do," Arliss retorted.

Philip took a breath and a hesitant step. "We move slowly. Have your weapons ready."

Arliss's every step was excruciating. She tried not to look at the snakes and hoped they were not looking at her. For whatever reason, the creatures lay still as corpses.

She breathed, stepped, breathed, stepped, as if she walked on thin glass. An ominous stillness ruled in the dark glade. Philip breathed heavily beside her.

Then, at the clearing's boundary a snake at the closest edge of the serpentine ring coiled up and hurled itself at Philip. Ilayda shrieked. Philip slashed his sword and hacked the creature in two. Black blood spurted from its dismembered form.

At this, the other snakes began sliding madly in circles, lines, and up and down trees. They did not strike yet, but acted as soldiers preparing for battle. Arliss felt she might be sick.

Philip, his voice strained and shaking, motioned to the others. "Quick. Run for the light, as fast as you can."

"But, Philip," Erik whispered, "That's the wrong way!"

"Can't you see the way to the river is blocked?" Philip said with the authority of an older brother. "Now go! All three of you, get to the light!"

"What about you?" The question slipped from Arliss's mouth before she thought about it.

"I shall be right behind you."

He did not make a very good liar. Still, she obeyed him, grabbing Ilayda's hand and dragging her away from the clearing. The snakes were still slithering around like strands of demoniac vines, strangling the forest.

Erik had his sword out as he covered them, and Arliss had an arrow on the string. Ilayda held no weapon. Arliss walked as fast as she could without making noise; even so, the space between them and the whiteness did not seem to be growing much smaller.

She glanced over her shoulder at Philip. He had stepped just outside the clearing and now stood with his sword toward the gathering serpents. His gaze met hers, and they locked eyes for a long moment. She did not turn away. She stood transfixed by the fierce care that permeated his gaze. He wasn't just acting the brother to Erik.

He was doing it for her as well.

She turned and marched on, not once looking back from then on. They neared the whiteness, an area comprised of several smaller parts. They came nearer still, and it looked like patches of snow. From within twenty paces of the white stuff, it resembled silvery paper.

Erik stopped her for a moment. "I'm going back to Philip. Stay here."

"I make no promises," she responded.

He huffed. With a stern stare, he turned and dashed back to his cousin.

The serpents must have been following them in the murkiness of the trees all the way, for one sprang from the darkening shadows of the surrounding forest and blocked their way. Ilayda shouted for Arliss. The snake preparing to spring on her was dead with Arliss's arrow through its open mouth even before Ilayda finished calling.

"Run!" Arliss grabbed her forearm and dashed for the white, open space.

The serpents raced along just behind them, hissing through curved fangs. Arliss released Ilayda's hand just before they reached the whiteness. Drawing an arrow—her last arrow—she stepped into the mysterious white stuff and turned to face the serpents. She would cover Ilayda to the end.

With a serpent hissing at her heels, Ilayda tripped over a root and tumbled into the milky expanse of the clearing. Arliss stretched her bow all the way.

She did not release the arrow. There was no need to. The snakes had stopped their pursuit and lay wriggling at the borders of the pale clearing. The creatures refused to come any farther. As unnatural as the serpents' aggression had been, this new development seemed even more unusual.

"Arliss, look," Ilayda whispered with an awestruck voice. "The flowers."

Arliss let the tension out of her bow and took in her surroundings. Gentle white flowers swirled the forest floor around her, covering a space about the size of her own bedroom at the castle. The petals shone pure white, with the furthest edges of them graced with a pale purple. They had appeared in the book about Reinhold, the book which she carried in her satchel. That book seemed to carry many secrets. It had even given her the name of the flower: Lasairbláth.

So they weren't just legend. They were *real*.

On the fringe of the grove lay a snake, writhing and convulsing. Its skin had turned from striped green to an ashy grey, and it rolled to and fro. Finally, it ceased all movement and lay limp at the border of the flowering clearing.

"Do you know what this means, Ilayda? The flowers kill the snakes. We can beat them!"

She gathered up an armload of loose petals and stuffed them into her satchel. She knelt and turned her head back toward the now-distant clearing of snakes. Somehow, she would retrieve her other two arrows.

She would need them.

Philip lunged with his sword, trying to fend off the serpent that was seeping down from the branches above him. It hissed, enraged, and slithered through his legs, trying to attack him from behind. He slashed the thing in half before it even rose to strike.

He wasn't fond of snakes. No sir, especially not ones this enormous. Repulsive creatures with neither arms nor legs.

Erik, on the other hand, cut through snakes left and right with little apprehension. Philip dashed over to join him. Their swords scythed the vile serpents like sheaves of wheat, yet more still came. Their numbers seemed to be increasing rather than the opposite.

With sweat streaming down his face, Philip put everything into the strength of his sword. He pivoted left to slice a wayward snake.

"Philip!" Erik yelled. A snake had attached itself to his forearm.

Philip grasped the tail of the snake and wrenched it from Erik's arm. Erik gasped in pain.

The scaly tail of the serpent felt disgusting. It sent chills up and down Philip's arm. But it all happened within a splinter of a second.

"Erik, grab your sword!"

Erik nabbed it from the ground, and they raised their blades. Philip swung the snake up and released it. The two swords met against each other and split the snake in two. The halves flopped onto the ground in a slimy mess.

Philip and Erik backed towards one another. The remaining creatures were once again encircling the clearing. How could there be so many? And would even more be coming?

Philip kept a wary eye on the snakes and stepped backward until he collided with Erik. "We have to get to Arliss."

"Looks like we need her to get to us," Erik remarked. "I'm sure you'd agree."

Heat rose into Philip's cheeks. He kicked his cousin's heel from behind. "I'm not sure what you are thinking, but I'd probably stop thinking it anyway." Philip quieted. He thought he had heard a scream: a distant, almost inhuman call. Was it...

"Arliss!" Philip raised his voice for the first time. The snakes twitched at the noise. "Arliss!" His voice strained with tension. No, she had to be safe. Yet still she did not answer. An orangish snake slithered nearer to him. "Arliss!"

An arrow stuck the creature as it sprang to attack. Arliss burst into the clearing, one last arrow on her string. Ilayda hurried behind her, carrying a torch.

"Philip!" Arliss called. "I'm here!" Her golden hair flying, she spun toward the gathering of snakes. She didn't shoot her arrow, though. Instead, she cast whitish petals all around. Her open satchel was full of them.

"What is this?" Philip asked, bewildered, as he joined her.

"Lasairbláth—a powerful and ancient flower. It's poison to the snakes."

A flash of light exploded behind them, and the snakes fled into the darkness.

"When the petals are burned, it seems that they snap and flare in an unusual way," Ilayda explained. "Quite convenient, don't you think?"

"Come on." Erik beckoned to the others as he strode toward the edge of the clearing. "Let's get out of here."

"This way," Arliss nodded as she yanked two arrows from coiled corpses.

Philip's chest sank heavily as he followed her—farther into the forest, farther from the river, farther from the castle, and closer to the heart of Reinhold.

Ilayda filled her lungs with the air that smelled deep and dark—like the purple edges of the flaming sunset. She could barely glimpse it now above the tangle of silhouetted trees.

She crossed her arms tight across her chest and let her breath shudder out. Adrenaline still prickled her skin and refused to let her pulse normalize. It had been *that* close. She had stared death in the eyes—its shiny, serpentine eyes.

She squeezed her eyes shut. If it wasn't for Arliss, that snake would have devoured her.

She opened her eyes and stared at Arliss's shadowy form up in the lead. If it wasn't for Arliss, they wouldn't be on this adventure in the first place.

It wasn't safe. But they had made it across the river, and the snakes seemed to be fully behind them. Who knew? Maybe the heart of Reinhold lay just beyond.

Erik slowed and let her catch up to him. He eyed her a moment, then reached into his bag.

She glanced briefly toward his rummaging hands. She didn't want to seem too interested in such a standoffish peasant.

He drew a sheathed hunting knife from the bag, flung it into midair, and caught it with his other hand. He tilted the handle toward her. "Here."

She reached cautiously for the hilt. "A...knife."

"Astute observation."

She narrowed her eyes at him. "But why?"

He snorted. "This forest isn't safe. You shouldn't be unarmed."

"I thought you were our guide, not our bodyguard."

He shrugged. "What about both?"

They had almost come upon the circle of Lasairbláth again. Surely, surely, they would stop now and rest. It had been the longest day of her life.

Ilayda accepted the knife from Erik, undid her thin belt, and strung the weapon around her waist. "Thank you."

"We *are* going to camp here for the night." Erik halted and dropped his knapsack on the petal-strewn floor.

Arliss was too tired to argue. She knelt down among the flowers and began to undo her satchel, drawing out the pork and oranges. The fruit had been somewhat squished during the incident with the snakes, but it would be edible. It had to be. Their stores might not last even another day. Somehow, they would have to recross the river and abandon their quest.

Her quest. That's what it had turned out to be, hadn't it? Ilayda complained about her every idea. Erik criticized each move she made, much like the king did. Yet she did not want to think about her father—about facing him once again. If she found nothing on this mission, she would return to the castle as a lawbreaker and a reprobate, with no spoils to show for her heroism.

She clenched her eyes shut. That would not happen.

Philip had forced Erik to lie down and was tending to his snakebite. The wound had not torn deeply, only scarred the outer flesh. Philip tore a strip of fabric from a spare tunic in his bag and wrapped it around Erik's forearm. Erik winced as Philip tied it in place.

Arliss felt her senses blurring from tiredness. Her hands moved mechanically through tasks: passing out victuals to the other three, taking careful sips of water from her flask, spreading out a blanket. As her eyelids began to drift shut, she could glimpse Philip sitting up at the edge of the forest, keeping a vigilant watch.

They would be safe that night.

Chapter Thirteen:
The Master of the Forest

Someone shook Arliss's shoulder, awakening her from uneasy dreams. Her eyelids fluttered open as she rolled fully onto her back, feeling the stiffness from the previous day's escapades.

"Good morning," Philip said.

She grunted and closed her eyes again.

"Erik caught some breakfast."

She yawned. "I knew I brought him along for a reason."

Philip grinned. "He found something else, when he was hunting."

She was awake now. "What?"

"A light. In the woods. He saw it from afar."

Her hair rippled off her shoulders as she sat up, staring at him. "A light in the woods? But that means—"

"We're not alone."

Erik tapped his small, iron pan with a stirring spoon. "Come on, you three sleepynuggins. Breakfast it is."

He took the tiny pan and scooped out meat into four even tinier bowls. The meat looked gristly but digestible—rabbit, if Arliss wasn't mistaken. Well, couldn't have venison every day.

As Erik continued his spoon-tapping, Ilayda simply moaned and moved her left foot. He slid over to her and banged the spoon again, holding the pot right next to her ear.

This time she rolled off her blanket, getting a mouthful of Lasairbláth petals.

"Stupid princess!" she protested, rubbing her eyes.

"I'm not a princess," Erik said.

Ilayda glowered at him. "Oh, you."

Arliss rolled her eyes at them as she stood and strode over to Erik's simple meal. Some fish would have been quite an improvement over tough wild rabbit. Yet it didn't really matter. Too much else pulled at her mind. The dark trees—had they been caused by the snakes? It seemed likely. But what about the snakes? What had caused them?

"You saw something, Erik," she said between chomping bites.

"Yes, I did." He nodded. "But I do not think you ought to see it."

"I know what you're going to say. That I've led us astray, that I shouldn't be allowed to go any farther on this quest. Maybe you're right. But I know that we must continue while we still can."

Erik swallowed. "I phrased it differently in my head. If you see the light and its source, you'll want to explore it, and you will not give up until you have."

Arliss smiled. "I suppose you can put it that way, too. And you're right—I am going to finish this quest, no matter the cost." She winced, her last words having come out harsher than she had anticipated. "What is the source of the light?"

"A house."

The ramshackle house was a poorly constructed affair—Arliss could tell that much even from far off. The wooden door looked too big for the doorframe, and the cloudy windows were unevenly spaced. The interweaving trees so enveloped the building that it seemed to almost blend into its wooded surroundings.

"The lights have been lit since early this morning. I never saw any movement," Erik whispered as he and Arliss stole along. Philip and Ilayda crunched on dead leaves behind them. Of all seasons to travel silently, autumn certainly wasn't the best—though it was the most beautiful.

Arliss fingered the three arrows which remained by her side. Only three.

They were nearing the shack already. Erik stopped her and stared at the building from behind a thick tree trunk. "What do you think is in there?"

She shook her head. "I don't know."

"Arliss, you have to tell me. There's something about your quest you have been hiding from me this whole time. I can see it in your eyes. Please, as a friend, tell me. Why did your father forbid crossing the river?"

She sighed and closed her eyes. Erik was clever, too clever. He could read her too well—all three of them could, in truth. She had no choice but to tell them.

"Five years ago, my father and many of the men from the village went hunting in the woods. For the first time, they crossed the river and hunted on this side of its banks. One of the men was lost that day. He went scouting on his own, and never returned to the company. His coat was found bloodied and torn, but they never recovered the body. After that, my father forbade anyone to come here."

"And you've dragged us right back?" Ilayda glanced around. "This place is downright creepy."

"It's more than just creepy. According to her," Erik said, "it's dangerous."

Arliss's arms tensed. "But that was five years ago! Why should one man's death cause an entire country to cease exploring?"

"But, how—" Philip began. A stark, terrible noise cut him off. A piercing, inhuman cry sliced through the murky silence of the misty woods.

It had come from the house.

Philip gripped his sword hilt.

She put a hand on his arm and felt the muscles ripple through his sleeve. "Please, Philip, don't go in there."

"I have to. Someone's in there, and it sounds as if they are in trouble—dying, even." He shook her hand off his arm.

"We will come with you, then." Arliss pursed her lips and set an arrow to her bow. Erik nocked an arrow on his longbow as well, and Ilayda gripped a hunting knife. The sight of Ilayda holding a weapon was rather amusing.

Philip took the lead and strode to the door of the dilapidated cottage. The being within groaned like a wild beast. The door stood locked. Philip drew his sword and hacked at the wood without hesitation. The thin, warped door buckled, and they entered the house over a pile of huge wood splinters.

Inside, the furnishings were sparse: a tiny table with two chairs, a brass kettle over a makeshift fireplace, and a shelf with various vials and gourds on it. In the far left corner, a creaking bed supported the weight of a moaning figure.

Philip and Arliss eased toward him.

"He will not offer much fight, it seems," Philip whispered, his boots clamping softly on the floorboards.

At the sound of his footsteps, the body on the bed moved, his unsteady breathing normalizing.

"Master..." the man coughed. "Master, there is a disturbance—a great disturbance. I don't rightly know what's caused it. Beat me not, please, for I haven't a thought as to what has disturbed 'em. Please..." his voice muffled off into nothingness.

He turned his head toward them and opened his eyes. A ruffled mop of graying hair framed a haggard face with wild green eyes. He might have been a handsome young man once. Now, he seemed barely human.

His eyes widened. "Who...the master...I didn't do it..." A strange look of recognition took over his face. "Arliss? The princess?"

Her heart jumped. How did he know her name?

He shook his head. "You should never have come here. Never, never. He knows. He is coming. He will find you and kill you."

"Who is *he*?"

"The master," was all he offered. "My lady, please. Run from here as fast as you can, warn your father, do anything! Do you not know me?"

She knelt beside the bed. "I am not sure, sir."

"My lady, I am a man of Reinhold—or I was. I am Áedán."

"Áedán?" she gasped. "It cannot be. You are alive?"

Philip knelt beside her. "Who is he?"

Arliss turned, tears forming in her eyes. "He is the one who was lost. He is the reason it is forbidden to cross the river." She clenched her fists on the edge of the bed. "All these years, you have been here, and my father's foolish laws have prevented us from saving you. Curse him!"

"Arliss!" Ilayda rebuked.

"No, princess!" Áedán grasped her hand. "Your father is right not to come here. There is nothing in this forest but death and decay. I tell you, there is no time, you mustn't stay here a moment more! Leave!"

A sudden fit of coughing seized him, and his body writhed as he spat blood upon his pillow. His grasp on her hand weakened.

"No, Áedán, please," she begged tenderly.

"There is no more life in me, my lady," he managed. "Nor for the land of Reinhold. A dark fire is coming and has already come, and it will eat away at your people until there are none left. Do not ignore the evil of lust—the lust for power, for possession. It has destroyed the heart of the master."

"Who is this master you speak of?"

Áedán's voice had so weakened, she needed to lean toward him to hear. "Thane! Thane has come!"

Arliss had no time to take in his words. Window glass shattered. A javelin slit through the air just by her right ear, embedding in the wall above Áedán's bed. Ilayda shrieked. Erik snatched at his quiver.

Philip tackled Arliss to the floor as another javelin flew through the place her head had been moments before.

She leapt to her feet just as two shadowy soldiers burst into the hut, trampling splinters of the wooden door beneath their feet. Each held a massive, ugly sword. They had sinewy arms with blue paint smeared on their forearms. Their clothing was dark fabric and aged leather, with little metal armor. In the dark forest, they must have been invisible.

Arliss nocked an arrow in an instant, but that wasn't quick enough. The first warrior closed the distance between them and arced his sword in a wide semicircle, as if trying to swipe off all four of their heads at once.

Erik and Ilayda ducked down, and Arliss backed just out of sword's length.

Philip stood his ground and brought his sword to bear against the grim warrior's.

He slowed the course of the blade's arc, but the momentum and power behind the sword were too great. The glowering soldier swept his sword clean, and Philip barely held onto his own. The second man began approaching the fight.

Arliss's heart pounded as the first enemy's weapon cut down at Philip. Philip blocked the blow with stunning skill. He parried and sent a thrust which nearly pierced the warrior's left breast. He sidestepped at the last moment, and Philip's sword caught his shoulder. The warrior snarled in pain.

"Who are you, you who dare to enter the dominion of the master?" The warrior's voice rasped, rough and chilling, as if his words were filled with pebbles.

Arliss found her tongue before Philip did. "Who are you, who dare to enter the dominion of the crown of Reinhold? I am…" She stopped, realizing how foolish it would be to reveal her full identity.

The warrior roared and swept his sword as he and his comrade advanced towards them.

Arliss glanced towards Áedán's dead body on the bed, and her face contorted in anguish. These men and their master had killed a man of Reinhold. They would pay. Justice had to be done. She had three arrows left—so she couldn't miss more than once. She wouldn't miss even that one.

The four travelers edged to the back corner of the shack, nearing the window which had been smashed by javelins. Smirking, the warriors retrieved the javelins from the wall, then turned to face Arliss and her company. Death was in their eyes. One blocked the door, the other blocked Áedán's body. Arliss's company could neither escape nor protect the corpse.

Erik slammed the point of his bow into the already shattered window. The rest of the glass crushed and fell to the ground outside. Gripping Ilayda's hand, he half led, half lifted her to the window. She leapt outside, rolling away from the glass shards. Erik followed.

Arliss and Philip were still trapped. With a nod to each other, the warriors separated. The first rushed from the building as the second readied to finish Philip and Arliss off. He stood barely taller than Philip.

"You shall die this very hour," the warrior snarled as he raised his sword.

"All men die," Philip responded, raising his sword like a beam of light, "but we shall not die today."

The swords clanged like lightning, scintillating in the vague sunlight which fought through the dense trees and into the cottage's window. Arliss dropped to the floor, rolling over to the doorway. She stood, gripping the unsteady doorframe.

Outside, Erik was engaging the first warrior while Ilayda gazed into the woods behind the cottage, fear painted on her face. She gripped the long knife. Arliss followed her line of sight to the three other warriors who emerged from the eastern treeline. These were armed like the first two, and two of them had blue paint not only in lines on their forearms but also on their faces.

Arliss's eyes narrowed. She was about to die, largely due to her own foolishness, but she determined to die fighting for herself and her companions. Perhaps some of them would live. Her mother needed to be warned.

"Ilayda!" she shouted. Ilayda ran to her. "Stay beside Erik, no matter what happens!"

"That's a cruel order, silly princess."

"Obey." Arliss spoke more with the love of a sister, and not the demand of a ruler. Ilayda complied.

Erik had downed his man—Arliss had not seen the moment of his victory—and now he stood, readying for the three new combatants.

Behind Arliss, the shaky wall which once held a lone window collapsed to the ground, the warrior falling atop it. Philip came running through the doorway just as the entire structure collapsed outwards. Neither he nor his opponent were carrying swords. Now the warrior stood, blinking as Philip rushed at him and landed a fist in his face.

Arliss drew back her first arrow, aiming it at one of the three reinforcements who came ever closer. Just as she released the string, the arrow transformed from a tool of practice into something darker: a weapon of war. The realization of it pierced her, and she could see every moment of the arrow's flight as it sped towards the foremost of the blue-streaked warriors.

The arrowhead found its mark quickly. The warrior dropped to the ground, and the princess of Reinhold became a warrior herself in that moment. It was her first kill. Never before had her bow been used on anything but tree targets and flying fowl. Never again would she be the same. Even in all the adventures she had afterwards, she found that moment was among the most difficult she ever experienced.

Chapter Fourteen: The Quest is Over

Ilayda's fingers trembled about the handle of the knife as she tried to hold it steady, pointing it warily toward the approaching warriors. She edged closer to Erik, who was just nocking another arrow on his string. His eyes shone with the fierce fire of battle—and Ilayda hated it.

"We have to leave!" She gripped his shoulder. "There are too many."

"There are only three—rather, two." Erik didn't even look at her.

Four fresh warriors burst through the thick treeline almost as he spoke the words.

Not sure whether to smirk or to scream, she yanked on his shoulder again. "All right, now we really have to run for it!"

Glowering at her, he lowered his bow and searched the clearing. Ilayda followed his gaze and saw that Arliss had moved and was now helping Philip to engage his foe. The warrior—somewhat smaller than the others—raged against the two, his flesh streaming with sweat and his left arm streaked with blood.

Arliss ducked to the side and fumbled in her bag for something. Whatever she was doing, there couldn't have been any use of it now. They needed to flee—Ilayda was certain of that.

"Arliss!" Erik shouted. "We have to get out of this place, now!"

The first drop of rain struck Arliss's cheek just as she turned to answer Erik. "We cannot abandon the quest!"

"The quest is over!" he shouted.

She shook her head and gripped her bow. The quest could not be over.

The six other warriors charged toward them. With just two arrows left, that would leave four against their two swords and one knife. If only she had brought one of her father's swords!

Rain began falling in sheets. It drenched the entire clearing, and within moments Arliss could barely see Philip near her, much less Erik and Ilayda in the distance.

Philip gripped her arm. "Erik is right, Arliss. We have to leave."

"What about your man?"

"I do not think he has the strength to follow us now. We must go!"

She followed him as they pushed their way through the blinding rainstorm, grasping each other's hands. Ilayda shouted her name from somewhere to the right. Swords were drawn, boots trampled the soggy ground. The other warriors were approaching.

"Erik, we're over—"

A hand grabbed her throat from behind and she fell, rolling out of her assailant's grasp. She lost her grip on Philip's hand.

The rain lightened up and she got a clearer view of the man: Philip's opponent, heaving for breath and glaring death at them.

Philip stepped in front of her and tilted his sword in front of his body. "Get Erik and Ilayda out of here," he ordered.

It was too late. The reinforcements had arrived.

A blue-armed warrior with an iron-tight grip clamped Arliss's arm and tore the bow from her grasp. She twisted and kicked and tried to claw the ugly sneer from his disgusting face. But he caught her other arm and forced them both behind her back, sending shards of heat darting up to her shoulders. She howled against the pain and rage permeating her body. She lashed out with her foot, but landed on the rock hard muscle of his thigh. He was too strong for her. She couldn't wriggle free.

"Erik! Ilayda!" she shouted, her voice finding new power from her anger and fear. "Get out of here! Go to my mother! Tell her everything!"

One of the men slapped his hand across her mouth, and she could say no more.

Almost as quickly as it had arrived, the rain departed, leaving the clearing drenched but quiet. Arliss had only a moment to take in her soaked surroundings—the seven dark-armored warriors, one struggling to stand, surrounding her and Philip—before she was dragged away to the left of the collapsed cottage, into the darkest part of the forest. The last sight she saw before they reached the trees was Áedán's body, lying upon the bed in the middle of the glade.

Adrenaline coursed through Ilayda's veins as her heart pounded like a drum. It couldn't end this way. She couldn't lose Arliss. Somehow or another, she would have to rescue the princess.

She took two steps towards Arliss's kerfuffle with the warriors, but Erik yanked her three steps back. She tore her arm from his grasp and whirled on him. "Stop! Just stop! We have to help them—or are you just going to let them be dragged away?"

"We don't have the strength or arms to overpower them alone. They would simply add two more to their captives." Erik rubbed his shoulder as he leaned against a nearby tree.

Tears dribbled down Ilayda's cheeks, but she lifted her chin. "I will not forsake them. This whole time, I've followed and done as I've been told. Now I cannot anymore."

"Ilayda," Erik said, his eyes softening.

Then his look changed. He reached for her arm and wrapped his around hers, slamming her into the ground. An arrow thunked into the tree trunk right where she had been standing. He rolled into the forest, tugging on her arm.

"Quick!" he whispered. "We have to run!"

He leapt up, and Ilayda stumbled to her feet, darting forward to match his swift pace. A throaty roar erupted several paces behind them. One of the warriors must have been sent to finish them off.

Another arrow whistled past their heads. Ilayda dashed through the forest, trying to suck air into her burning lungs. Beside her, Erik was placing an arrow on the shaking bowstring even as he ran.

He stopped running.

The warrior stood just twenty paces off, his bow put away, his sword now raised, his blue-painted face wild.

"Get behind me!" Erik shouted at Ilayda.

She slid behind his tall, slender form, then immediately stepped out to the right. She had to see, no matter what he said.

He drew back his longbow, fingering the string for a split second. The warrior saw his doom, but it was too late. Erik's fingers relaxed their grip. The arrow flew spiraling toward its mark. Ilayda turned her head at the last moment.

They stood a moment, panting amidst the trees.

She spoke first. "We have to go back, don't we?"

"Back to the village? Yes. That's exactly what Arliss told us to do."

"I know it is, but still…I've grown a little bit wary of what Arliss tells us to do."

"You are not alone in that regard."

She let out a sigh of frustration. "How can we get back? We can't retrace our steps—the snakes, the river!"

"We'll have to."

"Could we try rafting the river?"

Erik shook his head. "It doesn't flow the right way for that. The river we crossed—I am certain it's the same one that flows by our village, the one that feeds the moat. It flows down out of the mountains in the north, curves by the village, and then curves again through the forest. I assume it feeds into the sea farther south."

She curved an eyebrow. "And why is this helpful information?"

"It means we cannot raft back to the village." He rolled his eyes. "However, it means you could ride a raft from the village straight into the forest."

"Why didn't we try that?"

How much had Arliss really considered the practical aspects of her plan? For such a level-headed person, she had acted quite hastily, probably because her emotions were moving independently of her reason.

Ilayda shrugged. "I guess there's nothing for it but to go back the way we came." Then she smirked up at Erik. "Wait a moment. I have a new plan. For now, I'm going to be in charge."

Erik folded his arms. "And what does this plan of yours involve?"

Ilayda's smirk turned into a smile. "Lasairbláth."

Arliss could see nothing, but her other senses were tingling. The air smelled thick and sweet from the rainshower, and the leaves beneath her feet had lost their brittle crunch. Instead, they slid beneath her wet, worn boots. She thought she could distinguish Philip's clear, careful footfalls just in front of her, but she couldn't be sure. How long had they been marching? Was it twenty, or thirty minutes?

The woolen blindfold itched her nose. The itch was maddening; the fact that she couldn't scratch it made it even more infuriating. She tried to ignore it, as she had no other choice. Eventually it subsided into a vague tickle.

One of the warriors—it sounded like Philip's opponent—gripped her wrists behind her back.

Without warning, the marching came to a halt. Someone lifted her up and placed her on some sort of wooden seat. The seat wobbled uncertainly. A boat? It couldn't be. Yet the wood beneath her feet couldn't be doing anything but *floating*. She hadn't ridden in a boat since their escape from the isle twelve years ago, but she still recalled the sensation.

"Here, Cahal," a gruff voice ordered. "Help me with the boy. Not quite as dainty as the girl, it seems."

Arliss stiffened at the mention of *dainty*, but at least he released her arms. For the moment she was free. She fingered the rectangular bulge in the pocket of her underdress and tore the pocket open wider. Smart thinking to have held on to this—the old book. It might come in handy later.

She heard grunts and low curses, and her seat teetered side-to-side. When the man called Cahal did not return to take hold of her arms, she tore off the blindfold.

They would blind her again as soon as possible, so she took it all in: the long rowboat with the curved prow, the seven burly warriors preparing to embark, Philip's opponent—who seemed to be the one called Cahal—bruised and bloodied from the fight, and Philip being hoisted into the boat.

She leapt to her feet, not considering the implications of being on a floating piece of wood. The boat trembled beneath her, and she nearly fell over the low stern.

Cahal and another man had almost dragged Philip all the way into the boat, despite his resistance. The second man now saw her, standing and unblindfolded, and he dropped Philip onto the wooden beam. The boat rocked again. Water splashed up into her face and washed over the side of the vessel.

She grabbed an oar which lay nestled in its hook on the back right side of the boat, and strained it up in front of her. The makeshift weapon was heavy in hand, but she didn't care. She glared at the warriors—Cahal in the boat, the other six on shore.

"Release us!" she demanded.

"What authority do you have?" The man who had helped lift Philip stuck out his goateed chin at her. His eyes flickered as if he knew he was goading her to reveal her identity.

She glowered at him. "What authority do *you* seven have?"

The man laughed, his snicker almost a cough. "We seven? You think we are seven? We are a multitude. We are a legion. I am asking again, what authority do you have?"

She invoked a name that would not reveal herself. "I have the authority of the one, true God."

Apparently they didn't think much of her answer. With a careless flip of his wrist, the leader coughed and spoke to his men. "Tie her hands, and tie his hands as well. Do it quickly."

She gripped the thick oar and swung it toward the shore. It slammed into one of the warrior's shins, knocking him to the ground. Gravity yanked it out of her hands, and it toppled downward, spanning the gap between boat and bank. She scrambled across the thin bridge no wider than one of her feet.

Two of the hulking warriors grabbed an arm each, jerking them behind her back. She glared at the coughing fellow, then at Cahal, then at the rest. She could kick one of them in the groin…but no, that would do nothing. She was too heavily outnumbered. Better to leave that trick for later use than to have it expected.

They slammed her back into the boat, the beam seat cracking painfully into her rear. Her last sight before they covered her eyes again was of a blindfolded Philip, his mysteriously colored eyes hidden. Yet she could see his mouth.

He was smiling.

Chapter Fifteen: Captives

Arliss slumped as the boat cast off into the river. Where were Erik and Ilayda? Were they even alive? The coughing man had sent a warrior to finish them off, she knew that much. Had the assassin returned to the company while she was marching blindfolded? She didn't know. Erik had a longbow, she tried to assure herself. And Ilayda had…well, Ilayda was Ilayda. She would think of something clever.

She herself stood in the more dire situation at the moment: captured, blindfolded, soaking wet, in a strange boat with strange men whose intentions were far less than amiable. At least she had Philip, though he was also captured, blindfolded, soaking wet, and in rather the same situation. She hoped the rain hadn't soaked all the way to the book in the torn pocket of her underdress.

'Tis all your fault, Erik said inside her head.

No, she snapped back. *It's these evil warriors. The quest was working just fine until they barged into everything.*

Silly princess, came Ilayda's voice.

I will follow you as long as it is right to do so, Erik insisted quietly.

You do not understand. You cannot even comprehend your own quest! Philip upset her fragmented thoughts.

She struggled to fit the pieces of the past three days together: her birthday, the ball, dancing…the conversation between Lord Adam and Lord Brédan, the dance with Brallaghan, the angry talk with her father…Philip. The book. The swordfight. Ilayda not wanting to wake up, Erik not wanting to believe her, Philip telling her she didn't understand. The river. The snakes. Lasairbláth. And then...the shack, the body, the warriors, and Áedán dead.

What good was there in any of that? How had any of it been a quest, much less a quest that was working?

What had she done wrong to deserve any of this? To save her people from their own prejudices, and to lay bare her father's bigotry: those were her only goals. Those, and to obtain a brother. Despite all her best efforts, she had failed miserably. Her spirit sank lower than the dense, wet air. Now everyone in the village, her father not least among them, would look upon her as a failure and a child. And as for Philip, she did not see how he could want anything more to do with her after this.

If an "after this" even existed. Perhaps they would not even escape this captivity alive.

Someone suddenly clasped her hand—a strong hand, but not that of a berserking warrior. This hand had gripped swords and hacked logs, engraved pommels and carved bedposts.

She released her breath. Philip must have been moved to be sitting beside her. She stretched her bound hands and intertwined her fingers with his.

All at once, the forest sounds became thick and echoey. A heavy darkness encroached overhead. Less and less light penetrated the thin blindfold. Arliss knew the boats were passing under something thicker and denser than the canopy of trees which had crowded above them thus far.

The strange, warm feeling of an empty belly saturated Ilayda's body—no longer a dull ache, but a sharp pain. Her stomach felt like it was being gnawed and pulled downwards by some wide-mouthed beast.

She halted, grabbing Erik's arm ahead of her. "Stop. We need to eat." Without waiting for a response, she crumpled into a sitting position. "And what about that snakebite from yesterday? It needs to be cleaned."

He offered his hand. "I'm fine. For now, I am going to be in charge. We have to keep moving. Arliss and Philip would do the same if they were in our place."

She groaned, but only from hunger and worry. She accepted his hand and allowed him to jerk her onto her feet.

"Besides," he said, "We're almost back to the Lasairbláth. We can rest there while we gather more flowers."

"And then?"

"We light torches and scare a path through the snakes."

"And then?"

"We cross the river, swimming if we must."

"And then?"

Erik curved an eyebrow at her. "Ilayda, you're the one who invented this plan, are you not?"

A throbbing ache burned in her lower back. She swiveled to stretch. "I am. But I have neither ideas nor abilities to rescue my best friend." Her hands trembled as she gripped her murrey-colored dress and took a step forward. "We need the queen."

Even with a blindfold on, Arliss could tell the fortress (or was it a cave?) stretched across a wide opening of space as they were herded through it. Noises clamored all around in the near distance: voices, boots clamping, the sound of a blacksmith's hammer banging hot iron.

Her captor jerked her to a halt.

A new voice spoke—probably another of these warriors. "Excellent prizes you have found."

"Shall I bring them before the Master?" the coughing man rasped.

"No." the other replied. He had a strange accent, just like all these grim warriors. "The Master is troubled, Damian. There was a great disturbance among the creatures, no thanks to these two." He kicked their shins viciously, and Arliss winced. "He will want them in the morning."

"I shall put them in a cell straightaway, then."

"What of the other two?"

"I sent Connal after them."

"He has not returned."

"You shall not worry about them," Damian rasped. "Now excuse me."

Damian jostled her along into some sort of dark corridor. A lock grated; metal scraped along stone. One of the warriors jabbed her ankle with his foot.

She tripped and staggered onto the stony floor as someone tore the blindfold from her face. She landed on her side, palms slapping against cold stone as she darted a glance up to the open doorway.

Damian shoved Philip into the room, and he stumbled to the floor beside her. With a final glare, Damian slammed the heavy door into the frame. Keys jingled as the lock clattered and finally clicked.

Then, silence—deep, terrible silence, the sort of quiet that only comes from a place which ought to be filled with noise. The noises she'd heard earlier now died away into the distance. And now she sat in a dungeon in her own realm—where in the land, she had no idea.

Behind her, Philip paced the cell. It was half the size of her bedroom at home, and neither blanket nor pillow nor any piece of furniture graced the bare stone floor. The rocky walls stood devoid of any window. The cell's lone light flickered from a small candle in the far corner.

Arliss hugged her knees to her chest, staring into the stone. How had it come to this? She'd wanted adventure, to discover what lay at the heart of the land. And now *this*—whatever it was—turned out to be her only reward. Philip was probably angry at her, and he had every right to be. After this, he'd never trust her again.

From somewhere deep within her chest, a sob formed and stuttered out. She restrained the second cry, but could do nothing to hide the streams of tears on her cheeks.

She covered her face with her right hand to hide the tears. She couldn't weep like this—not in front of Philip. But what did she have to hide? Especially now, what could she withhold from him?

He knelt beside her. He must have read her thoughts. They'd only known each other for these few days, yet already he read her mind better than even she could.

He brushed aside the hair that had slipped onto her cheek and gently peeled her hand away from her face.

She blinked through the tears and straight into the eyes that had haunted her from the moment she first looked into them. Now, in this dungeon, they were her only comfort.

"Well, Arliss, we're in quite a strait." He attempted a smile. "We've been across a river and through a forest infested with snakes. Maybe you have a good idea for getting out of this one?"

"No." She sniffed and dried her cheeks on her sleeve. "No, I can't get us out of this one."

He released her hand and shifted to the side. "I am sorry that I can't get us out either."

"It certainly isn't your fault, none of it." Her face grew hot. "The blame is mine. Everything that has happened to us is all my bloody fault."

"You aren't exactly wrong about that," he said. "Why, though, Arliss? You wanted to change our people. You wanted to change the way they looked at you and at me and at each other. Then you wanted to change your father's mind, and make him see things the way you saw them. But then you wanted something more: to explore the heart of Reinhold and find the places the legends speak of."

"And I have done none of those things."

"But why? Why drag me into all those goals?"

She turned to him, fresh tears watering her eyes. "Because they were never what I really wanted. What I wanted was..." She held back another gasping sob.

"Me?" His stared at the stone floor.

"I wanted a brother. Always, I've wanted a brother, and when you stepped across my path—in the fields, in the Bronze Lion, at the ball—I thought perhaps you could be that brother."

"I suppose I wasn't quite what you expected from the quiet carpenter's apprentice."

"Not at all." She almost smiled.

"Everyone is deeper than you realize, Arliss. Everyone has hurts. Everyone has stories. I not least of anyone." He looked at her again. "You pay a price for friendship, because you get more than a person. You get their hurts and their histories, too. A brother is no different."

"You don't understand," she said. "I realize that more than you know."

"What do you mean?"

"I have hurts, too. You may think I want a brother because I never had one, but that's not exactly why. I *did* have a brother." Trying to tell Philip the thing she had never told anyone else proved harder than she'd expected. She forced down the pain that burned her chest. "My mother gave birth to a son when I was eight years old. She almost died in childbirth. We buried my brother the next day."

Philip sucked in air, but he said nothing.

She closed her eyes to shut out the world, the pain. "His name was John Joseph."

Philip stood. "So this is why we're imprisoned—because you wanted a brother, and decided I was the one."

"I'm sorry. Deeply." She stared at the floor.

"In all those eight years, you've never once found someone to call your brother?"

"Never."

"But what about Lord Brédan's son—Brallaghan? I've seen you with him many times."

She lifted her gaze from the stone and faced him. "You've noticed me?"

"Of course. You're the princess. How could I not notice? I've watched you for a long time."

All this time, she had scorned the barriers of her city, not realizing that she herself was entrapped by them. He'd been watching her for years. For her part, she hadn't even known he existed.

"We've all been so blind," she finally exhaled. "Except for you."

"I've been blind, too. Until a few days ago, I never even tried to approach you." He placed his hands on his hips and lowered his eyebrows, but she thought she detected a flicker of a smile on his lips. "Maybe I'd have been better off if I hadn't."

"I know you want to tell me that I should have never left the village and disobeyed my father's orders. And I suppose you're right. But for now, this is our fate. Whatever happens here, I cannot let the darkness and snakes continue to brood."

"You think it's our fate?" he asked. "I think it's destiny."

She scrunched her brow together. "What do you mean?"

"I mean that we are here for a reason. You are meant for something important, Arliss. Something only you can fulfill."

Tilting her head, she looked at him. The tears had stopped for good. "You're right. We must find the Master these warriors answer to, and stop him from poisoning Reinhold."

With a harsh scrape, the wooden door slid open, scratching its way along stone and releasing dim light into the room. Damian stood on the threshold, and as he stepped into the room, the younger warrior Cahal limped in beside him. A bloody bandage wrapped Cahal's right forearm, and his face was dashed with cuts and bruises. Glaring at Philip, he followed his superior into the cell.

"I am sorry to intrude upon your lovely conversation," Damian said, "but I have need of the young swordsman here. He has a different cell waiting upon him, yes."

They moved to yank Philip to his feet.

Arliss leapt up. "No, don't take him—please!"

"It is the Master's orders." Cahal sneered and shoved her away.

She sent a swift kick into his injured leg. He stifled a yelp and skipped onward.

Even as they dragged him out of the room, Philip said, "It's going to be fine." His grim eyes pierced hers as the guards hauled him from the cell.

The door crashed into its stony frame. The draft flicked out the candle's light. Arliss shuddered in the darkness.

Chapter Sixteen:
A Fortress of Stone

A trickle of morning light oozed beneath the door—just enough for Arliss to squint at the book in her lap. She ran her hands across the words of the story she'd read so many times before.

> While the attacks of the Great Terror that rose up out of the East grew ever stronger, the resistance to them became ever emboldened. The enemy's fury was a wildfire; their will was as a hurricane. As the armies assaulted and even occupied the lands around Eire, the stoutest of hearts trembled at the power of the Great Terror of the East.
>
> Hope was not all lost. Although the times were dark, some stood against the tyrannical assaults.
>
> In one great castle, nestled in the highlands that overlooked a vast field of corn which the king harvested for food and profit, the king heard tidings of the wave of wild enemies which was taking the island by force. This forewarning gave him fear, for his defenses were few, and he held a premonition that his people would fall. Still he rallied his troops.
>
> The enemy army came sooner than expected, and the king's army was not yet prepared. But the queen began to make a plan of her own. Even as the enemy was a few miles

off, preparing to march across the king's cornfields, she sent out her bravest spies. Carrying heavy buckets of oil which threatened to yank their arms to the earth, the spies flew across the fields, hiding behind the tall plants. Everywhere they spilled trails of oil.

The enemy army began to march across the fields, trampling the corn. Seeing one of the spies, they shot him through the heart and prepared for an all-out ambush. But none came.

The queen stood in the tallest tower, her bow in hand. In the courtyard below, the royal army was tense, straining for the moment when they would flood through the castle gates and begin their hopeless attack on the enemy. The enemy soldiers were already halfway through the cornfields when they began firing their war machines—catapults and ballistae—at the castle. Still they were out of bowshot, so the army still had time to prepare without worrying about a volley of arrows. None could shoot accurately, if at all, from that distance.

None, that is, in either of the two armies. But the queen, an innately skilled archer, could make the shot. There, poised on top of the tower, she readied her arrow. The arrow for this shot was no ordinary arrow.

It was a fiery arrow.

The queen had dipped it in flame from the tower's torch, and it now blazed bright as she knocked it in the string and aimed. With the dancing flames reflecting in her eyes, she drew back the string. She released the arrow.

Heavy footsteps smacked the stone floor in the hall.

Arliss slammed the book shut and stuffed it back into the tattered pocket of her underdress. She barely had time to right the slit skirt of the blue woolen dress before the door creaked open. Damian stood in the doorway sneering at her, a squashed fragment of bread in his hand.

"Here, have breakfast." He threw the deformed piece of loaf at her.

She wolfed it down and instantly wished there was more. She'd eaten nothing since the morning before, and her stomach was complaining riotously.

"It is time." His accented voice was sharp and rounded in the way he pronounced vowels. "You shall come to the Master. He demands to see you, now, yes?"

"What if I don't want to see him?

He drew a long, ugly dagger. "Then you shall not see your companion again, either."

Her heart beginning to beat its drum, she rose and followed him out into the hallway. Who was this Master? Why did they not address him by name?

Áedán's final words burned in her memory: *"Thane! Thane has come!"*

Thane. The name stirred something deep within her memory, something which had long been forgotten and unused by her mind. Damian grabbed her arms and pushed her along as images flashed and flickered in her head before fading into darkness: the Isle of Light, the volcano erupting, her father leading, fighting…

Fighting a man with a bloody gash on his jaw and a treasure chest beneath his arm.

Somehow, this memory had remained neglected—no one had spoken of this moment in all her life. It seemed like a dream which was real and vivid in sleep, yet faded away the moment she wakened.

The dark hallway spilled out into a huge clearing—an open cavern of stone. It was like being inside a hollow mountain with the peak cut off. Walls of stone, ground of hard dirt dotted with boulders. And all around there were soldiers and guards, clomping about in silence.

She was in a defensible structure—a castle of sorts. A turreted wall spanned the width of the stony clearing behind her, and guards patrolled its crenelated heights. In the middle of the wall's base hung a large door beneath which flowed a small, slow river. It trickled straight across the entire clearing, disappearing beneath a tall stone platform which overlooked the entire fortress.

Short stone embankments had been erected to help contain the water's flow. But there must've been some other dam concealed beyond the guarding wall. The river flowing through the forest was much too vast and raucous to be limited to this thin, trickling stream. The stream was at least seven feet wide, but the water slithered along, as if its flow was being dragged from behind.

This master clearly wanted a hideout both defensible and camouflaged. Only if someone followed the river all this way into the forest could they find this place.

So *this* was the heart of the land. She hadn't known what to expect to find, but it certainly wasn't a dark mountain fortress. The old legends described this land as beautiful, wild. But the land of Reinhold around her was dark—mysterious.

Had Erik and Ilayda escaped? Were they even now getting help? Even if they were, could they find her? Erik had proven his skills as a tracker and a woodsman, but not even he could uncover this castle built into the heart of the mountains.

And where were these warriors keeping Philip?

Arliss expected the men to shove her into one of the long galleries which spanned the sides of the clearing, connecting to the front wall on either side, but they walked straight on, keeping the river beside them. They were headed for the stone platform at the far back of the rocky dell. The platform had been carved flat atop a mound of uneven stone, and staircases had been hewn on either side of the mound.

They reached the right hand staircase. On the opposite side, across the river, another guard was leading Philip up the stone steps.

At the top of the mound, on a throne-like chair, sat a pale, dark-eyed man. He fingered a gilded goblet in his right hand, and his left stroked an old scar on his jaw.

Thane had come.

CHAPTER SEVENTEEN: THE PLANS OF ELOWYN

Ilayda's lungs were burning. Another step, another stride, she told herself. Forcing herself to match Erik's sprinting pace, she promised her aching sides and pounding feet that the run would soon be over.

Over and over and again, her worn boots smacked the alternating grass and rock that carpeted the plain between the forest and the city. Already they were nearing the city itself—the singular stone tower shimmered in the brazen morning sun—but still Erik did not slow down. Not until they reached the drawbridge and burst through the open gates did he pull back, his pumping legs halting. Unable to stop her own momentum, she slammed into him.

"Sorry." She swiped brown hair out of her face.

Erik nodded at her apology. "We made it. Time to find the queen."

Ilayda took a step ahead. "She often lingers in her garden in the early mornings. Sometimes Arliss and I have joined her. Come on, I'm sure she'll be there."

He hesitated. "Do you think we're allowed in the royal gardens?"

"You forget I live in the castle."

The first tier of the city was almost empty but for the few craftsmen who had their doors wide open for business. Most were out in the shaded western fields, harvesting as much of the potato crop as they could before the busyness of the day began in earnest. They rounded the corner up into the busier second tier, then Erik hesitated. "Perhaps I should go to my house. My parents will want to know that I'm all right, and…"

"And that Philip isn't? Erik, we have to get to the queen without delay. Parents will slow us down. They'll want to talk, want to know everywhere we've been, and why only half of us have returned. There is no time for any of that."

"Ilayda!"

She whirled in the direction of the voice.

Her father.

Erik nodded at Adam's swift approach. "Speaking of parents slowing us down."

She groaned, covering her eyes. "Not now!"

"Ilayda, what *have* you been doing?" Adam had almost reached them.

She whispered to Erik. "Distract him. I'll run to the castle."

He crossed his arms and curled an eyebrow. "You're going to talk to him. You have to."

As her father closed the distance toward them, clouds slipped over the sun and blotted out some of its burning light. Ilayda shivered. November would be upon them in no time at all, and any remnant of the summer's heat would be long gone. She shivered also not from the cool but from fear—fear that her best friend could be dead or dying.

Stand strong, she told herself. *For Arliss.*

Her father clasped her shoulder and pushed the hair off her face. "Where have you been?"

She forced a smile. "It's a long story, and all very interesting."

"Tell me—no subtractions or additions from the truth."

"Of course." She nodded. "But, one moment. You see, I had something pressing I was about to do."

Erik stepped forward.

"Who are you?" Adam eyed Erik's shabby tunic. "No knight of Reinhold, I'll bet. What are you doing with my daughter?"

Ilayda stood between them. Erik probably wouldn't defend himself. "He's my friend, Father, and a decent fellow in his own right. He's the son of the carpenter."

He pulled her back. "You would do well to leave my daughter alone. Who are you to run off with her like this?"

Fires lit in Erik's eyes, and his neck tensed. "Who am I? I am the one who scouted our journey, found our way, fought off assailants, and saved your daughter's life. That is who I am, Lord Adam." He grabbed Ilayda's wrist. "Now, if you will excuse me, we need to get to the queen."

"The queen?"

"Yes, and it's urgent. Let us go!" Ilayda pleaded.

He scowled at them. "Two days! Two days you stole my daughter from me, and now you both return expecting to get off without telling me what you were up to."

"I didn't steal your daughter." Erik's voice dropped low. "You don't know the half of it. None of this is my fault."

"Then whose is it?"

Erik and Ilayda exchanged glances. Should they tell him? Her father already disliked Arliss enough. The conversation from Mrs. Fidelma's shop rushed back into Ilayda's mind. Goodness, it seemed a lifetime!

"Speak!" her father demanded. "You're not going anywhere if you ignore me."

Ilayda exhaled. "Arliss. It was Arliss's idea, her plan."

Adam huffed. "I should have known it was her fault, foolish princess that she is. Is she not traveling with you? I assume she decided to show up late again."

"Father, please stop. Stop being so cruel to her. She is my best friend—my sister—and I beg you not to speak of her like this. She's in trouble, and we have to help her." Ilayda nodded to Erik. "We're going to the queen, and I do not care what you say about it."

She stepped away from him and strode up the hill. Uncertain as she felt, she swallowed and tried to keep a confident poise.

Behind her, Erik turned to her gobsmacked father. "She can be quite difficult, can't she?"

The wind that whispered through Elowyn's hair spoke of change: not only the change of seasons, but a change in the realm. The mountains stood tall in the distance, keeping their own secrets. The plains lay quiet. The village sprawling on the tiers beneath her had been stirred up by something, and a restless feeling pervaded the very air. The queen closed her eyes, adjusting the silver circlet whose jade stone dripped down her forehead, encircled in tiny sterling vines. Her bare feet stroked the soft grasses and silken flowers which carpeted the small garden in green, crimson, and lilac.

Beside her on the stone bench, Nathanael cleared his throat. "Two days without the king and the princess. Reinhold is quiet."

"Yet they are screaming on the inside. Something is coming to Reinhold, something which even I cannot see." She sighed. "These past two days, I have felt the presence of God's Spirit about this city more than ever before. But there is something else. Something dark lurks as well, trying to find a way in."

She opened her eyes and faced him. "I am worried about them."

"Kenton's company will be fine."

"Oh, not him. I am worried for Arliss and Ilayda. Two days it has been since they left, and two days was the allotted time I allowed her to be gone."

"It is unlike you to worry, Elowyn," he said.

"I know. Perhaps it is foolish of me to worry, but I do want to know that my daughter is safe."

The wooden gate to the garden clicked open and Ilayda rushed in, dragging a tall young man behind her. She almost tripped over a grove of bloodleaf as they both stumbled towards her, winded and unable to speak. The look in Ilayda's eyes offered a flicker of the ill news she was about to share.

"Sit." Elowyn motioned to the bench.

The young man bowed. "I am Erik, your majesty."

Elowyn nodded at him, but her eyes were on Ilayda.

Nathanael stood to make room for the other two on the bench. "Some tea, my lady?"

Ilayda shook her head. "No time for tea. Have...to go back for Arliss."

"Go back where?" Elowyn grasped the edge of the stone bench.

"I don't know." Ilayda collapsed on the bench.

"Where is Arliss?" Elowyn demanded. Something horrid had happened, she could see it in Ilayda's eyes. Her throat constricted. "She is not with you, is she?"

Ilayda shook her head. Erik looked grim.

Kneeling, Nathanael implored Ilayda and Erik. "Where is she? Tell me—I will go after her! I could not bear for something to happen to her."

"She and my cousin were captured by a band of dark soldiers who claimed allegiance to one called *the Master*," Erik said.

"Who are you?" Nathanael demanded. "Who is your cousin? And bloody *why* were you in the forest with the princess and the Lady Ilayda?"

Ilayda sat tall, her chin tilted back. "Lord Nathanael, please stop accusing him. We've already been through that with my father. Arliss may be my best friend, but I am unashamed to say that everything that went wrong in our quest was entirely her fault."

Nathanael still looked suspicious. "Your quest? What do you—"

"Nathanael, let him speak." Elowyn faced Erik. "Where did this happen?"

Erik stood. "I am not certain of everything—we were in unexplored territory. Please, my lady, my cousin Philip was captured as well. I will guide you. I know most of the way."

Elowyn stood. "You will do nothing of the sort. Both of you are to stay here at the castle and help Adam oversee affairs until we return. But first, you must give us an account of your entire venture."

Erik smiled. "I can do even better than that. I can draw you a map."

Ilayda also stood, a confused look painted on her face. "You can't be leaving now, without us and with no knowledge of your way? And how d'you expect us to 'oversee' the castle without you here?"

"We *are* leaving now, and without you, but not without knowledge of our way." Elowyn strode toward the back door of the castle tower. "Come, follow me to the council room. I am sure you have much to tell us in such a little time."

Erik touched her arm. "Wait, my queen. There is something you need to know."

"What?"

"Just before Arliss and Philip were captured, we found a dying man of Reinhold. His name was Áedán."

"Áedán? How is that possible?" She gaped at him. "Then he was alive all this time…"

"He died even as Arliss was speaking to him. But before he passed, he spoke one name—Thane."

Elowyn scrutinized Erik's eyes, but could find nothing but truth within them.

How? How could this name—this person—still haunt their lives? She had left half her heart on the Isle when they fled. Yet, somehow, she thought she had also left this name behind forever.

Nathanael stepped close to her, his face so close to hers that she could feel the heat of his nervous breaths on her cheek. "Sister, you know what this means. We thought we were safe here. We thought we were alone. But after all these years, our old enemy has returned."

Chapter Eighteen: Identities

"Who are you?"

The question jabbed Arliss's ears for the third time, and this time she wanted to throw the same inquisition back at her questioner: who was he?

The ebony-haired man, pale as paper, fierce as fire, sitting atop a stony dais in a fortress which looked not unlike a castle. Of course, she knew his name—or had a confident guess; but as to his character, his intentions, she was blind.

She would tell him nothing. If he knew who she was, he might uncover more secrets. Who knew what could become of the village if such a man attacked it!

She cast a glance in Philip's direction, but he was glaring at their questioner. Philip looked like he'd had a rough time of it. His eyes narrowed, lids dark. What looked like a bruise mottled his forehead. What had they done to him? Would he have sense enough to keep his tongue as well?

Thane set his golden cup down on the ornate side table beside him and folded his hands. "You are becoming quite tiresome, O silent one. Answer my question, please, for I do not have all day to waste on interrogating you."

His voice was a smooth as silk and as sharp as poison. A raven-black tunic, belted about his waist, did little to conceal his powerful body. The deep black of the snugly-fitting garment contrasted starkly with the shimmering silver edging around the sleeves and collar.

Arliss spoke. "I don't want to share my identity with you, but suffice it to say that if you keep me prisoner much longer, you will regret it."

He laughed. "Of course. So you have friends in high places, then?"

"High places, low places, strange places, normal places. I have many."

"And where are your many friends now? They have not come to your aid."

She bit her lip and said nothing.

He turned to Philip with a sneer. "And what about you, sir? Do you have friends in high places as well?"

Philip's eyes narrowed, his jaw tense. "Well, she is my friend, and we're standing upon a pretty tall mound of stone, so I suppose you could say so."

Thane stroked his jaw. "You have a witty companion, my lady."

She smirked. "Guests who are witty must make up for hosts who are not."

He stood. "So this is what you are, a traveling troupe of wits and riddlers? Tell me, did you outwit and riddle the snakes to death as well?"

Arliss shuddered at the thought of the vile creatures.

"No, we used a different method," Philip said. "More along the lines of hacking them in half, shooting arrows through their heads, spilling their guts on the ground, and blasting them with poisonous exploding flowers."

Arliss added, "And those are our preferred methods with anything or anyone who apprehends us against our will."

"And what do you call the flower which exploded in your fight with the serpents?"

"It is called Lasairbláth."

Thane stepped over toward her, his black boots clamping the smooth stone of the dais until he faced her. His eyes shone with flickering green, in places almost yellow. He studied her until a light of recognition gleamed in his eyes.

She lowered her gaze. What had he recognized? Her doubt? Her foolishness? Her rebellion?

"Send everyone else away. Take the young man back to his cell." His voice echoed off the fortress's wide stone walls which bracketed the flatness below them.

Arliss watched the guards depart, dragging Philip with them. He caught her eye before they jerked his head back around.

Thane sat again. "I am sorry to stall like this, asking the same question over and over, but I needed to know who you really were and how strong your allegiances may be. Now that we are alone, there is no need for any of that, princess."

"What exactly do you mean—wait! *Princess?* Why do you call me princess?"

He laughed. "Sit down, O princess of Reinhold. See, I have brought a chair for you, my guest."

She refused to sit. "How do you know who I am?" she asked through clenched teeth.

"I know much about you, Arliss, first princess of the realm of the clan of Reinhold. You are the daughter of Kenton and Elowyn, and you are sixteen years old. You shoot a bow often in the forest. You have escaped without your father's blessing or knowledge. But your fiery speech and recognition of Lasairbláth alone prove you have been well-educated—that you are royal."

She scowled. "I know some about you as well—Thane, enemy of Reinhold! You fought my father on the Isle of Light. You were wounded, but escaped. Now, you are inflicting your revenge on me."

He released a heavy breath.

"You may find questioning me harder than you thought." She tossed her hair back behind her shoulders.

A wry laugh escaped his lips. "You know nothing of hardship. Of what I have done to your friend, of what I can still do to him." His eyes burned into hers. "I know who he is as well."

"What do you mean, you know who he is?"

"He is Philip, son of Carraig; yet he is that no more, for Carraig is long dead."

She scanned the uneven walls of the stony fortress. What lay beyond the other side of the sheer cliffs? "If you know so much about both of us, why are we being interrogated? Clearly you know everything already."

"You are mistaken in that regard. I am not so omniscient as it may seem." He stood and edged closer to her. She stole a step backwards.

"What do you want with me?"

"I shall be frank with you. You are the princess of Reinhold. Thus, you must know something about your father's army—how many men he has, what sort of weapons, and so on. Give me that information, and I will release you."

"And Philip?"

Thane's eyes were steel. "Yes, and Philip."

"And if I will not tell you what you want to know?"

"If you will not, then I will kill him."

"Why would you kill him? What could you possibly gain?"

"You know nothing of the harm Philip's line has done to me."

"That's absurd! Whatever harm his forebears may have caused you, Philip himself did none of it."

Thane stepped so close his voice was only a whisper. "Well, then, I suppose you can be my excuse. If for no other reason, I will kill him because of the pain it will cause you."

"And you think I would tell you these things then?"

"Yes."

"Why?"

"Because—why would you still defend the one you do not love when you have lost the one you do?" He paused, letting his statement sink into Arliss's mind.

She shoved away from him and stepped back.

Her foot plunged into nothingness. Flailing, she tried to grip something—the platform—the sides of the mound—anything, anything that would stop her fall. Yet there was nothing she could do, nothing to hold onto. She braced herself for the impact fifteen feet down.

But Thane grabbed her left forearm. Her book dislodged from her hidden pocket and tumbled to the ground by the river. As she watched it fall, she slammed against the rocky mound. Pain shot through her side as a rib cracked loudly enough to be heard.

Grunting, Thane hoisted her up and laid her upon the dais. "Goodness, Arliss, be careful. A fall from this height could stun or kill a man—or woman."

Arliss tried to speak but found she could not. Her side burned. Her face tightened with anger. Why had he pressed so close to her earlier? He'd made her back away. Yet he'd also saved her life. Perhaps that meant something.

No, she told herself, *it doesn't. He's evil. Tell him nothing. Tell him nothing.*

Philip lay on the floor of his cell, alone with his thoughts centered on Arliss—what was being asked of her, and what was she telling? Would they spare her the treatment he had received earlier that morning? She didn't know about it. And it would be better if she didn't.

The memories from that morning rushed back into his head. Shouting. Screaming. The leader, the Master, pacing the stiff chamber. Blows, pain, blood.

That Cahal fellow was a real fiend. Even after the scuffle in the forest, he hadn't learned his lesson. Philip had promptly fixed that. But then…the Master…the pike slamming into his head…

Still, he hadn't let anything slip. Unless Arliss broke down during her interrogation, these ruffians would know nothing of Kenton's army—or his current absence from the city. If their captors knew Reinhold was without a ruler and without much of an army, they might attack straightaway.

He clenched his eyes shut. *Please, Lord, let Arliss stay strong.* She could not accidentally divulge that knowledge. Despite her rashness, she had a loyal streak in her, a steadfast strain. Plus, she had a decent head on her shoulders. He hoped they could both keep their heads that way.

His temples pounded as he lay on the hard-packed dirt floor. Arliss's cell floor last night had been stone, so he knew this dungeon lay somewhere else along the walls of the fortress's wide mountain bailey. His stomach burned with hunger. He hadn't had even a halfway decent meal in over a day. The sagging bread and unfiltered river water didn't amount to very much, especially after the beating and questioning he had just been through.

Boots clamped in the hallway, and the door jiggled open. Cahal stepped in, smirking. "Time for the midday feast, sirrah!" He dropped the squashed mass of bread on the dirt floor. He bent and set down the glass of water, letting it drop the last foot to the ground. It hit, toppled a moment, and tipped over, creating a patch of mud on the dusty ground.

Philip stood, gripping the metal cup. "Would you mind getting me another cup of water, Sir Cahal?"

"I already brought you some."

Philip's jaw tensed. "Really? Yet not a single drop made it to my lips."

"That is not my problem." He shrugged and started away.

Philip grabbed his shoulder, pulling him back into the cell. "I may be in this prison, but I'm not your subject. I'm your ward. So that makes it your duty to keep me alive, eh?" He shoved Cahal closer to the wall.

"The princess we are to keep alive and well. I have no orders to keep you that way."

"Then you shouldn't have any problem with me leaving this cell." Philip released his shoulder and stepped to the doorway.

Cahal drew his dagger and plunged it toward Philip's upper back. Philip ducked, grabbing Cahal's wrist and twisting it around his back until he dropped the dagger.

Philip pinned both of Cahal's arms to his sides and slammed a boot into his chest. Spluttering, Cahal tumbled to the floor.

Philip dashed out into the hallway and studied the layout of the fortress. He stood on the opposite side from the cell where Arliss had been kept last night. That dungeon appeared to be carved into the mountain itself. The building with his cell had been built from wood and stone—a two-story structure which bordered the mountainous fringe of the dell and met with the outer wall at the front of the fortress.

Cahal approached, his boots clobbering the ground behind him. "*Tá an príosúnach éalú!*"

Guards on the opposite end of the glade saw him and shouted. They ran and leapt the thin stream which separated them.

Philip ran to the stone mound, his legs pumping as he darted a glance at Arliss's interrogation. Anything could have happened in the past few minutes. Anything.

On the ground before him lay her thick leatherbound book. At the top of the dais, the Master was bending over a body, removing her torn outer dress. Philip's breath lodged in the middle of his throat as he stifled a shout.

As if to assure him, Arliss's chest fluttered with a faint breath. He collected the book and vaulted up the rocky stairway.

Chapter Nineteen: Realms Beyond Reinhold

"What are you doing, you scum?" Philip shouted up the stairs. He leapt the last three steps and strode across the platform to Thane, his fists clenched. He couldn't let Thane harm Arliss, even at a cost to himself.

"I'm saving her life, imbecile." Thane didn't bother to look at Philip, but instead focused on Arliss. He wrenched off the rest of the blue woolen fabric and tossed it aside.

She groaned softly as the dress came off. Beneath it, her white chemise was in little better state. Her pocket sagged in tatters. She must've stuffed the book inside it.

Philip stuffed the book beneath his arm.

"Help me," Thane ordered. "Take her head."

Still scowling at him, Philip did as ordered and gently lifted her shoulders and golden head into his arms. Thane snatched up her legs, and together they began to make their way down the staircase. The book felt like it was trying to escape from Philip's clamped armpit. He clenched his arm tighter as he tried to carry both the princess and the thick book at the same time.

"What did you do to her?"

"I did nothing to her. She was stupid enough to push herself off the dais, and I happened to be close enough to rescue her."

Her eyes fluttered open and her eyebrow curved as she gave Thane a suspicious glance. Still she said nothing.

"How close?" Philip demanded.

"Does it matter?"

"Yes."

Thane ignored him as they reached the bottom of the stairs. The two guards roused by Philip's escape still stood at attention, rather befuddled by the whole situation. Thane nodded at them as he shifted Arliss's weight, carrying her legs as if they were the most awkward bundle in the world. "Here," he said. "Can you hold her on your own a moment? I need to find a place to lay her down."

"I can hold her on my own as long as needed." Supporting her by the shoulders with one arm, he slipped the other under her knees and accepted her full weight.

"Good," Thane snapped as he strode toward the guards.

The moment he had stepped out of earshot, Arliss opened her eyes and looked up at Philip.

"Are you all right?" he asked.

"Yes. At least, more than he thinks at the moment."

"Did you tell him anything?"

"Philip, he knows so much already. He knows all about who I am. He even knows who you are—rather, who your father was."

He frowned. "What did he say?"

"He said that he had some quarrel with your ancestors, and he wants to take out his revenge on you. But—Philip, I know who he is."

"What do you mean? How?"

"Aédán was right, he is Thane. He lived on the Isle of Light before our people fled, twelve years ago. He was one of us, but he did not flee with us. He escaped alone."

"And why has he come back?"

"I think he intends to take over Reinhold. Why else would he question me about my father's army? And why else would he be raising an army of his own?"

"But where did he get—"

Thane's voice shot across the wide bailey of the fortress. "Come, son of Carraig, bring the princess over here."

How did Thane know his father's name? The mysteries were piling up thicker and thicker around this hidden fortress.

Philip walked to where Thane stood, close to the front wall of the castle. He motioned for Philip to follow him into the long structure that joined both the outer wall and the side of the mountain. The same building which housed his own prison cell.

Cahal loitered inside the simple stone building. Philip's muscles tensed.

"Open the door for us, Sir Cahal." Thane lifted the candlestick he had retrieved.

Cahal gaped at the procession and the princess lying in Philip's arms.

"*Now*, guard."

"The door to Sir Orlando's chambers?"

"Yes, that door!" Thane growled. "Now hurry up about it!"

Cahal yanked the door opened.

As they entered, Philip couldn't help but offer a smug "Thank you, Sir Cahal."

The chamber within was undoubtedly the most beautiful room Philip had seen in the entire fortress, if not the only one. Fine silk covers draped over a simple bed without frame or curtains, and beside it stood a small table with an ornately carved lamp. Old wax clumped up the sides of the lamp, but Thane now offered its wick the flame from a candle he was holding. The lamp flicked to life, its curious curves and contortions magnifying the light throughout the entire room. A full-length mirror spanned the height of the far wall.

"Here, on the bed." Thane pulled back the outermost cover.

Philip set Arliss down gently. She let slip a small smile as he released his careful hold on her. He inhaled tightly. She was beautiful—really, truly. She was also an idiot. But her quest was begun with good intentions.

Now, in this place, he was all she had to protect her.

Thane's face turned suddenly sour. He raised his voice and glanced at the door. "Come, now, seize him!"

Cahal and the other two guards entered the room and grabbed Philip's shoulders, herding him through the door. Cahal snatched the book from beneath Philip's arm and tossed it to Thane.

As Philip was dragged away, Thane sat on the bed, a pained expression creasing his hard-set face.

The same muggy wetness pervaded the room, but the bed felt cool and dry beneath the silken covers. It seemed the loveliest thing Arliss had ever felt—or, at least, the loveliest thing since she left the city. How many days ago was it? Two? Three? Ten? Her brain spun from the pain in her side and the gnawing hunger in her stomach.

"Well, are you all right or not?" Thane demanded.

She opened her eyes and shifted her weight. Pain pierced her ribs. "I'm fine, but I'm hungry."

Thane threw his head back and laughed—a true, lilting laugh. "You just fell off a cliff and fractured a rib, and all you're thinking about is that you are hungry?"

She sat up, sucking down the pain with a massive breath. "I hope you don't think the pitiful excuses for food I've been served have been anything like a real meal."

"No, indeed."

"Look, Thane." She leaned forward earnestly. "If you have these sort of fine room decorations, then you must also have equally nice food from wherever that came from—wherever you got this bloody army, no doubt. As you see, I catch on quickly."

Thane appeared thoughtful. "Indeed, you do."

"So, why? Why me? Why am I here?"

"You encroached on my borders."

"No, I pushed the limits of *my* borders."

"That is debatable."

"I don't think so. Just because you want to own the realm of Reinhold doesn't mean you already do."

Thane motioned around the room as if to signify the sheer size of the fortress. "What do you think this means? While you have built your fortress—your city on a hill—I have build mine within a hill. You build upon rock and stone. I have built within rock and stone. Did it ever occur to you that when a person builds a castle and seizes an area—and is utterly unchallenged—he owns that area for all intents and purposes?"

Arliss rolled her eyes. "I have read a few books in my life. I'm not an idiot. Which brings me back to what I was talking about earlier. Where does it all come from—the men, the lamps, the weapons, and the food which I am waiting for you to bring me?"

He went to the door and signaled a guard. "Luncheon for the princess and me, forthwith." Then he returned and sat upon the bed, resuming his focused glare.

"Arliss, you say you've read books. Surely you can figure out where it all comes from."

She looked down, searching the depths of her memory. "I'm afraid I can't. To be quite frank, I do not know what in the castle library is fact and what is fiction. To me, they are all wonderful stories, even though some may be more history than legend."

He shook his head. "Your father never taught you anything."

"He certainly did teach me! He taught me the bow, the sword, and the pen."

"You sound grateful indeed to the one from whom you just ran away. I'm sorry to tell you, but your father's education was terribly lacking in two subjects—true history and real geography."

She hesitated. "I know that our clan escaped oppression from another clan with much more land and power. That was why we took refuge on the isle."

"Correct."

"And there was some sort of war or at least a battle about the whole thing, involving a third clan that was as big or bigger than the oppressive one."

Thane lifted his hands. "And what do you question?"

"But that was so long ago—"

A knock sounded on the door just before it swung open. A guard rolled a table set on wheels toward the bed. Cheese, bread, smoked fish, a flask of dark wine, and a pitcher of cool water with which to wash it down. Arliss's mouth began to water, and her stomach groaned. She couldn't wait to curb her hunger.

After the guard left, she pointed to some curious round berries. "What are these?"

"They're olives." Thane shook his head. "This is what I mean about your education. If I told you all about this world you live in, you would be shocked mute."

She tore at a hunk of bread. "I've been through a lot of shocking things these past few days. You might be surprised."

"What if I told you all you take as legend and lore is actually history? Would that make a difference? You see, I have been flipping through this book—" he lifted the leather volume from his lap so she could see it "—and it is no collection of stories. Yes, there are legends and outdated prophecies and apothecarial instructions, but much of this book is the story of our realms."

The wedge of cheese Arliss had just swallowed felt as if it lodged in her throat. She gulped. "How is that possible? If you're telling the truth, then the old realms from the stories are all still in existence?"

"Indeed."

"Ikarra? Anmór?"

Thane closed the book. "You are pressuring your mind too much for one who has suffered such an injury. Come, have some rest. I will leave you."

"I want answers." Arliss licked her lips.

"If you will not give me the answers I want, I will not give you any answers either."

Then he left, gliding through the door like a dark specter before she could say another word to him. She poured some of the water into a glass. If she told Thane what he wanted to know, he might perhaps tell her what she desired.

And, perhaps, he would keep his promise to free her and Philip.

Chapter Twenty: Body and Blood

The instructions flowed through Elowyn's mind with every step she took through the ominous forest. Although the sun still had several hours to reign in the heavens, the thickly clustered trees blocked and filtered its light, allowing a few scattered rays to penetrate the leaf-covered ground. Elowyn's ever-subtle footfalls still crunched the fallen leaves as if they were burnt paper.

Nathanael trudged beside her, but she barely noticed. Erik's instructions flowed through her mind, repeating themselves.

For half a day, journey through the forest. Start at Arliss's secret clearing, which lies just within the forest exactly across from the city in a straight line. That much had been quite easy.

Your half-day's journey will bring you to the riverbank. You must either swim across or create a bridge. We found no ford within a hundred paces in either direction.

Elowyn's indigo traveling dress still dripped with water from the dicey crossing.

Then, you will come to a part of the forest where all the trees seem dark and sickly. Here you must beware. Prepare torches, and make ready the Lasairbláth.

Elowyn stifled the uneasiness that rose in her chest. Dark trees—dark as midnight, dark as hate—already surrounded her.

They had come to that part of the forest.

The door to the sumptuous room creaked opened, dousing Arliss's bed in flickering light. She squinted and sat up. What time of day was it? Perhaps she had slept through dinner—in which case he would be bringing her something to eat.

"Hello, stranger," she said as he turned and shut the door behind him.

He came towards her, and the light from his candle cast curious shadows on his face.

"Hello, Arliss." Philip's face seemed grimmer and more determined than ever. He lit the curved glass lamp which sat on bedside table.

The light flickered upon a tall chest of drawers and reflected on a fiddle. The instrument's glossy surface had clearly been collecting dust for some time.

Philip knelt by the bed, taking one of her hands in his. "I'm so glad you're all right. I begged to check on you all last night and all this morning. Finally Thane relented."

"Of course he would do that. He's not quite as bad as I supposed."

Philip snorted. "Not as bad as you supposed? He's a bloody villain, Arliss."

"You sound like me. I suppose I must sound like you now."

He raised his eyebrows. "What makes you think he's not as bad as he is?"

She wriggled up higher on her pillows. "He offered me a deal—tell him what he wants to know, and he will free both of us."

"And you actually believe him?"

"What other choice do I have? I sent Erik and Ilayda for help. No help has come, although we've been here for an age."

"It's only been three days since we left the city. I have kept a very careful count."

"Only three days! It...it seems like a week, a month. I feel as if I have not seen Father—" She stopped herself. Did she really miss him that much? He was half the reason she'd left the city in the first place.

Philip gave her a knowing look.

She hesitated, choosing her words more carefully. "I miss my mother very much. And my Uncle Nathanael. And Ilayda. That's why I have to tell Thane. I know it might be dangerous to tell him things about our city, about our army, but that may be our one hope for getting out of this accursed place."

"And when we are free?"

"We will return to the city. If Thane comes, I will protect our people. My father will see how wrong he was about me, and in turn I will apologize for stirring up this great evil. I will not, however, apologize for saving Reinhold."

"Reinhold isn't saved yet," Philip murmured. "But I forgot why I came. Here, let me see that flask of wine. I hope you have not drunk it all."

"Actually not." She smirked. "I tend not to drink while sleeping."

He poured a little of the dark wine into her cup. Then, seeing another cup on the richly carved dresser, he took that and poured wine into it as well. After that, he pulled a crust of bread from within his shirt and tore it in two.

"What's this?"

"It is Diescrol," he said, "the Sabbath. Surely you didn't forget it was the first day of a new week?"

"I told you, I have lost track of all the days in here."

"Well, we have neither minister nor chapel, but we do have this bread and this wine, the symbols of the Lord Jesus. And we have each other. I suppose that is what matters, isn't it?"

His words and act of making the sacrament pierced her heart. "Yes, that is what matters."

"It is said that two are better than one, because they have a good reward for their toil."

"I wonder why that is?"

"The passage tells us—if they fall, one will lift up his fellow."

He had not quoted the end of the Scripture passage. She spoke it solemnly, her vision blurring as she stared into nothing. "But woe to him who is alone when he falls, and has not another to lift him up."

He took her hand. "Know this, Arliss, if you fall, I will lift you up again."

"I know."

They lifted the bread and the wine, and they ate and drank.

She motioned with her cup towards the patch of freshly disturbed dirt in the corner of the room. "I planted some Lasairbláth over there. There were a few dried flowers left in my pockets. I don't really know why I did it. Just don't tell Thane."

He looked thoughtful. "Speaking of the devil, where do you think he gets it all from?"

She looked around. "The fortress?"

"No, the soldiers. The weapons. He's even got a blacksmith's shop and a small garden in here."

She set her cup on the side table. "He disappears from our clan for twelve years and shows back up rich and powerful. I suppose the only explanation is that he conjured it from thin air."

"He's obviously dabbling in dark magic. I mean, just think about the snakes." He shrugged. "But realistically, things don't just come out of nothing."

The door slammed open, and Thane stamped in with his usual leather boots and silver-embroidered tunic. However, today he wore a long oilcloth coat which reached to his ankles and flapped as he walked.

"You've been in here far long enough," he barked, striding over to the bed. "Get out!"

Arliss glared at him. "I would love to get out and have some fresh air. What a lovely idea, Thane!"

"I shall talk with you in a moment, O witty princess." Then he turned on Philip. "Get out, now. Cease your petty observances of ancient customs."

Philip stood. "Sometimes the ancient customs are the best."

"I hope you're not hanging your hopes of getting out of here on some miracle from God," Thane spat. "Such things do not happen, so I would suggest you squelch your hopes of them at once. Your escape from my prison depends solely on whether the princess here will tell me such things that are expedient for me to know. As such, I would appreciate for you to leave us in privacy as we talk."

Thane shoved Philip, who bristled but did not push back. He walked out of the room. No doubt half a dozen guards were waiting in the hallway.

When Thane turned back around, Arliss glowered at him. "You will be used by God. Either as a son, or as a slave."

"Of course." His voice was bitter. "I wonder, which will you be?"

Chapter Twenty-One: Concerning the King

King Kenton walked alongside the sandy shoreline which lay between the ocean and the natural wall formed by the massive Cliffs of Aíll. He sucked in his breath and took in the view—the eternally blue ocean cloaked in a thick morning mist, the gulls screaming merrily as they darted up and down, the monumentally tall cliffs standing like guards to the land of Reinhold.

The first time he'd taken Arliss to see the seaside as a child, she'd been six, blue eyes even wider and more curious than they were now. The vast cliffs had struck her dumb as she had wandered the beaches in a state of wonder.

Not he. He had a quest, a job, a duty. His task was not like that of the men who were even now constructing new buildings to attach to the lone square tower high upon the cliffs. All had been decided: the seaside outpost would be expanded. It would surely become bigger and greater than the city upon a hill which lay twenty miles inland. Perhaps ships could be built, the ancient lands across the sea explored…

His task. He rushed his mind back to its base. Why was he this easily distracted so suddenly? Was he really so unfocused? Perhaps, perhaps not. He blamed the cliffs and the waves for his distracted mind, and he continued to set aright his thoughts.

Somehow, he would have to convince Adam that he had chosen the best course. Brédan had been easy enough to convince, but he knew Adam would put up more of a fight, even after the council's decision. How easy it had been to make a decision without Adam here! Already foundations were being laid for the newborn city.

Leaving Adam at the city had been best, but the rash lord might stir up trouble in his absence. At least Elowyn was there. As long as she remained in the city, no harm would come to it.

"My king, a few words with you, p'raps?" Brédan asked.

Kenton nodded as Brédan changed his stride to match his. Waves crashed on the shore a few feet from their boots. A few handbreadths beyond the waves, a wall of cloudy mist encroached upon the coastline. The mist hid the endless ocean separating them from the Isle of Light.

"These cliffs were of old regarded as a gateway to lands of faerie and mystery," Brédan said. "Yet for us they are a gate from the inside out, a portal to the whole world."

"The whole world, indeed. It's quite a mysterious place."

"Not half so mysterious as the mysteries which lay unexplored within our own borders, sire, if you ask me."

Kenton let a smile crease the edges of his mouth. "I did not ask you. Though you are no doubt right." He frowned. "You sound like my daughter."

"A true forthright lass, she is."

"Perhaps too forthright for her own good."

"Yet none can be too true for their own good."

"Only those whose truth is a lie, my good lord."

Brédan slowed his pace. "You doubt her loyalty?"

"No, I simply doubt *her*. It is not her loyalty alone that I impugn."

"She may be a fiery archeress, but whatever flaming spirit she has comes from her father."

"Do not compare me to her!" Kenton sucked in air as he wished to suck back in his words. Why did he with his every thought and word prove himself wrong?

Brédan pursed his lips. "I shan't say I told you so. Still, she's a right fine maiden, and a right fine maiden will sooner or later attract suitors—some noble, and some not so much."

So that was where this conversation traveled. Kenton nodded. "I think your Brallaghan would make a good husband for Arliss. He is a skilled swordsman, an aspiring knight, and a learned student of many honorable arts."

"You pay me a great compliment by saying so, my king." Brédan seemed a bit too enthusiastic. "You do know that Brallaghan has long been among Arliss's good friends. I'm sure she is quite fond of him as well."

Kenton sighed. "Indeed. Though most all maidens take some persuading."

"Brallaghan can be quite persuasive. No girl in Reinhold would resist him long, once they saw him truly."

"Perhaps you do not know how stubborn Arliss can be."

The words hung in the air between them unanswered.

Something emerged from the fog, many yards out upon the ocean. At first it looked like a massive wooden spear, until the spear dragged an entire ship out of the mist. Had he seen it in a book, Kenton would have deemed it a beautiful craft, with its ornately carved wooden prow and high, gilded stern. Yet seen in these circumstances, appearing so strangely from the mist so close to the shores of Reinhold, it made his blood boil.

Heading north, the ship disappeared back into the fog almost as quickly as it had come.

Kenton pressed against a heathery rock for support. The people of Reinhold had never made such a ship. Yet the vessel appeared young, as if on its maiden voyage. It had come from somewhere other than Reinhold, and that somewhere was alive and well enough to produce elegant oceancraft.

"Sire, are you all right?" Brédan's brow knitted with concern. "That ship, where—"

"It's going to try to land farther north. There are many places where they could disembark. If they found the river flowing from the mountains…" Kenton lost his voice for a moment. "They could be at the city within a day."

He headed toward the steep hill on top of the cliffs. Over his shoulder, he shouted at Brédan, "Stay here at the outpost, and make sure someone stays with you! I cannot leave this place unguarded."

"I shall do as you ask, my king."

Kenton reached the camp of a dozen other men. "We must leave at once! A foreign ship has been spotted sailing north. We have to return to the city." *To Elowyn.*

To Arliss.

Chapter Twenty-Two: The Son of Carraig

The ancient pages crackled as Arliss turned them, carefully revealing each one. Some of the brittle pages had not been turned in many years and remained obstinately stiff.

She had skimmed the book many times before, so many that she could recite some of the stories from memory. Yet Thane's words had somehow enlivened the leather volume and transformed it into something new. If many of the book's collection of stories, poems, and notes were true, which ones?

She had just come to the entry on Lasairbláth when the heavy door across the room creaked open. Cahal stepped in.

"The Master requests your presence at luncheon upon the dais, please." His voice sounded calm and courtly. He almost reminded her of Brallaghan, in a strange way. Yet Brallaghan's kingly behavior was genuine. Cahal, on the other hand, had to have something up his sleeve.

"You may tell Thane that I do not wish to come to luncheon upon the dais, please." She glared at him, and he stiffened. Did he speak as civilly to Philip as he did to herself? Likely not.

He waited as if to be dismissed. She arched her eyebrows and waved him off. "Go on, let me get back to my reading."

He smirked, stepping back into the hallway. "Of course. And do allow me to go back to my torture of the other prisoner."

She leapt to her feet, allowing the book to tumble to the floor, but she could not reach the door in time. It slammed in her face as she collapsed against the uneven wood, sobbing. The lock clicked, and Cahal's footsteps receded.

"Come back here, you snake!" she shouted through the cracks in the wood. She pounded on the door until her hands were raw and stuck with splinters. No one answered.

She rubbed the back of her hand across her cheeks to ebb the tears. Oh, Philip! None of this had been his fault. How could he endure? How could he not hate her—with every horrid thing Thane's men did to him, how could he not hate her? If she would just tell Thane the things he demanded of her, she could spare Philip this agony.

Philip would tell her not to give in, not to tell Thane a single thing. Yet if she could save his life, what would it matter? Her father could deal with Thane's army. *She* could deal with Thane's army. She could be the prophesied heroine.

Perhaps her father's life and her own life would be endangered if she told Thane. What did it matter? Philip had to live, or she felt she would die of guilt and grief.

Another blow bashed the side of Philip's face. Pain shot through the side of his skull. He grunted, trying to stay upright and on his feet. Not that he had to try: the ropes tied to his wrists ensured that he would be held upright, no matter what.

He clenched his fists and strained against the ropes until his wrists bled. If only he was freed from them! They were wrapped around the beams of the ceiling of the stone-backed room, giving him barely enough leeway for his feet to touch the ground.

Damian prodded him in the stomach with the but of a spear, then jabbed harder. His empty stomach churned. He coughed, and Damian let loose a rasping laugh.

Other warriors skirted about him, punching and kicking him, cracking him in the back of the head with spear shafts, as if they took pleasure in having a prisoner to pummel. But he could not give them the pleasure of seeing him lose his footing.

Could he bring the beams down? No, he wasn't near strong enough for that. However, if there was enough weight yanking the ropes downward—

Damian approached again, brandishing his spear. Philip glared at him. Here came his chance.

"Does our poor young knight tire of the torture?" Damian feinted a stab with the head end of the spear. He flipped the weapon back over, raising it over his shoulder. "Does he grow weary of the pain?"

"Your sort of pain is hardly worth being called by that name."

Flaring his nostrils, Damian pulled the spear even farther back, ready to thrust its dull end into Philip's unprotected stomach.

Philip held his steely glare.

The butt of the spear hurtled towards his abdomen.

Philip shifted to the side. The spear slammed into the stone wall behind him. The wood splintered against the mountainous wall.

With a roar, Damian charged. Philip braced against the wall behind him and slammed both feet into Damian's gut.

The other guards rushed to the coughing commander's rescue. But they came not soon enough.

Sputtering from the kick, Damian grabbed Philip's legs and pulled.

With a yell, Philip thrust himself forward with as much force as he could muster. The ropes chewed into his wrists. Damian kept pulling. Philip slammed his forehead into his opponent's face and hurled them both to the ground in a final effort. The ropes snapped free under the weight of their bodies and the force of his pull.

The falling bodies knocked Cahal off his feet, and the three rolled about on the floor.

Philip found his footing first, then Cahal. Philip's fist smashed into Cahal's chest, sending him sprawling. Philip raced to the door and came just short of slamming into Thane.

He could not leave. Thane consumed the doorway with his presence. He wielded no weapon of iron or steel, yet his weapons seemed more deadly and terrifying than any other Philip could face. Philip grabbed the pointed end of the spear Damian had shattered on the stone wall and hid it behind his back.

Coiled around either of Thane's arms, writhing and contorting their bodies hideously, were two long, striped snakes. He readjusted his arms and stroked their slick bodies. At his touch, they relaxed, wrapping themselves further about his arms until little more than their horrible heads were free to move.

With a smooth, hissing voice, he whispered strange words to the creatures: "*Codladh anois, agus stailc nach bhfuil.*"

At his command in the peculiar language, they settled down, as if asleep.

He smirked at Philip, letting his snake-cloaked arms fall to his sides. "So very clever are you, O son of Carraig, to find a way to destroy my implements."

"It wasn't that difficult to do, no thanks to your idiotic torturers." Philip jerked his head at Damian on the ground.

Thane threw his head back and laughed—a great, cold laugh that sounded stale and out of practice. "Ah, yes. I suppose torture is not Damian's strong suit. But, you, son of Carraig, are no simple peasant farmer are you?"

Philip bristled. "Of course not. I'm a carpenter—apprenticed to my uncle. At least I was until a few days ago. No doubt he'll slaughter me when he finds out where I've been." He lowered his brows. "But let me ask you something."

"Please, ask away." Thane tensed, and the snakes also tightened their coils.

"Why do you keep calling me by my father's name?"

Thane's eyes narrowed. "Is it not custom for children to be known by their father's name in Reinhold?"

"Sometimes," Philip answered, edging closer to him. "But better yet when a child makes his father proud by making an even better name for himself. A more honorable name."

Thane pursed his lips. "And no doubt that is what you wish, to make the name of Philip greater than the name of Carraig, to rise above the weakness and death of your father."

What did Thane know about his father? Philip clenched his fists, his wrists still bleeding and braceleted with the ropes which had eaten into his skin. "My father was a good man!"

The simple statement pushed Thane over the edge. His subtle, crafty visage cracked as he lashed out at Philip. "No, he was not a good man! He was a greedy weakling, afraid of change, afraid of Kenton, afraid of me!"

So Thane knew something about his father's death—it was written in his eyes. But what?

Glancing around at the handful of guards gathered in the cell, Thane lifted his arm and waved them all away. The snake on his arm flicked its tongue in and out.

"Leave us in peace, please." His words took instant effect as all the others exited, Cahal glaring and Damian coughing.

Once they were gone, Philip pointed his broken spear at Thane. "How can you claim to know so much about my father?"

"Because I knew him, of course."

"How?"

"Didn't Arliss tell you anything?"

"She told me you escaped from the Isle of Light the day we all left, but that you did not come with the rest of your clan."

"It was *never* my clan."

"And she told me that you had returned after all these years in order to take over Reinhold."

"Curse it all," Thane muttered. "That lass is perceptive indeed. No doubt she has also determined the specifics of my battle plans?"

"How would I know? I've been suspended from a ceiling beam all this time." Philip continued to glare, brandishing his shattered spear haft. "Now tell me about my father."

"What is there to tell? He hated that Kenton ruled over our island, but he also hated that I ruled over the treasury, so he decided that amity with Kenton would get him farther. Thus he hated me, I hated him, and when the plague struck the island, each of us waited for the other to fall dead."

"And I suppose you got your wish." Philip's voice tottered between a hoarse shout and a trembling whisper.

"Of course I did," Thane drew out his long knife.

Philip tensed, readying his own weapon.

Thane continued. "The plague took so many. What would be one more among the dead, no matter how he died? Now, fate has brought Carraig's son to me, and you will also die. But I'm afraid I shall not be so subtle this time."

"This time?"

"Yes." Thane's dagger flashed in the torchlight. "It was indeed I who killed your father."

Philip let out a fierce yell and threw himself at Thane.

The snakes awoke and unwound themselves from their master's arms.

Cahal returned to Arliss's cell two hours later, this time bearing another request from Thane.

"Master Thane wishes for your presence at tea in his private chambers."

His private chambers? Arliss stiffened. These invitations were becoming more and more cordial. Ought she accept and haggle with Thane to release her and Philip? Or should she ignore this ignoble villain who continued to try to torture an answer out of Philip?

She tilted her chin, fixing Cahal with a gaze that she hoped was queenly. "Tell Thane this—until he ceases torturing Philip, I will not consort with him, not for luncheon, not for tea, not for dinner."

"And if he accepts your demand?"

She tilted her head and smiled. "Then perhaps I will be willing to talk."

He trudged out of the room without speaking another word, and the door grated into its jamb behind him. Silence prevailed in the outer hall for a long moment.

Just as she had picked back up the book to continue exploring its contents, the door scraped open again. Cahal reentered, pushing one of the rolling tables on which he had brought her so elegant a lunch the day before.

A silk brocade cloth, rippling with curious designs, draped over the top of the table and halfway down to the wheels. Perched in the very center of the tablecloth stood a tall, narrow pitcher of tarnished silver; arranged around it, like the petals of a flower, sat a cup, saucer, cream pitcher, honey jar, and a few thin biscuits upon a plate. No doubt Thane considered this a simple tea, but to Arliss it seemed one of the most lovely teas she had ever enjoyed. A cup of tea was never so good as after two days of interrogation.

Cahal released his grip on the rolling table, grimacing as he poured Arliss a cup of tea. "Cream? Honey?" He practically choked on the words.

She squared her shoulders. "I can serve it myself, but thank you."

Cahal nodded, then backed away, glancing askance at the corner of the tea tray.

She noticed the slip of paper tucked under the saucer of her teacup. Carefully lifting the saucer with its filled cup, she picked up the note and unfolded it.

Arliss,

Be informed that no more harm will be done to Philip's person this day. However, if you will not meet with me and tell me such things as I have been requesting these past few days, I will continue torturing him until one of you speaks.

Your friend is safe until sunset.

Cordially,
Thane, your captor and cousin

The closing sentence held a sense of finality: *your friend is safe until sunset.* Her pleas had won Philip half a day of reprieve.

The sickening pit in her stomach colluded with her pounding heart. If she didn't reveal the specifics of Reinhold's military force to Thane before sunset, Philip would die. And no doubt Thane would force her to watch every moment of his long, painful death. He would revel in the pain he caused by snatching from her the closest thing she'd ever had to a brother.

She reread the note's closing. Suddenly her heart froze over. She clenched the piece of paper as she brought it closer to her face, trying to ensure she read it rightly. There could be no mistaking it.

Thane, your captor and cousin.

Aye, his name was Thane. And aye, he was her captor.

But her cousin? What was the hidden meaning of that?

She set down the note and gulped a sip of tea. She sputtered a moment, finding the tea hotter and stronger than she had expected. It was a deep, heavy tea, almost fiery in its flavor; she felt as if smoking coals were being poured down her throat. In an unusual way, it tasted most delicious.

Thane, her captor and cousin.

Her cousin. Thane.

How many secrets could this one man possibly possess?

CHAPTER TWENTY-THREE: THE VISITOR TO THE CASTLE

Ilayda grimaced as she wound the bandage tighter around Erik's lean forearm. She tried to ignore the blood that began to seep from the reopened wound.

Erik sucked in a breath through visibly gritted teeth, but he allowed her to yank the bandage taut and tie it off.

"That ought to do it," she said.

Filtered by scattered clouds, the afternoon sun streamed through the huge window of the castle library. Erik was sitting in a reading chair—the king's reading chair, no doubt—as she bent over him and tended his wound. After the queen and Nathanael had left, pain had seized Erik's forearm as the scarred flesh began to fester. Thankfully, the bite had been a superficial one, and easily enough doctored.

Standing up straight again, Ilayda squeezed her eyes shut as she stretched her tense back. How unusual the last few days had been! Never in her life had she dreamed of these sorts of things happening.

The sun flashed through the clouds and into the open window again, and she squinted. A gust of wind upset the heavy curtains. She pulled them over the blazing light of the window.

Erik let out a massive sigh behind her. "I should have gone with them."

"You? Don't be silly. With your wound still untreated and unbound, you'd have slowed them down."

"I suppose. I mean, I actually *wanted* to go with them. I want to make sure my brother is safe."

"Your cousin," Ilayda corrected.

"Philip's both of those to me."

She slumped into a chair by the window. "So is Arliss to me."

They held the silence for a moment. Ilayda savored the quiet. Such peace had been scarce the past few days. She sat still, relishing each slow breath.

Shouts from the village below pierced the silence.

What was the ruckus about? Ilayda leapt up and pulled the curtains open just a crack. People bustled about in both tiers—probably finishing the midday meal before they continued with the events of their day. From up here, the lowest tier was just a blur of homes and workshops.

A foreign sound stirred the city, pounding the hard dirt road which wound through the tiers. To Ilayda it sounded like a pair of giants running up the city.

The creator of the sound rounded the bend from the second tier to the third, approaching the castle.

It was a man, his deep burgundy cloak streaming out behind him in the autumn breeze. Ilayda squinted. *That* was unusual enough, but he was just a man, after all. Her attention was more drawn to the majestic creature he rode. It looked rather like a tall, shaven dog, yet it walked too nobly and its face stretched out too long. The creature's feet (if they could be called that) seemed to be hard, as if carved from obsidian, and created the strange clamping noise that had puzzled Ilayda a moment before. She fumbled through her memory for the creature's name. This beast galloped through the pages of many books.

Erik appeared beside her to look through the window. The creature's name came to her mind just as he spoke it.

"A horse."

Ilayda bounded down the castle stairs and across the great hall. The hoofbeats were getting louder, which meant one thing: the visitor in the burgundy cloak wasn't stopping until he reached the castle.

She flung open the double doors and found her father standing outside, his arms crossed.

Adam glanced nervously at her. "Someone's coming—riding some thunderous beast."

"A horse," Ilayda corrected.

He shrugged one shoulder. "You should get back inside."

"You really think I'm going to miss the first horse to ever ride through our village?"

He looked at her again, his face perched on the edge of amusement. "It isn't safe. Take one of your secret passages, get to the market, and find your mother and Arden. I want to make sure they're safe."

She bit her lips. He couldn't do this to her. Everyone *always* did this to her—sent her away just when things were getting exciting.

But he was her father. And she'd been brash enough the previous day. She nodded stiffly and turned for the path down to the second tier.

The horseman rounded the main road and cantered up onto the flat hilltop of the third tier. He pulled his horse to a halt and dismounted.

Ilayda froze, waiting for her father.

Adam greeted the stranger. "Welcome to Reinhold, sir."

The man bowed, slipping one leg forward slightly. The burgundy cloak hid him in a muddy mystery. Dark fabric also stretched across his face, revealing only his eyes—shimmering brown.

Erik stepped out of the castle, and his eyebrows twitched slightly. "Who are you, and—"

Lord Adam held up his hand. "Let me take care of this." He stepped toward the visitor. "Who are you, and where do you come from?"

"I am a weary traveler," the fellow's voice was young but hoarse, "and I seek refuge."

Ilayda sent her father a subtle nod. A tired traveler seeking refuge—that was what all the Reinholdians had been when they came to this land. Surely her father could not deny this stranger a place of rest.

"Weary traveler, indeed." Adam placed his hands on his hips. "Show me your face before I show you a place to stay."

"I am diseased, and the long ride did nothing to help my condition."

"Father!" Ilayda strode back over to him. "Let him come in and rest. He needs water and food."

Adam leaned close so only she and Erik could hear. "We don't even know who he is or where he's come from. He must be connected to Thane's return."

"How do you know that?" Ilayda hissed.

"I just do. I am a lord."

Her eyelids twitched as she resisted the urge to give her eyes a good roll.

Erik glanced over at the burgundy-caped man. "Perhaps he's telling the truth. Either way, we can keep a better eye on him in the castle. If it winds up he is connected with Thane, then at least he won't have wreaked havoc on the whole city."

"Perhaps you're right." Adam grunted. "But I want you to watch him. Guard him. Don't let him leave until the queen returns. I must go and inform the rest of the city to be on guard."

Ilayda stole another look at their guest. If he wasn't a citizen of Reinhold—and he clearly wasn't—then who was he? Arliss hadn't mentioned there being any others lost other than Áedán.

So where had this fellow—with his horse and burgundy cloak—come from?

Arliss had made her decision. No matter what it would cost her father, she would tell Thane what he wanted to know. Losing Philip's life—and her own life, for that matter—was not worth securing a temporary truce, a mere delay of Thane's imminent attack.

When Cahal brought Thane's final invitation of the day, she accepted, informing the young guard that she would be ready within five minutes. That gave her just enough time to do something about the dreadful state of her clothes.

Her dress couldn't be helped. Thane didn't have any women's clothes in the fortress, and her old blue woolen thing was in shreds. Still, going to dinner in a simple chemise did not seem suitable.

She paced about the fancified room, her bare feet slapping against the hard-packed dirt floor.

She glanced at the far corner and froze when she she saw the thin, budding sprout that had sprung up. It could be nothing but an infant Lasairbláth plant. So it had sprouted—and so quickly! She'd never seen any flower grow—much less bloom—in so little time. Perhaps it possessed some sort of magic.

On a standing hook near the fiddle on the dresser, thick and long and dark, hung a deep red cloak—almost a muddy red. It draped nearly to the floor.

The richly lined cloak was a perfect length for her, and she fastened it about her shoulders. She caught a glimpse of herself in the tall looking-glass which spanned the height of the far wall, and gaped at what she saw. She had not glanced in a mirror since the night of her birthday ball, when she was dressed in all her finery and her hair had shone golden in the lamplight.

Now, her hair tangled and waved its way down her shoulders, weighed down by dirt and sweat from the past few days. Her face was flecked with scratches, and her underdress could hardly be called white anymore. Yet the burgundy cloak somehow transformed her whole reflection. She looked like a queen in disguise.

A princess on a carven throne, clothed in simple raiment.

Chapter Twenty-Four: Heirs to the Throne

"This is the first time I've entertained royalty here." Thane lifted his glass and sipped its contents.

Arliss, too, took a sip from her goblet. A sharply acidic wine bit her throat, and she coughed as the swig traveled down.

"Hopefully," she managed, sputtering slightly, "I won't prove too demanding."

On the dais, a fine table had been set for them. All six feet of its length which separated the two of them was filled with all manner of fine food and drink: meat, bread, wine, cheese, and those curious olives of which Thane seemed so fond.

"This is also the first time I've hosted a woman here, as a matter of fact." He took another sip of the bitter wine.

It would be impolite to refuse the drink, wouldn't it? She again lifted her glass and took a sip—a smaller one this time. It still made her sputter.

"I wonder, have you entertained any guests here at all?" She tried to stifle the burning sensation in her throat.

He didn't seem to notice her trouble. "Ah! Now you have hit the nail upon the head! Perhaps you now see why I have pressed to entertain you at my table."

"Because you want me to tell you all I know about Reinhold's military forces?"

"Mayhaps." He stroked his short beard. "But that is not the only reason."

She inspected him, considering again the note he had sent with the tea. That, more than anything, seemed impossible to explain.

"I think I have a guess as to the other reason. But it confuses me." She leaned into the table, her voice lowering. "Why did you sign your note 'cousin'?"

"Does it not make sense to you?"

"One often calls their close friend or relation 'cousin.' Yet the way you have treated me proves you are neither my friend nor my relation."

His expression twisted with anguish, and he reached for his face, his hand gripping his bearded chin with pale knuckles. "I—I'm sorry, Arliss."

She tilted her head. "After all this, you're asking my forgiveness?"

"No. I dare not do that. But I have to admit that no cousin should treat their relation as I have treated you."

She gripped the stem of her wine goblet, her own knuckles going white. "Why is that relevant, pray tell?"

He let his hand drop into his lap, and something like a groan escaped his lips. "Is that also among the many things your parents never told you? Don't you understand? My father was your grandfather's brother. We are cousins—or second cousins by generation, as they say in some books."

Arliss's mouth dropped open. She released the goblet for fear she would knock it over with her trembling hands. She and Thane were cousins? It could not be. Her parents would have told her. Then again, why would they resurrect the name of one they presumed dead?

"Why did you not tell me this before?"

He sighed. "I assumed that if you knew my name, you must have known everything else. I did not know how ignorant you were—rather, how ignorant your parents had made you."

"But that means you are our family! You ought to be guarding the royal castle, not scheming in this hole."

"It means, Arliss, that I ought to be heir to the throne of Reinhold."

Indignant fire burned in her chest. "You are nothing of the sort."

"Why do you say that, *pray tell?*" Thane stressed the final words, clearly mocking her.

She set her jaw and glared at him. "I am the heir. I am the daughter of Kenton, the king, the direct heir descended in a line from Reinhold himself, a line which has never been broken. And it never will be. My mother told me the line of Reinhold always endures. I believe her words."

"Your mother is a fool!" He spat out the words. "She fueled Kenton's mistrust of me. Their marriage only solidified our enmity."

"My mother is no fool!" Arliss pounded the table with her fist. "She is wise, wiser than any man or woman in Reinhold."

He laughed scornfully. "So Elowyn continues to play at being a seer and a prophetess? She always was a mystic—and a fool."

"She is neither a mystic nor a fool. She is simply a very wise queen."

"Your mother claims to see the future." Thane smirked, twisting an olive between two fingers before popping it in his mouth. "I doubt she has seen what is coming upon her and her city. Which brings me to another of my many reasons for inviting you to dine with me. Let us plan our revenge together."

"Our revenge?"

"Yes, of course. We both have a score to settle with Kenton, do we not?"

"How do you know about that?"

"Why else would you run away? Why else would you be in the woods with a peasant carpenter's apprentice? And you forget that I knew Kenton for many years. I know how his mind runs in circles upon itself. And I know how he can so easily drive others away with his stubbornness. You and I are both stubborn as well. We have that in common. Do not think you are the only one who has been driven away by Kenton's single-mindedness."

"I will not tolerate this sort of talk about my father!"

"So you're defending him now, eh?"

"Well, I am his heir, after all." She swigged the wine and erupted into coughing. She continued to wheeze as Thane exploded with laughter.

As her chest slowly calmed its heaving, she glared at him. "It isn't really that funny."

He continued chuckling. "Arliss, the pitcher of water is there for a reason. This wine is meant to be mixed with water before being consumed."

"The water pitcher is almost empty, if you hadn't noticed. Perhaps you could send for your servant Cahal to fetch us some more."

"I do not subscribe to Kenton's elitism. There are no servants in this fortress, only comrades with varying levels of skill and authority." His face became grave once again. "You may be trying to defend your heirship and your life, but do not forget it was you, O Arliss, who fired the first shot in this war. You had the first kill."

She cleared her throat, lifting her chin. "No, it was you. This war began the moment Áedán died."

He held her gaze, not answering.

She searched his eyes. What did he want? He was a Reinholdian—her cousin—but he had been gone for so long (only God knew where) and he had changed. How long had he hidden here—and why did he choose to make his move now?

Then she swallowed the truth that rose in her throat. It was because of *her*. By going on her quest, she must have triggered his realization. Unless, of course, she had walked straight into a plan already in motion.

He placed his eating utensils on the plate. "Have you eaten well?"

Arliss glanced at the full platters on the table. "I have eaten enough, I suppose."

"Then shall we go down to Orl—to your chamber for some tea? I have ordered it to be prepared for us after the meal."

She stiffened. "Why in my chambers? Why not up here?"

"Because in your room you can properly answer my questions. You can draw me maps of your city. You can tell me the truth about your father."

Yes—and she could free herself and Philip. The pit in her stomach deepened. "Yes, let's. I'm certainly not hungry for food any longer."

Arliss sat upon the bed, sipping slowly on a sweetly spiced tea and fingering her side. The lower ribs still throbbed with soreness, and climbing the steps to the stony mound for dinner hadn't done them much good.

A few steps away, Thane paced, sipping his own tea and examining a map Arliss had drawn of the city. She swallowed. Hopefully he wouldn't pick up all the details she had intentionally left off. At least, not yet.

While his back was turned, she slipped to the chest of drawers and lifted up the dusty fiddle. She positioned it under her chin and plucked the strings almost silently to check the tuning.

Thane spoke. "So, you say there are hardly more than a score of able knights in the city? What about bowmen? Surely all—"

She filled the room with gentle, flowing music and drowned out his voice. He stopped talking and pivoted to face her.

With a practiced skill, she pulled the bow across and through the strings and began to recreate the melody Philip had been singing in the woods. The melody which accompanied the poem. The poem which accompanied the prophecy. She began to sing the words as she played the song a second time, her voice blending with the high clarity of the fiddle's notes.

"A princess on a carven throne," she began. "Clothed in simple raiment."

"A queenly look is in her eye," Thane intoned, surprising her. "And grace is on her forehead." Then he continued, singing the second verse. "A princess on a smooth-hewn throne, clothed in linen raiment—a queenly look is in her eye, and grace is on her forehead."

Together they finished the song. "A princess on a gilded throne, clothed in silken raiment—a queenly look is in her eye, and grace is on her forehead."

She let the bow slip silently from the string and held his stare.

"We have not had music in this fortress for a long time." His eyes burned with sorrow.

"Why then do you have this fiddle?"

"It belonged to one of my men."

"And what happened to him, if it is not too forward of me to ask?"

Thane sighed. "He is on another mission, perhaps far away, perhaps not."

"You speak as if he were like a son to you."

"He is rather like a son—or perhaps more like an apprentice. I am quite fond of him."

"And you wish for him to return?"

"With my whole heart."

"Perhaps now you will also let me return. My father, too, will be expecting me. I have told you everything I know of his army, and the maps I have drawn ought to more than describe the city. Can you not now release me and Philip?"

Thane clenched his eyes shut. "I cannot."

Her heart pounded as she set the fiddle back down. "But you swore you would!"

His broad shoulders creaking as he stretched them, Thane stepped closer to her. "Perhaps I did. But I also made another oath, to your father, twelve years ago on the Isle of Light. You were there, do you not remember?"

"I was but four years old. My memory of the Isle is hazy."

"I swore to him that I would take the blood of his house. I have sworn an oath, in my own blood, that I will destroy the house of Reinhold." His voice trembled barely above a whisper. "That is why I cannot release you. Either I kill you, or I wait for your father to come, and I kill him."

"You will not kill him."

"Then would you rather me kill you?"

"No!" she shouted, then tempered her tone. "No, I would not rather you kill me. I am the heir to the throne."

He released an angry yell and swept his hand in an arc in front of his body. Arliss ducked, and he bashed one of the four curved glass lamps. Its pieces shattered onto the floor, and the room's flickering light grew dimmer. "You are not the heir! You are a woman—how could you be the heir?"

"How does that make a difference?"

"Kings want sons to carry on their lines, not daughters."

"I don't see why either is preferable. A prince still needs a princess to produce heirs." Her heart fluttered in her chest. "And a princess still needs a prince."

His fists clenched. "You will never be the heir. I will crush you until you are alone, beyond alone."

"No one is alone."

"Of course." His voice stung bitterly. "No one, except the boundless numbers of those who *are* terribly, indubitably alone. I was alone until I gathered my army, built my fortress. And you, Arliss, will be alone when I have finished. You will be alone when I have killed your father, your mother, your uncles, your friend Philip. You will wander the wilderness, lonely and alone, because there is none, no one, not a single person on this earth who can quench your grief."

Tears streamed down her cheeks. "What about my faith?"

He snorted. "You think God will keep you from this lonely fate?"

"I do not know what the future holds. I know he has allowed my captivity for a purpose. But no matter what happens, I will not let you destroy Philip. Nor my father."

"What power do you have to stop me?"

"Love. My love is stronger than your hate." She quivered. "I'm not afraid of you. The love in my heart—the love of God—casts out fear."

"Hah! Your *love*. Arliss, you are sixteen, barely a woman. He is barely a man. Perhaps in time things shall change, and you shall then see that what you mistook for love was only childish emotion."

"It will never come to that," Arliss insisted.

"And your love for your father? Indeed! What great love you have shown him! You, the daughter who rebels and runs away and gets herself captured and drags others down with her! You know nothing of love."

She stared at the ground. Maybe Thane was right. She had been foolish—too careless to make plans or to think of her own father. And she had trampled over all of her friends this whole time. Now, because of her rashness, she and Philip were permanent prisoners.

But she *was* doing this for a reason greater than herself. It had gotten lost somewhere along the way, trampled down in the depths of her mind. Lines cut between the people of Reinhold. She meant to erase them. Yet by leaving, by forsaking her father, by dragging her friends down, she had drawn more lines.

She looked up at Thane. "Perhaps I was blind in what I did. But I think I can see more clearly now. If only you could also understand."

"There is nothing to understand, only this—I will destroy the line of Reinhold battle by battle, and you will watch your city burn."

She closed her eyes, at first seeing nothing but the reddish glow within her eyelids. Then it transformed into a vision of her city: the three tiers burning, the castle tower collapsing, the moat filled with wreckage and debris. She shuddered at the vision as it burned in her mind.

No. She could never let that happen. The city was her home—the very foundation of Reinhold itself. Someday she would even rule the city herself—when she felt ready. And when she was ready, she would need a king to rule with her—someone as close or closer than a brother.

She glanced up into Thane's face, her eyes pleading.

"Even if you will not release us, allow me to see him. Let me go to Philip."

Chapter Twenty-Five: The Price of Liberation

The night was dark in the roofless canopy of sky which spanned the top of the mountain fortress. As Arliss hurried across, pulling the burgundy cloak about her shoulders, she glimpsed one lone, shining star among the clouds. The clouds had gathered in a multitude. The air smelled of rain.

Thane did nothing to restrain her as she hurried across to the row of half-wood, half-stone buildings and galleries built into the side of the mountain. No one had told her which door was his, but the instinct of friendship guided her. She came to Philip's cell room and opened it with surety, not trying any others.

He looked up, clearly stifling a groan as he forced a small smile. "Arliss."

She dropped to her knees in front of him. He'd been bound with ropes which hung from planks on the ceiling—some of which seemed to be broken. Blood streaked his forearms and forehead, and his chest shuddered as he exhaled. She looked away, too ashamed even to weep. "Do not forgive me. I cannot ask you to do that."

"What is there to forgive? You haven't done any of this."

"I brought you here, Philip. If only I had left you in the village. If only I had gone alone, or not at all."

"You mean, if only you had obeyed your father?"

She glowered at him, but did not argue.

"Maybe you should have obeyed him, and maybe you shouldn't have dragged me into this adventure." He licked a cut at the corner of his mouth and grimaced. "But why think about that now? The past is behind you. Your destiny is ahead of you. And, while you cannot change your mistakes, you can mend them. You can make things right."

Her laugh sounded like a sob. "You think my father will let me fix things, even after all I've done?"

"He will have no choice. Yes, you're the one who started this mess. But all that means is that you're the best one to fix it."

"People often fix mistakes which they themselves didn't make."

"This is not one of those times." He tugged at the ropes that restrained him. "So tell me, princess, what are you going to change when you return to the city?"

Tossing her hair behind her shoulders, she crouched on the dirt floor beside him. "I don't know."

Thane's voice resounded outside the door. "Hurry up, Arliss. We still have things to discuss. The sun has long set. Your time is expiring."

She leapt to her feet. "I have to go. Thane may have promised to release us once I spoke with him, but now it seems he will not keep his promise."

"Does that really surprise you?"

"Yes." Arliss sighed. "He is more than you think."

The blue flecks in Philip's eyes turned to steel. "I understand that now more than you know. He is the one who killed my father."

"No." She didn't want to believe it. But she could see the truth in Philip's eyes.

"It is true. And now, if he can, he will kill me as well. But as long as I am bait for you, he will spare my life, no matter how much he tortures me. I hope you've put together why he built his fortress in this place."

"I must admit I don't really know."

"He's found it," Philip whispered so low she had to strain to hear. "He's found the heart of Reinhold—the oasis which all the old books spoke of. The only thing keeping it hidden is this fortress."

"Arliss!" Thane's tone verged upon anger.

She reached for Philip's bound hand and gripped it. "I promise you this: I will do whatever I can to get you out of here."

"And promise me something else. You will not forget the bow I was making before we left the city, and you will not forget your promise to make things right." Philip smiled. "Perhaps—"

Thane bellowed for Arliss again, his voice fiery. Then, Damian's voice exploded from the battlements of the fortress wall, a warning frantically shouted in their strange tongue. A massive crashing sound, as of wood splintering and cracking, rumbled from the entrance to the fortress.

Arliss glanced worriedly at Philip, who nodded back at her. She was free to leave him.

Outside the cell, Thane's attention had been completely distracted. "What is it, Damian?"

"*Ionróiri!*" Damian shouted.

"What did he say?" Arliss asked.

Thane's fingers slipped to his sword hilt. "Invaders."

Arliss then saw what had produced the cracking sound. The wooden portcullis, which overhung the river as it passed beneath the wall, had been destroyed and its beams now floated down the slow stream. Two figures emerged from outside of the wall, drenched from their waists down. One brandished a long sword, and the other had an arrow on string even as she carried three more shafts in her draw hand.

Arliss's heart leapt into her throat with a shock of joy.

Queen Elowyn and Lord Nathanael had come to liberate them.

Elowyn took in the fortress—the high mountain walls, the long buildings which ran down the sides and attached to the front wall, the thin river which flowed like syrup towards the high stone platform—even as the rich scent of alder trees and mountain air filled her nose.

Nathanael leapt out of the river and onto the fortress's flat inner bailey. She followed him, drawing back the arrow of her bow even as her feet found dry land.

Two people rushed out of the colonnade of rooms built into the rock on the right. Torches hung in brackets at intervals around the clearing, casting grim light on the figures. The first—a tall, muscled man who was just drawing a long, curved sword—Elowyn recognized at once. Twelve years hadn't changed him much, unless it was that his shoulders were broader and his forehead more crisscrossed with lines.

Then the second figure emerged all the way into the moonlit keep. Elowyn's muscles clenched. Thane stood between her and her daughter.

Arliss. Her hair cascaded over her shoulders in its usual waving tangle of gold. What appeared to be a tattered chemise was cloaked in a burgundy cape fit for a king and draping to her ankles.

Elowyn wet her lips. No matter what happened, Arliss would make it out of this fortress alive.

"Good evening, Elowyn!" Thane called, twirling his sword in his palm. "It's been a while! Twelve years is a long time to go without seeing such close relatives."

She flexed her fingers on the bow. "I cannot say that I have the same pleasure at seeing you again after so long."

"You thought me dead—or hoped it, no doubt?"

"Whatever I thought or hoped, it matters not, since you are clearly not dead." She scanned Arliss's face for some sense of worry or agitation, but she saw only surprise and determination. That was well; they would need every bit of her wit and will if they were to get out of this predicament.

"Where is Kenton?" Thane spoke bluntly.

"Kenton is his own man. I am not his governess. I am only his queen."

"He's not here, is he?"

"If he was, do you think we would still be having this conversation? We'd be fighting already."

Nathanael leveled his blade. "In my opinion, that might not be a bad thing."

Thane ignored him. "Doubtless Kenton would be giving us all one of his long-winded speeches. There's something I have noticed—of all the things Arliss inherited from her brash father, she didn't receive that trait. She's quite the conversationalist, as I have been able to experience on a number of occasions. Right, dear Arliss?"

Arliss's middle three fingers clenched as if holding an arrow. "One must make the best use of even the worst of conversation partners."

Thane laughed, the sound of it echoing off the sides of the mountain. "See, here it is! A right fine wit she has, eh, Elowyn?"

"Shut up," she ordered. "And get away from my daughter."

Thane took a step back toward Arliss. Elowyn raised her bow.

"You would not kill me, Elowyn."

"If you continue to stand between me and my daughter, I will not hesitate."

"Nor I," Nathanael butted in.

"Nathanael, be quiet. Your sister and I are talking, and we did not give you any say in this matter."

Thane turned and leapt the distance between himself and Arliss, pinned her arms to her side, and held his blade to her neck.

Elowyn prepared to shoot.

Arliss watched her mother and uncle approaching, tense and wary. Farther behind them, Damian and Cahal waited for a command from Thane. Where the rest of the guards were, she didn't know.

"Do forgive me for this, Arliss." Thane's bearded cheek scraped against hers. "But in order to catch the game, you have to offer the bait."

"Release her," her mother commanded, "or I will stick an arrow in your forehead. I hope you don't think Arliss received her archery training from Kenton alone."

"If you release that arrow, I slit her throat. I think you know how this works, Elowyn, so I shouldn't have to tell you."

Arliss grabbed Thane's sword arm, then slammed her foot back into his groin.

His grip on her arms weakened, and she used the leverage to pull his sword arm away from her neck and slip out from under it. Somersaulting out from beneath him, she jumped to her feet and stood between her mother and uncle. Nathanael reached out to grab her shoulder, but Elowyn didn't flinch. Thane edged closer to Philip's cell.

"My brother in arms is behind that door. We must save him." She looked over her shoulder towards the fortress wall. Cahal and Damian were circling, pacing, blocking their escape through the destroyed portcullis.

But she needed to retrieve the ancient book. She couldn't leave it behind. "There's something important in the chamber across the hall. I must fetch it."

"Do it quickly. Nathanael and I will deal with Thane." Elowyn tugged at the bowstring as Thane—at least ten paces away from them—stepped backwards to fill up the doorway of Philip's cell.

"And you must get Philip out of there," Arliss whispered.

Elowyn nodded. "We will do what we can. Now go, and get what you need. We will cover for you."

Arliss sprinted to the river, leapt over it, and bolted toward the exquisite chamber—ignoring the pain that shot across her ribs. The book would be lying on the bed, right where she left it.

Cahal split off from Damian's side and leapt after her. But she had been too quick. By the time he reached the river, she was already rushing inside the colonnade.

She pushed into the room and grabbed the book off the bed, then scoured the tables and dressers for a bag of some sort. What had Thane done with her own leather satchel? She hadn't seen it since they'd been captured in the woods.

She found an aged knapsack of thin, cracked leather, and stuffed the book inside.

Footsteps smacked the earth just outside the left colonnade of rooms. She narrowed her eyes. She needed a weapon—any weapon, but preferably a bow. In fact, it would have to be a bow. Her blood was coursing too fast right now for her to use anything else.

The shattered remains of the lamp still lay on the dirt floor. She could use some of the larger shards as makeshift knives. But those could only be used at extremely close range.

She gripped the knapsack with the book inside. There was nothing in this chamber. Thane's chambers, though, were probably farther down the hall outside. Surely his room was stocked with weaponry.

She started for the door just as Cahal burst into the room.

"You," she spat. This fellow had played a clear hand in Philip's torture. Her body burned with the desire for vengeance.

"Me." He drew a long knife. "And you are unarmed."

She wound the strap of the knapsack around her fingers. "Move out of my way. Now!"

"No." He pointed the knife at her. "You should not even be in this room. No one else is even allowed in this chamber. Why should Thane treat you with such favor? You should be in a cell. I should've been torturing you with the other prisoner."

"Go ahead." She spurred him on, edging him to charge her.

He did, knife slashing.

She ducked out of the way, swinging her knapsack. The book clobbered him in the side of the head. He staggered to the side and fell palms-down in the pile of glass shards.

His cry of pain echoed in her ears as she rushed out of the room and down the dark hallway.

A tall warrior—Damian, as Thane had addressed him—rushed from the wall at Elowyn. The world slowed down as she turned her arrow toward him. She watched his every move: the rise and fall of his feet, the tottering of his sword as he closed the distance between them.

Thane and Nathanael had drawn swords behind her and each waited for each other to make a move.

Her fingers twitched. There would have to be blood. Thane had ensured that, no matter what happened, it would not finish without the cost of many lives. Still she hesitated as she lifted her bow. If she had the power to prevent it, no blood would be spilled this day.

But she would get Arliss out of here at any cost. Arliss was the line of Reinhold. She had to survive.

Her fingers released the arrow almost against her will.

Damian ducked, and the arrow whizzed an inch above his shoulder.

Elowyn cantered to the side, sidestepping his momentum. He swept his sword in a wide arc where she had been standing. She slipped off to the side again.

"I am not wanting to play games," he said. "If you are compliant, I know Thane will take you alive as a prisoner. He will add you to those for which he demands ransom."

"If you want me as a prisoner, come and catch me." She took to her heels and ran, heading for the frontal wall of the fortress. The more she could split up this fight, the better chance Nathanael would have.

Nathanael and Thane began their fight by the entrance to Philip's cell. The sound of clanging metal erupted in the mountain fortress behind her.

She reached the wall and strained for a decent grip on its stones. The gaps between the huge, hewn stones were just thick enough for her to insert her booted toes into. Just as Damian reached her, she hoisted herself higher, and the flat of his blade pressed against cold stone.

She kept climbing. Why weren't there more guards? There had to be more. But Thane hadn't called out reinforcements, and she wanted to keep it that way.

The wall must have been twenty feet high, and she was panting when she tugged herself over the side of the upper crenels and into the battlements. The walkway spanned the top of the wall and had about five feet in width. From here, she could behold the entire fortress—and fire arrows upon it.

Besides Nathanael's duel, the fortress was eerily quiet and empty. The thin river flowed below her, across the fortress and beneath the stony mound at the back. What was beyond that mound—beyond the other side of the mountains? If the legends were true...

A warrior sprang from the shadows of the far side of the wall, dislodging her bow from her grasp and slamming her to the ground, her cheek sliding against the callous edges of stone. She jutted her foot into his stomach as he grabbed at her. He gasped and doubled over. She had just enough time to retrieve her weapon.

Her mind raced. She backed up against the edge of the wall. He cut down upon her with his sword, but she ducked beneath him, and his blade and arm slammed down into the nearest crenelation. Elowyn used his momentum against him and shoved, tossing him over the side of the wall.

Thane roared. The fight had moved to the center of the fortress, with Thane forcing Nathanael away from Philip's cell. But Thane seemed to have stumbled. He now stood in the river, up to his chest in water.

Nathanael turned and ran toward Philip's cell.

Thane shouted something in a foreign tongue that made Elowyn's neck bristle.

She dashed to the center of the battlement, finding the staircase which cut back down to the wide bailey. She rushed down the stairs and into the darkness.

Once back on ground level—still inside the wall itself—she saw that the only way in or out, besides the river entrance, lay through the doors which sat equidistant from the center of the wall. Because of the staircase and the arched river entryway which lay between them, the doors could only be reached from the side of the stream on which they stood.

Her hands shook as she unlatched the door on her side of the wall. She burst back out into the wide expanse of the mountain fortress, hurrying toward Thane.

Thane clawed himself back onto dry ground and strode forward, brushing hair out of his face with a dripping palm. He stood between her and Philip's cell—between her and Nathanael.

She nocked at arrow. "Stand down. I will not say it more than once."

He glared, but he sheathed his sword. She cocked her head. What was he doing? It was never like Thane to listen—to avoid a fight.

He inhaled, his huge chest expanding. "It's too late for me to stand down, Elowyn. Surely you realize this is bigger than that. It's bigger than you. Bigger than me."

She lowered her arrow. "*What* is?"

"This place. My purpose. Reinhold could be mine. I believe it should be mine. And I have the aid of forces beyond you."

What forces? Everything Erik and Ilayda had said about the snakes pointed to dark magic. Was Thane simply implying his dabbling with sorcery? Or was there something deeper?

"Reinhold is not yours," she said. "Reinhold will never be yours."

He snorted. "You think you know many things, Elowyn. But even you know nothing of who I am and what I can do. I have the power of legends on my side—ancient power, the power of the heavens, of the moon itself."

She tensed. His mind had become very dark indeed. Only the darkest and most twisted of legends worshipped the heavens, or the moon. He didn't know what he was speaking of.

Or perhaps he did. And that was somehow more frightening.

"The moon merely reflects light. It is but a glimpse and a shadow of the true sun. Sometimes the moon is not at all what she seems."

Nathanael and Philip burst out of the prison cell. Nathanael had his sword ready, and Philip—though unarmed and unsteady—had clenched fists.

"You cannot protect them from me, Elowyn." Thane reached beneath his cloak and pulled a bow and arrow from its folds. "You cannot protect Arliss from me."

Arliss squinted down the dim hallway. The dark doorway at the end had to be Thane's room. She lowered the handle and slipped inside.

A lamp lit the interior just enough for sight. It left the room dark enough that the cluttered piles of books and papers seemed even more chaotic. Thane had been studying, it seemed.

She sidestepped a tower of stacked books and ventured into the shadowy corners of the stone-walled room. A richly carved desk spanned the whole right-hand wall. She could hardly see the top of the desk for letters and maps.

Weapon. She needed a weapon. But this room seemed to be empty of sword, bow, knife, or otherwise. She had expected Thane's bedroom to be an arsenal. Instead, it seemed like a philosopher's library.

A glint of metal on top of the desk flashed in her eyes. She stepped closer and peered at the thing.

It was a necklace, weighing down a stack of letters written in a fluid script. The thick silver chain was coiled carefully, like a sleeping snake. The large pendant curved in a metallic arc. A crescent, almost.

Rather like a moon.

She gathered up the necklace in her hand. Its edge brushed against her palm, and she realized the edge was fine—and sharp. It wasn't just a necklace.

It was a knife.

She gripped the necklace and whirled to leave as Cahal entered the room.

"You can't get out now." He smirked. His hands were scathed with bloody scratches from the glass shards.

She held the chain and spun the necklace, slinging it through the air toward him. It caught him by surprise just enough for him to jump out of the way.

That was all she needed. She ran out of the room and down the hallway.

The change of air from the stale passage to the open bailey filled her lungs with a sort of freedom. But when she looked around, she felt like she was being choked.

Philip was freed from his cell. But was separated from Nathanael and Elowyn—caught in a battle of wills.

Next to the river, Thane had an arrow ready.

Closer to the wall, Elowyn also tensed with her own arrow. She was clearly aiming at Thane.

But Arliss could read the body of an archer too well for Thane's eyes to deceive her. He wasn't aiming for her mother. He was aiming for Philip.

"Mother!" She waved her arms as she ran toward the river. Surely Elowyn had to realize what Thane was doing.

Cahal tottered out of the stone hallway behind her. Arliss ran, but she knew she wouldn't reach them in time.

Thane released his arrow toward Philip's heart.

Elowyn released her arrow toward Thane.

Chapter Twenty-Six: If They Fall

The two arrows pinged off each other in midair and whirled back to earth.

Thane froze for a split second, and that was all the time Arliss needed. She bounded across the river and ran toward Philip, her head pounding from the fierce conflict.

Thane dropped his bow and rushed at Philip from the other direction, flashing his sword, driving him back toward the cell.

Halfway between the river and Thane, Nathanael grabbed her shoulder and yanked her back.

"Go. Follow your mother. Now!" He shoved her toward Elowyn.

"I'm not leaving without Philip!"

"Go!" he shouted.

She held up the burgundy cape and ran to where her mother stood beckoning at the left-hand door. Elowyn yanked her through the door and out the other side in one swift motion. Arliss collapsed on the mossy riverbank as her mother reentered the door.

Arliss squinted into the shadows. Water flowed into ditches along either side of the mountain. How—and why—she couldn't tell.

Elowyn hurried back through, helping Nathanael along. His bare left forearm held a nasty gash.

Arliss leapt to her feet. "Where's Philip?"

"If I had tried to get into that cell again, I would have died. Now we must go."

Nathanael and Elowyn strode past her toward the fringes of the mountain which jutted out on either side of the outer wall.

"Come, they'll be after us in an instant!" Nathanael untied three unusual creatures which Arliss had not yet noticed. She squinted at them in the dimness of the moonlit midnight. She felt she had seen such beasts before, but anger at her mother and uncle burned in her head, clouding her vision.

"I am *not* leaving without him," she hissed.

Nathanael grasped her and practically forced her to mount one of the curiously noble beasts. "Yes, you are!"

"Arliss," her mother said, "your father must be warned. If we try to save Philip, there will be no one to warn him."

"You didn't even try." Arliss made no attempt to inhibit either the tears or the anger in her voice.

Voices and swords mingled in the wall behind them. Had Thane summoned more of his men?

"We're leaving—now!" Nathanael slapped the rump of Arliss's mount as he vaulted onto the back of his own steed.

The beast lunged forward as she grasped at its mane and the leather strap which lay across it and tried to hold on. She jostled up and down as the animal's hooves pounded the mossy forest floor.

Elowyn urged her horse into the lead, and Nathanael took up the rear.

Horse—that was it. Of course, she'd heard of such creatures, though they always existed only in books and drawings and her own imagination. No longer, it seemed. Thane had been right: all the things she thought to be stories and fairytales were becoming more real than she had ever envisioned.

Thane was right about so many things. And he was even now doing just what she herself had always wanted to do: explore the heart of the land. A thousand secrets lay over the mountainous walls of the fortress. How, then, could he also be so wrong?

Her mount dodged a thicket, and she wobbled back and forth in her seat. She clenched her legs tight around the horse's back.

Thane was wrong because he was set on deception—on usurpation—on vengeance.

A cry stuck in her throat. "Thane may kill Philip now," she shouted to her mother. "He said he would. He was holding Philip for bait, and now that I'm gone, he'll kill him."

Elowyn turned her head to look at Arliss and nearly slipped from her mount. She turned back around, and her words were almost lost in the wind. "Perhaps he still needs the bait."

Arliss grasped the horse's rein in one hand and gripped the cloak about her with the other, trying to block out the chilly midnight air. Stifling a sob, she whispered to herself, "I'm sorry I couldn't save you, Philip. But I have a duty—a duty to my father. I promised you I would make things right, and I will do it if God gives me strength. And I will come back for you."

Philip's wrists burned from hanging so long in the bonds which stretched his limbs. The sharp smell of blood blurred his senses as Thane struck him again, roaring with an unquenchable rage.

"You fool! Your insolence, your insistence on silence, becomes very dull after a time. What do you think—that she will return for you? That I will spare your life on her account? Hah!"

Philip looked up. "If she returns, she won't be alone."

Thane stepped back, the veins in his neck taut with anger. "I won't deny that you make masterful bait for luring the princess into a trap. But that is too much of a gamble on my part. I will destroy her utterly, and you will never see her again. Trust me when I tell you this: I shall save you as bait for the princess, but that measure will prove unnecessary. She will give you no thought once I crush her city and destroy her people—even crush and destroy her, if it comes to it."

"You cannot break her." Philip's gaze held, unflinching. "Her spirit is more powerful than you know."

"Is that so? And what makes you think she will come back for you?"

Blood trickled from Philip's nose, tickling his lip. "Because two are better than one."

Thane took a step away, his eyebrows undulating with scorn. "Precisely what do you mean by that?"

"If they fall, one will lift up his fellow." Philip strained, trying to get a truly deep breath. "But woe to him who is alone when he falls, and has not another to lift him up."

Thane's fist struck Philip's temple, and hazy blackness clouded his vision, overtaking him as his mind withdrew into darkness.

Chapter Twenty-Seven: Return to the Castle

The breeze that circled about Arliss, tugging at her cloak and tossing her hair, did not simply warn of change. It seemed to say, "Reinhold will change, Reinhold has changed, Reinhold is changing!" They had been riding hard ever since leaving Thane's fortress, with only the briefest stop for food, and throughout it all the winds had refused to silence their whispering. But their backs had become tense from the long riding, and it was time for a short rest.

She stopped circling the little grove. She had come to her favorite tree, the bent and gnarled one—doubling as both a seat and an archery target. As she stroked and traced the tree's wrinkled bark, her mother spoke from a few feet behind her.

"I don't pretend to comprehend what goes on in your head, Arliss. I gave up on your father years ago, and you are quite similar to him." Arliss's cheeks grew hot as her mother continued. "But perhaps you can explain matters to me. Why, my dear, why? Why the running off—with two peasant boys you barely knew? And just when your father was also leaving!"

"I'm sorry I worried you, Mother. I am also sorry for endangering both of your lives."

Nathanael snorted as he patted one of the grazing horses.

Arliss ignored him. "More than anything, I am also horrified at what has become of Philip. But I am not sorry for doing what I did. Perhaps it was done hastily, without much sense, but it needed to be done." She pulled herself up to her full height, her eyebrows raised as she addressed her mother. "You are wrong, my dear

Mother. They are not peasants. They are not lower. In fact, I'm ashamed to inform you that Philip—the supposed peasant, the orphan, the carpenter's apprentice—has more sensibilities than your daughter."

Elowyn smiled. "I did not mean it that way. I simply meant they were less well off than the lords' families."

"Perhaps they are. Yet if that is so, I fear it is Father's doing. He created lines and divisions which he cannot erase."

Elowyn's eyes flashed. "I think you forget I am married to your father. Choose your words carefully."

"I am choosing them carefully, Mother. I see the truth now—my father is a good man, a noble man who wishes to do what is right. He deserves to be defended. But he is blind. I, too, was blind, but I have been given sight."

"And what do you see?" Nathanael asked. "Your father is not at home. Thane is coming. He knows now that Kenton is not at the city. How can you stop him?"

"I don't know." Arliss shook her hair behind her shoulders. "I don't know what to do. I'm almost afraid to trust my own skills, my own instincts. But I know I must be the one to set things aright."

She clambered onto her horse, smacked its rump, and vaulted out of the forest, towards the castle sparkling in the midday sun.

The sound of clomping hooves alerted the city long before the mounted posse of royalty arrived. As Arliss urged her horse on, gripping its ginger mane to steady herself against the pounding of the creature's gallop, she gazed up at the city before her. Her city. Less than a week ago she had left it, planning to come back in triumph, to lead her band of adventurers through its streets and denounce the king and his ways.

Now, she was returning, separated from her three companions and on a mission to protect the king, his city, and his name.

The horses ran swiftly across the dry, rocky fields, and the castle itself rose into focus. Atop the lone tower a flash of brown caught her eye as it swished about and vanished. Ilayda. How Arliss had missed her friend! In truth, she had missed everything—her mother and her archery not least of all. She also longed for the little things: the scraping of the gate as it opened, the flickering of the candlelight as she and her parents read far into the night, the hubbub of villagers taking dinner at The Bronze Lion. Strange as it was, she missed Brallaghan, even for all his annoyances.

She didn't have much time to miss him. The moment the gates swept open and the guards called "The queen has returned!" Brallaghan himself hurried over and offered a hand to help her off her horse.

"Are you all right, Arliss?" He gripped her hand as she dismounted.

"No." She leapt off and slipped her hand from his the moment she hit the ground.

"And what might be wrong?" His brow scrunched as he examined the horse. He ran his hand across its hide, curiosity creasing his face.

"Everything." She shoved her horse's reins at him and started up the hill to the castle. "Thane is coming, and I have to stop him before he destroys this city."

"*Who* is coming?" Brallaghan called after Arliss, but she had already hurried out of earshot.

Elowyn passed close to the young knight. Her indigo dress brushed against his legs as she leaned close and whispered in his ear.

"A great evil is coming upon this city. If we are not united against it, we may all fall. The king is not here, and I only have so much physical power over the people. Already I am drained because of the past day's events." She stared at him. He had always been a kind fellow—one of the few young men in the city she deemed worthy of Arliss's friendship. "No matter what happens, make sure the people unite to serve their princess. I feel I can trust you."

Brallaghan nodded, but his face betrayed his befuddlement. He smoothed out his tunic and bowed to her as she nodded her head and handed him the reins of her horse.

Just behind her, Nathanael also placed his reins in Brallaghan's hands. "I suppose you don't know how to care for one of these."

Brallaghan shook his head. "What *are* they?"

Elowyn stroked her mount's mane. "Surely you'd recognize a horse when you saw one."

He arched an eyebrow. "It's not like I've seen one before—not in real life, at least."

Elowyn caught his eye.

He checked his brash tone. "Where did they come from?"

Elowyn exhaled, closing her eyes. "Not from Reinhold."

Arliss stopped in front of the castle, hesitating before she opened the huge door which led into the great room. She bent her head. Was this—her life, her home, her friends—worth the decisions she had made? She had told herself that her father's prejudice had driven her away.

Now, she saw that she had driven herself away by her own hatred. When he forbade her friendship with Philip, she had hated him for it. Yes, he was wrong to forbid it. But wasn't what she had done far more wrong?

The door to the castle swung inwards. Ilayda's chocolaty brown hair flashed in the shadows of the doorframe. "You're extremely late, silly princess."

Arliss stumbled through the doorway and into the sunbathed hall, collapsing in her friend's embrace. Ilayda squeezed her tightly, running her fingers through her hair. "Look at you! Your hair's a mess!"

"It always is."

"And your dress! Good gracious, running about in naught but a cape and chemise! It'll be the talk of the village for weeks."

Arliss's smile melted. This beautiful moment could last no longer.

Ilayda tilted her head. "What's wrong?"

Elowyn and Nathanael burst through the open door. Unstrapping her quiver, Elowyn cast it and her bow to the ground as Nathanael slammed the door and collapsed into a chair beside her.

Ilayda stretched her neck from side to side, as she searched the other faces. "Philip?"

Arliss shook her head. "He is still Thane's prisoner. I think Thane will hold him as bait until he is no longer useful."

"And when would he stop being useful?" Nathanael questioned, running a hand through his brown locks.

Exhaustion nagged at Arliss, but she refused to give in to it. She couldn't, not while Philip was still in captivity.

"He will cease to be useful the moment this city is destroyed or I am killed. If Thane achieves that, he will need no bait." She settled onto an adjoining chair. Desperate as the times were, she wasn't going to toss etiquette to the wind.

"So you think that is his next move?" Nathanael asked. "Attacking the city?"

"Everything he told me, all the questions he asked, they all pointed to that goal."

"And how is he planning to attack it? What tools does he have?"

"What tools does he need? He knows the king and half our guards are gone. All he needs to do is break through the moat and the outer gate, and the city is his."

"The river is at its autumnal peak," Nathanael said. "It's practically flooding the moat."

"That will do nothing to stop Thane," Elowyn said.

Arliss turned to Ilayda. "Where is Erik?"

"I had to dress and bind up his snakebite. He's resting in the library."

"No, he's not." Erik's voice echoed from the staircase which led down from the second floor of the tower as he descended into the great hall. "Did you tell them about the visitor, Ilayda?"

Ilayda's eyes widened. "No, I didn't."

"Visitor?" Elowyn's eyes were sharp. Arliss's breath felt sharper.

Erik strode closer to them. "Yesterday afternoon, a man galloped up this hill on a creature straight from a storybook—a horse. He showed up at the castle doors exhausted from hard riding. Lord Adam wished to turn him aside, suspicious as to who he was and where he came from. He wore a dark red cape and refused to show any of his face but his eyes—he claimed he had a disease of the face. Ilayda insisted, so we welcomed him and made him a cot in the pantry. He's still resting in there."

"That's unusual," Nathanael remarked.

The front doors swung open, and Brallaghan entered the hall, letting the doors collapse into the jamb behind him. "Your majesties, pardon me, but there's news which I have to share."

"Technically I'm not a majesty." Ilayda jerked her head at Erik "And he definitely isn't."

Arliss rose to meet Brallaghan. "What news?"

"An army has been seen exiting the edge of the forest. They're marching across the plains as we speak, coming straight for the city. A few of them are on horses."

"How many are they?"

"At least three dozen men, from the looks of it."

Arliss closed her eyes as everyone in the room burst into discussion, plans, desperate ideas.

"We must have a council." She looked at her mother. "A council of war."

After a quick bath, Arliss hurried up the tower steps.

In her room, she tossed aside the burgundy cape and tattered chemise. She opened her wardrobe, remembering the times she had hidden within it as a child. She had always secretly believed the doors of the wardrobe led to some secret room or portal, but she never found anything behind the clothes but solid wood. Now, with the weight of her sixteen years piling on her shoulders, she searched the wooden closet for the dress she wanted.

A flash of fire caught her eye. She tugged out the dress, holding it up into the stream of light flooding through the window of her bedroom. This would be the dress in which she would confront Thane—the flaming red dress, the same in which she had streaked tardily across the fields to her uncle's knighting, in which she had been kissed on the head by Nathanael, in which she had entered the fields and worked with the commoners.

The linen fabric tickled her bare skin as she slipped the dress over her head, thrusting her arms through the sleeves. She tucked a few handkerchiefs in her pocket. Then, strapping her quiver about her waist like a belt, she left her room and marched downstairs to the council chamber.

As she rounded the staircase, she caught a fleeting glimpse through a thin window: far away, at the edges of the forest, a dark mass like a cloud of land-traveling gnats was moving steadily west.

In the council chamber, Arliss found Elowyn, Nathanael, Erik, and Ilayda all sitting around the long table. So this was the royal council. Kenton and Brédan were gone. Adam must have rushed to find Elisabeth and Arden, so only Ilayda remained from that family. And now Erik—not a royal—participated in the discussion.

Elowyn's usually confident eyes had widened with emotion. Arliss knew it was not fear, but worry—and not worry for herself, but for her people.

Arliss's brain was still tossing about its ideas, so she sat in a chair between her mother and uncle, trying to keep her face blank. She didn't want to be asked what she was thinking about until she was ready. The plan whirled and congealed in her mind, but it refused to fully take shape. Better to keep silent than to speak before her time.

Erik rested his bandaged forearm on the table. "We sent Brallaghan to rally the city guard. Not that there are enough men in the city to bother with. The king has two dozen of our best guards with him."

Nathanael grimaced. "We cannot go out to meet him, and we certainly cannot withhold him if he enters the city."

Erik fingered the longbow slung around the back of his chair. "Some of the best archers could go to the top of the tower and fire at him from there."

"But then you'll be exposed," Nathanael said. "So his warriors can just as easily shoot at you."

"Still, it might hold them off for a while," Erik said.

"Arliss," Elowyn said, "do you have any thoughts?"

"Your plans are usually better than mine. But…yes. Yes, I do have a plan."

"What sort?" Nathanael asked.

"The sort of plan you find in stories and legends." She took a deep breath. Then she began to sing. "A princess on a carven throne, clothed in simple raiment."

Her mother sang the next line. "A queenly look is in her eye."

They finished the song together, clasping each other's hands as they looked into each other's eyes. "And grace is on her forehead."

Arliss leapt to her feet, adrenaline rushing through her body. Her arms trembled with the thrill of adventure. All of the others also rose.

Nathanael stared, bewildered. "What are you going to do, lass?"

"I'm going to make another legend come to life. Thane has brought all the old stories back to Reinhold. I suppose it is my turn now." She reached for the door. "I need you all to cover for me. Keep everyone away from the lower tier, except for the guards. Make sure the little children and the elderly are safe. Bring them inside the great hall if you must. Just in case—"

"—it doesn't work." Erik finished for her.

Ilayda stomped on his toes. "It *will* work."

"I certainly hope so." Arliss hurried through the door, down the hallway, out of the front door of the great hall, and out into the harsh light of the sun.

Bo Burnette / 206

Chapter Twenty-Eight: The Fiery Arrow

Outside, the city had erupted into chaos. Guards rushed to assemble in the lowest tier as other villagers scrambled up towards the castle—the place of most strength and security. Arliss caught her breath at the sight of the fearful expressions painted on the children who rushed towards her. She pulled both castle doors inward and stepped through.

Ilayda hurried out behind her. "Come! All the children, come in here!" But no one marked her voice.

Arliss strode across the flat hilltop and leapt onto a rock which would give her an extra three feet of height or so. From here, she commanded the crowd.

"Help all the little ones get safely inside! The queen and Lady Ilayda will help you. Now hurry!" Several young men and a few young women—all near Erik's age—carried their own bows. Arliss called to them. "All you who have bow and arrow and courage, follow me!"

She bounded off the rock and began running down the city's tiers the moment her feet slammed into the ground.

She rounded the curve from the second to the first tier and collided with Lord Adam. His scowl spoke more of worry than anger. "You? What are you doing?"

"I'm trying to stop this mess."

"Leave that to others, princess. Aren't you the one who started it?"

"Yes. I did."

"Then back away. Go somewhere safe."

She shook her head. "I will not back away. I have my city, and my father's name, to defend. I will not allow you to stop me from saving either of them."

"The city can be saved, yes. But your father has already tarnished his own name—pressed on with his own goals and ignored mine."

Arliss stepped closer to him, her heart burning with indignation. "Whatever tarnish is on his name was placed there by you. Perhaps my father left you in charge of governing matters, but you still answer to me. Either you're on the side of Reinhold, or you're against it, but don't stand here blathering and wasting precious time."

She stepped free of Adam and left him openmouthed as she hurried to the guards Nathanael had assembled at the gate.

Brallaghan rushed forth to meet her. "Arliss, there're so few of us. I am afraid there isn't much to be done against such an army."

"I have a plan, which you must obey, no matter how absurd it may sound." She tried not to glance over his shoulder at the encroaching army. Steadying her feet, she lifted up her voice so that the rest of the guards could hear. "I need you to find oil, the oil with which we light our torches. Go to every house and take whatever you find there—you have my permission. I will repay them double later."

The guards already wore faces of utter befuddlement.

"Once you have the oil, I need you all to take it and dump it all around the city—in the moat, on the fields behind, on the plains in front. Make sure it all connects in one great trail."

"Arliss?" Brallaghan curved an eyebrow.

"Trust me, please." She cringed when she saw how tenderly he looked at her. He wanted something from her she felt she could not give.

"We'll be out in the open—exposed—if we go out of the city to dump oil on everything."

"I will have archers covering for you. But no more questions! If we don't do this now, there will be no time. Go!"

The guards scattered to do their duty to their princess, and Erik and four others appeared around the corner of the tiers.

"Your archers, Arliss," he announced.

"Very good. Stay here and cover for the guards. You must open the gate and let down the drawbridge for them. No matter what happens, keep each one of the guards alive."

"Do you have extra arrows?"

She pulled all her shafts out of her quiver except for one. "I'll only need this one. You take the rest. Two of you, get up to the top of the tower. The rest of you stay here and help the guards."

Leaving the band of archers to do their work, she headed for the one place which held the thing she needed most, yet the one place she did not desire to go.

Philip's home.

The small wood-framed home lay quiet and still, sunlight fluttering through thin window-curtains. In the front room, a wide square table held an array of half-finished carpentry projects. A gorgeously carved chair lay upon its back on the table, waiting for two of its legs. Two wheels, perhaps for a cart, sat stacked upon each other. Arliss scanned the house for the tillering contraption.

She found it within the door of the adjoining room—the very room where, less than a week before, she had sparred with Philip. Someone had finished the bow, and it lay propped against the wall, tall and unstrung. With thoughts of her friend weighing heavily on her mind, she reached for the bow.

"What are you doing, lady?" The hoarse voice shocked her, and she yanked her hand back, turning towards the speaker. The carpenter himself stood a few paces away.

"I do not mean to intrude, sir. I come on behalf of your nephew."

"Philip?"

"Yes."

"You're the princess, aren't you? You did all of this. My son Erik told me Philip is imprisoned because of you."

She hung her head. "He is right."

"Then why are you here?"

"Because he told me to come and get this bow. He said it was mine." She stepped closer to him. "I am sorry. Truly. And I will do whatever it takes to rescue your nephew. However, to do that I must have this bow."

The man closed his eyes. "Take it, and do what you must."

She gripped the bow and rushed from the house.

Ilayda rushed down the stairs into the great hall just as Erik and another fellow hurried through the door and across the hall crowded with children and their mothers. Where were *they* going so quickly? She tilted her head as she dropped a stack of blankets onto the floor for the little children to lie on.

"And where might you be going, silly fellow?" she demanded, her hands on her hips.

"To the tower, on Arliss's command." Erik strode around Ilayda.

"Be careful," she said coldly.

He disappeared up the stairs.

A few moments later, a cloaked figure emerged from behind the stairwell—from the hallway which led from the kitchen. Ilayda gulped. The mystery visitor, still cloaked and mysterious as ever, stood three paces from her.

"May I help you?" Ilayda asked.

"No, thank you." The cloth about his mouth muffled his voice. "I just need some fresh air."

"It might be dangerous to go outside. I'm just warning you."

"I make a living on danger," he said, and walked across the hall and out into the city.

Giving one glance to where Queen Elowyn knelt assisting with some babies, Ilayda dashed towards the door and after the unknown visitor and his burgundy cloak.

Arliss slipped her leg over the straight bow, stretching the string from one end of the stiff weapon to the other. She tested it with a few draws. Philip had crafted it beautifully.

As commanded, Brallaghan, Nathanael, and the other guards were dashing around the city, casting buckets and canisters of oil onto the half-dead crops, the barren plains, and the river-fed moat. On the horizon and drawing nearer, Thane's warriors approached. Thane rode at their lead, his head unhelmed, his black cape exchanged for a gaudier blue one which flowed behind him like a river. He rode not like an invader coming to sack a city; he rode like a king coming to retake his own.

Biting her lip, Arliss gripped the lone arrow in her quiver. She took a handkerchief from her pocket, wrapped it around the arrowhead, and tied it fast.

Torches burned on either side of the gate to the city. One of the flaming torches had been extinguished, likely in a gust of the autumn wind, but another still burned from its lighting that morning. Arliss approached the torch and held up her arrow. After a tiny moment, the cloth-wrapped tip sparked and caught the flame.

Her heart trembled as she set the arrow to her bow with steady fingers. She stepped left and centered her body with the open gates.

She took a look around. How did she look to everyone else? From high upon the tower, Erik could see her. Elowyn, who had joined Erik on the tower with her bow, would also see her. Ilayda, just rushing through the second tier, stopped short. Brallaghan, reentering the city with an empty bucket, gaped with surprise when he saw her. Nathanael, Adam, the guards—they all looked upon the princess and saw her, standing tall, bathed in flaming light. The sun, the fire, and her dress would all seem to blend into one, and she would shine like some legendary queen of old.

Thane, too, could see her as he rode ever nearer.

Arliss nocked the fiery arrow and drew it back with ease.

The line of oil traced a path around the city. She aimed her bow at one especially drenched patch of grass.

Just as she prepared to release the arrow, Ilayda's voice shouted, "Behind you!"

A shadowy figure crashed into Arliss, snatching at her bow. His burgundy cloak flashed as he gripped her arm and dashed the fiery arrow to the ground. She struggled against him, trying to wrench her arm from his clenching grasp.

Using his hold on her as leverage, she slammed her foot in his chest, and he tottered back. For a moment, she noticed nothing but the fierce look in his eyes as he lifted the extinguished arrow and snapped it in two. Then he drew his sword.

Yelling with excited fury, Brallaghan rushed in, his sword drawn to meet the strange visitor's.

Arliss scrambled for her arrow. The shaft had been cracked beyond repair, and the burnt handkerchief had dissolved into ashes. She tossed it aside with a groan. She darted a glance towards Thane's army and groaned again. By the time she could go to the tower and get another arrow from Erik, Thane would be marching up the tiers of the city, destroying everything in his path.

Her heart jumped within her as she remembered the arrow she had cast aside in the dust beside the gates, just before Nathanael's knighting. Every detail flashed back into her memory: her bare feet, her quiver still strapped about her, and one arrow remaining in it.

She ran the few paces to the gate and sifted through the dirt for that arrow.

"Arliss!" Nathanael rushed towards her. "We have to close the gates!"

"No! We cannot!" She shouted back, digging her fingers into the ground as dirt packed into her fingernails. Her fingers curled around wood. She gave the arrow a triumphant smile.

Brallaghan shouted. "Catch him!"

Scrambling to her feet, she saw the strange visitor running back up the bend between the tiers, with Nathanael and Brallaghan at his heels.

Arliss shook her head. She had to focus. Trembling from the tension, she tugged another handkerchief from her pocket and knotted it around the arrowhead. Her fingers barely wanted to obey her. Finally, she thrust the arrow into the torch. After an agonizing moment, the arrow kindled.

Thane's army had come almost within bowshot. She aimed the arrow to land several paces ahead of Thane.

She drew the string back to her ear, sparks from the flame flitting past her face.

She aimed carefully, tilting the bow slightly leftwards.

She breathed out, tensing her arms against her own exhalation.

Her last thought before releasing the arrow was of her father. Kenton's steady gaze and his knotted brow appeared in her mind as her fingers relaxed and the arrow flew from her bow.

Flying gracefully as the most delicate of birds, the fiery arrow arced through the city gates. Elowyn watched with pride as the arrow struck the dead center of the oily patch of dead grasses.

Flames consumed the patch as a trail of fire erupted around the city. From her vantage point on the tower, Elowyn could see all. She whirled back and forth to watch the flames that licked up the trail of oil on their journey around the city. In an instant, the recently harvested bean field turned orange with conflagration. The blaze spread until it created a fiery ring around the city, and even the oily surface of the moat flared with the fire.

Elowyn saw her daughter, standing far below by the city gates. A stirring realization rose in her chest.

One of the great prophecies of old had just been fulfilled.

Chapter Twenty-Nine: For Reinhold

The clatter of hooves woke Arliss from the dream she felt she must be walking through. She—Arliss, first princess of Reinhold—had shot the fiery arrow even as the queen in the ancient legend. Her shoulders felt both powerfully light from her triumph and weighed down with the burden of her own destiny.

A horse rounded the corner and pounded towards the castle gates.

Unable to do anything to inhibit its rider, Arliss threw herself to the ground as she ducked away from the horse's path. The figure in the burgundy cloak streaked over the inflamed drawbridge. Without hesitation, he leapt over the trail of fire and landed on the other side of the river. Then, instead of turning his horse to meet Thane's army, he reared the beast and galloped on in the opposite direction—towards the sea.

Through the flames which surrounded the city, Arliss could make out darkly cloaked warriors setting arrows to their bows. They would soon find them useless. The people of Reinhold were skilled archers, Arliss certainly not least among them. The fire obscured their view of the lower tier, and the second and third tiers had emptied of villagers.

Despite these advantages, her fiery arrow could not defend the city forever. At some point, the fire would burn out, and the city could then be breached.

The drawbridge collapsed with a sighing crackle of wood into the moat below, strewing boards across its surface. So, that entrance no longer existed, either. Perhaps that could also buy them some time. They would be severely outnumbered, but they would be ready.

A shout erupted from the castle. Ilayda, her brown hair streaking behind her, ran towards Arliss from the opposite side of the city's entryway thoroughfare.

"Arliss! You—you're—"

"Ridiculous?"

"Well, yes. But you're also incredible."

Arliss smiled, but her forehead still knotted together. "What are they shouting about up there?"

"I can't make it out myself."

Striding towards the upper tiers, Arliss craned her neck and held her hand to her ear. "It sounds like a battle cry—some shout of victory. I hope they know we aren't victorious yet. Thane is delayed but not defeated."

"Listen—they're saying that someone is coming," Ilayda said.

Nathanael rounded the corner into the first tier, with the rest of the guards behind him, Brallaghan and Adam in their midst. "The king is coming! The king is coming! The king has returned!"

The king. He was here. A strange mix of delight and horror twisted Arliss's breath from her lungs. She ran to the gates to get a better view.

Her father and his dozen men charged across the plains, straight towards Thane's forces.

Even through the smoke, she caught a glimpse of Thane. He jerked his mount around.

"Retreat!" he bellowed. His words produced an instantaneous, rehearsed action from his men. They turned on their heels and fled back towards the forest without needing another word from their commander.

Kenton's band raced after them in the same manner.

Nathanael thrust a long, narrow board over the moat, barely spanning the width of the river. He mounted the board, which easily supported his slender form. "I'm going to aid the king."

Arliss touched his shoulder. "Uncle Nathanael, no."

"Kenton needs every man on his side."

"Then what about the rest of the guards?"

"They refused to join me."

Arliss bit her lip, unwilling to look at those traitorous guards behind her. "I will see what I can do to persuade them." Not that they had much reason to trust her prior to now. But she had just saved their city from attack, if that counted for anything.

"You're a fine lass. Now you must let me go." Nathanael bounded across his makeshift bridge and ran towards the king with speed like a courser.

Her fist clenched around her bow, Arliss turned to face the city guards. Ilayda shuffled about behind them.

"I know many of you despise me," Arliss began, eyeing Lord Adam. "But I hope you see that, no matter what I did, and no matter what you think of it, I am doing everything I can to make it right. With God's help, I will uphold Reinhold as long as I have strength."

She looked at Brallaghan. His eyes shone in agreement with her. She smiled. "I know the king has been proud as well. He has created boundaries between our people. But now is not the time to let petty grievances and grudges separate us. We must fight for the king!"

Adam crossed his arms across his chest. "Why should we fight for one who does not fight for us? The king looks only to his own plans."

She motioned towards her father's now-distant figure, running towards the forest. "Do you think he cares only about himself, about his own plans? Look—he is fighting for you! You have a duty to him—all of you."

Adam scoffed. "Princess, surely you of all people know that your father is undeserving of our service. He forgets the ideas of the lords, forgets the commoners—forgets even you!"

Several of the guards murmured in agreement.

She stifled her mounting frustration. "I know he has allowed lines and divisions. I've seen them myself, and I know the evil that these schisms can produce. But believe me when I tell you this:

fight for the king, and I will fight for the rights of all honest, noble Reinholdians."

"But *you* brought this evil upon us."

She stared at the dust beneath her feet, then looked up into Adam's eyes. "Yes. I did."

Adam blinked in surprise, but he still appeared unconvinced. "We will not fight, for—"

"Silence, Lord Adam!" Brallaghan stepped forward and turned to Arliss, smoothing the front of his green tunic as he reached for the pommel of his sword. "We will fight for the king. But who will lead us?"

She lifted her bow and addressed the guards. "I will lead you, if you will follow me. Long ago, our clan of Reinhold fled from the oppression of a great evil across the sea. It seems that some of that evil has survived, and it is eating away at the heart of our land. Follow me—follow the king—and we can preserve Reinhold's freedom."

Brallaghan nodded as the rest of the guards also gave their consent. Even Adam dropped his cynical frown, and Ilayda slipped towards her friend from behind the others.

"Make ready your weapons!" Arliss commanded.

As if at her command, Erik came hurrying down towards the gates, a bundle of arrows in his hand. "For you, Arliss."

Such a true friend to think of her! How could she be worthy of him—of any of them? She restocked her empty quiver. Then she turned to Erik and Ilayda.

"I feel it is almost wrong to ask this of you, after all the misfortune and chaos I've caused you both." She paused, giving a hesitant glance at Erik's bound forearm. "But I will ask it nonetheless. Will you also follow me to aid Philip and the king?"

Erik nodded. "You are my princess. My duty and my bow are ever yours."

A playful smirk twisted the corner of Ilayda's mouth. "Silly princess that you are, I think I'll join you. As it's said, 'a threefold cord is hard to break'."

Arliss clasped each of her friends' shoulders—one a lifelong companion, the other a new comrade—and felt that she was the luckiest princess of any realm in history. Of course, Erik would say there was no such thing as luck. And he was probably right.

Brallaghan appeared beside them, gripping a long pole from which streamed a long, purple flag with an ornate "R" embroidered in its center. Behind him, the rest of the guards had assembled. Three of them held the reins of the three horses that Arliss, Nathanael, and Elowyn had ridden back to the city. Arliss mounted her ginger mare with an almost-practiced ease.

Erik swung a leg over his mount as Brallaghan hesitated with the reins of the other.

"May I?"

Arliss shrugged. "I don't see why not."

Brallaghan bounded onto the horse with grace, offering a hand to Ilayda. Her eyebrows curving suspiciously, she accepted and mounted behind him.

"Raise the flag," Arliss said.

Brallaghan lifted the pole into the air and it caught in the autumn wind, flickering out in a long stream.

Arliss reared her horse and shouted with every particle of air in her lungs, "For Reinhold!" Her horse whinnied and leapt across the moat, not slowing down once its hoofs clambered on the other side.

Erik, Brallaghan, and Ilayda took off after her, and all the guards rushed across the narrow board with fiery passion, all taking up the cry of "For Reinhold!"

Standing atop the tall castle tower, Elowyn beheld her daughter rallying the troops and taking off across the field. The gingery-brown mare, the flaming red dress, and the pure gold of Arliss's hair mixed together in a wild flash of color.

Elowyn exhaled. If only Kenton could see Arliss now, he would see the young woman she had become—that she was becoming.

She had truly taken up the mantle as princess and leader of her people.

But more than that, she took up that role out of love and honor to the king. Elowyn didn't need to have been on the lowest tier to understand her daughter's words and thoughts. Arliss rode for the king.

Her eyes closed, Elowyn drank in the thickness of the air. And she prayed that, if it lay within God's will, all those of Reinhold would return safely home.

Chapter Thirty: The Mountain River

Kenton's boots pounded the forest floor as swiftly as his throbbing heart. In the distance, he thought he heard the splashing of water, so he urged on his weary legs and straining lungs. Just a few more paces, and he would be upon them.

Finally he reached a place where the trees started to thin. The splashing noise grew ever louder—the army of warriors fled downstream in boats, with Thane himself at their head.

Heaving to recover the air he had lost in the run, Kenton studied the path of the boat in the rear of the entourage. If he balanced his weight right—

A hand clamped down on his shoulder. He reached behind him, grabbing the outstretched forearm and slipping his other arm around his assailant's torso to flip him to the ground.

"Easy, now, Kenton," Nathanael whispered.

Kenton released him and motioned toward the river. "Come. Follow me and do as I do."

He darted out of the trees and cast himself into the middle of the wide river, landing squarely in the aft of the last boat. The boat lurched. He stumbled against ropes and paddles as the boat's two passengers drew their blades. Drawing his own, Kenton brandished it, playing the offensive as he urged the two warriors backwards.

One of them, a young fellow not much older than Arliss, his eyes wide with fear, leapt into the boat ahead of theirs. Both boats wobbled, and Kenton and his other opponent stumbled to their knees, grabbing the sides of the small watercraft for support.

Coughing, Kenton's foe took a hasty step backwards, once again pushing the boat off-kilter. In his haste to rebalance the boat, Kenton dropped his sword. The coughing warrior snatched it up and pointed both swords towards Kenton.

"The king of Reinhold!" he hissed. "What a price Master Thane will give to me, I am sure. Do you have any final words?"

Any movement Kenton made would set the boat off balance, and he would be dead just the same. The coughing warrior brandished the two blades even closer. Could this truly be his end?

Suddenly an arrow whizzed by his ear, just missing him. But it was not intended for him. The point found its mark in his opponent's breast. Sputtering a last cough, the warrior collapsed over the side of the boat and into the river. Kenton's sword clattered in the bottom of the boat. He glanced in the direction from which the arrow had come.

Arliss stood with Nathanael by the edge of the riverbank.

The arrow had hardly struck Damian when Arliss snatched the reins of her gingery horse from her uncle. "Go, get in the boat. I have this taken care of."

Nathanael nodded and ran downriver to join the king.

Two more horses bounded out of the trees to join her just as she remounted her own. Ilayda held Brallaghan's waist as he struggled to rein his black charger to a halt. The horse whinnied, fighting its inexperienced rider. Arliss chuckled as both Ilayda and Brallaghan nearly toppled from their seats.

"What news, princess?" Brallaghan managed.

"Father and Uncle Nathanael have commandeered one of Thane's boats. They may reach the fortress before we do."

Erik urged his horse closer to the others. He rode as if he'd done it all his life. "The rest of the guard are far behind. They'll never make it in time. Plus, they'll have to cross the river, and you know that will take some time. The snakes might not be worth such a steep risk. Do you have any more Lasairbláth?"

"Very little, but here, take it. Anyway, how are the guards going to catch up?"

"They won't." Ilayda's face was grim. Was she worrying about her father?

"There is a way…" Erik's brow knotted as he thought. "I could ride back and forth—transporting one at a time farther along."

"That would waste too much time." Arliss groaned in frustration. "We have little enough as it is."

"It's the only way. Leave it to me. You three go on ahead." Erik let the slack out of the reins. "Arliss, you have to trust me."

"I do trust you. Now go!"

Erik turned his stallion around and galloped after the guards.

Arliss also turned her horse about. "We follow the river. It should lead us straight to Thane's fortress."

Brallaghan faltered. "Then what will we do? I mean, do you have some sort of plan to take this Thane fellow down?"

"Not exactly, but it's coming to me piece by piece. I know we must take down his fortress, but I don't know how. But there is someone who will know, I think."

"Whom?"

"My brother."

Bo Burnette / 224

Chapter Thirty-One: Sacrifice

The ginger mare quickly outpaced the steed carrying Brallaghan and Ilayda, and Arliss soon found herself surrounded by nature: trees on one side, the river on the other. She pressed the horse on in every way she could, unsure of what signals and touches were customary. The mare minded not, forgiving her new rider of her inexperience. As for Arliss, her thoughts went only to those parts of her heart where her father and Philip lay, making the tightness in her chest even heavier.

She arrived at the fortress—the mountains jutting up on either side, and the wall spanning the width of the mountains. Here the river, of course, flowed beneath the wall. The host of boats now lay in lines alongside the shore.

She'd wondered before why the river slowed to a thin stream in the fortress. The reason now seemed quite simple: the wall itself acted as a dam, inhibiting the river's flow and diverting it into long ditches on either side. If the wall had not spanned the mountain pass as it did, the wide bailey of Thane's fortress would be at least half full of water.

Tying the reins of her mare to a tree, Arliss dismounted and crept out of the woods. A lone guard paraded atop the battlements, guarding the open entryway where the portcullis once existed. Striding silently as a wood-maiden, Arliss reached the right-hand mountain, careful not to step in the ditch of redirected river water. She set an arrow to her bow and took careful aim at the unsuspecting guard.

Her arrow pierced his shoulder—just as she had intended. No more death than was necessary would be dealt this day. His pained cries erupted from the battlements. Thane could probably hear them as well.

It didn't matter. Every princess deserved a ready welcome. Gritting her teeth, she jumped into the front boat and pushed it forwards, and she steadied herself as the boat floated under the wall and into Thane's mountain castle.

"Welcome, cousin Arliss! We were expecting you'd arrive shortly." Thane's voice boomed towards her before her eyes adjusted as the boat floated out from the dark tunnel and into the afternoon light which flooded the mountain clearing. The sun's beams flashed erratically from behind threatening clouds. One of Reinhold's signature showers couldn't be too far off.

Clenching the bow in her left hand, she leapt from the watercraft and pulled together every inch of her height and her will. "I have come to bargain for the land of Reinhold."

The laugh which erupted from Thane's throat was almost as threatening as it was annoying. She stiffened, unwilling to give up her resolve to this mocking infidel. Thane motioned for the warriors to step aside, and he did the same.

Arliss froze.

Two warriors, struggling to hold down their prey, gripped Kenton's arms, holding him still even as he struggled. Two other warriors restrained Nathanael.

Her father saw her and stopped struggling. "Arliss…"

"Father." Her voice barely came over a whisper. She had to rescue them, and Philip, too. Yet what could she do—alone, against so many? Even a fiery arrow would do her little good now.

Two men gripped her arms and hurled her bow to the ground. Their calloused hands bit into her skin. Did it really take two apiece to hold down the royal family?

She glared at Thane, shaking her hair behind her shoulders. "If you release my father, my uncle, and Philip, I will withdraw my army. We can then parley sensibly and decide what must be done to have peace."

He rubbed the scar on his jaw. "There is no peace, no bargain I will accept. Anywise, what army have you to challenge me? You are alone."

"My army will come, and then you will want to parley."

He drew his curved sword and pointed it at her. "No—then, we will have war. But first, I will fulfill my oath for Reinholdian blood." His navy cloak flapped as he turned on his heel and faced her father's restrainers. "I will have my revenge."

Seeing the upraised sword, the determined glint in his eyes, she realized what was about to happen. "No, Thane, you can't do this."

Thane issued an order to those holding her. "Hold her down. She can watch him die."

Her father's head remained upraised, his eyes fiery.

She pulled at her captors, her heart pounding unrelentingly. Nothing she could say would prevent Thane from fulfilling this mad oath. The flickering sun, now almost smothered in storm clouds, caught the polished flat of Thane's blade. It flashed in her eyes.

Thane set the edge of his sword upon Kenton's neck.

She swallowed as a strange peace came over her heart. She lifted her head. "Take my life instead."

"Your life? You would sacrifice yourself for this wretch?"

"No—he's not a wretch!" Her voice commanded his attention, and he turned to face her as she spoke. "He is my king, and he is my father. You want Reinholdian blood? You want to end our line? Kill me! But promise me that you will release the other three, and you will spare their lives."

Thane turned his blade towards her as he strode forwards, the tip of the sword just a pace away from her forehead. "I wanted to make you suffer, watch you driven mad with grief and pain."

"Why?" She gritted her teeth. "Is this not enough?"

"You are right. The line of Reinhold is broken. Is that not suffering enough, for you to die with that cruel knowledge?"

Her father strained against the warriors. "No! Arliss, you cannot do this!"

Another warrior moved to help restrain him.

Thane edged towards her until he stood beside her. He put his lips next to the side of her head. His breath tickled her ear as he whispered to her. "I will release all of them. You have my word. Now you shall die. Your mother is not here to save you this time. There is no one to save you. I am the master of this realm."

"You are not the master." Arliss refused to look at him. "I know the true Master, and I serve Him. My life is in His hands, not yours."

Thane raised the sword and bared her neck of her hair. Strands slipped down beside her bent head, covering her cheeks as she closed her eyes, a silent prayer escaping her open lips. What would it feel like to die?

Her eyelids fluttered open. The sword arced toward her.

Chapter Thirty-Two: The Armies Are Unleashed

Philip thrust his sword beneath Thane's, barely missing Arliss's golden head. Using both hands on the pommel, he shouldered every bit of his strength up into his sword. It halted Thane's curved blade just one foot short of Arliss's neck. There they struggled for a long moment in a battle of strength and will for the life of the princess.

One of the warriors restraining her swatted at him, trying to dislodge his fierce grip on his sword. They couldn't break it. Not when Arliss's life depended upon it. She was his princess.

This realization pumped new strength into his aching muscles. He forced their swords up and batted Thane's blade down to his other side. It stuck into the dirt, lodged about a foot deep above the tip.

The warriors restraining Arliss released her and drew swords. Yelling, Philip swept his sword around and clobbered it into one of the opposing blades. Metal hissed. The blade spun from the warrior's grasp.

Two explosive thrusts, and both warriors lay dead on the ground.

Philip had freed Nathanael on his mad dash to rescue Arliss. Now Nathanael rushed at Kenton's captors, sword slashing.

Thane struggled to pull his sword from where it had been planted. By the time he readied his cutlass, Philip stood between him and Arliss, his sword pointing up, his forearms knotted both with muscle and the ropes which had bound him.

"You will not touch her again, snake!" Philip spat his words at Thane.

Thane's look darted toward the dais.

Philip readied his sword. If Thane made it to the dais, he could control everything in the mountain clearing.

Thane glared at him and Arliss, then fled towards the stony dais, his deep blue cape flowing behind him.

Philip started to pursue Thane, but Arliss held him back. "No—don't. We must spare his life if we can."

"Arliss, he just tried to kill you!"

She sighed, seeing the dark rings under his confident eyes, the coarse stubble which peppered his chin. "Yes, I know. But he is my cousin, and I would be ashamed to kill one of my own kin. Whenever such things happen in ancient stories, it's always because the killer has been cursed, or knows not who they are killing. I don't wish to be in either place."

"Very well." Philip's voice was almost a growl.

Ilayda burst through the open waterway, with Brallaghan behind her.

"Arliss! Philip!" she shouted.

Her joyous cries were cut short. Thane stood atop the stony dais, a shining steel breastplate now beneath his cloak.

"Let my warriors come forth!" he shouted. "*Lig do na nathracha teacht amach!*" The last command sounded so cruel and devilish that Arliss shuddered. What might *nathracha* be?

The warriors holding her father cast him to the ground. One of them remained to fight him, while the other charged at Arliss and Philip, a bloodcurdling scream bursting from his throat.

Thane's warriors, with Cahal at their lead, emerged from the side of the mountain in which Arliss had been kept in that beautiful bedchamber. All of them carried swords, and some wore faces streaked with blue paint as on that first day in the woods when

Arliss's company had first encountered them. One of the blue-faced warriors dashed to a small door in the right-hand wall.

Thane again called "*Nathracha!*" A dozen creatures spurted from the hole—long, wriggling, limbless things. Arliss realized with a sickening shiver what *nathracha* were.

They were snakes.

Arliss readied an arrow. It would take every one of her shafts to down all of these creatures.

Her chamber! The tiny Lasairbláth she had planted had been budding the day Elowyn and Nathanael rescued her. Surely there was enough to fend off these horrid creatures.

She gripped Philip's arm. "There's Lasairbláth in a chamber on the left. We have to get it."

"Arliss, come over here!" Brallaghan called behind them.

She looked to her father. Kenton had downed his man and now rushed towards Thane's platform, his boots pounding the dirt.

Philip's eyes were fixed on Thane's stony dais, surrounded by warriors. "I have to help the king. Cover for me however you can, and do what you must with the Lasairbláth. Or stay and help the others. Whatever is most necessary."

Brallaghan's voice came again. "Arliss, I have a plan! The dam—we can break the dam!"

Her heart jumped at Brallaghan's idea—the same she had stumbled upon earlier. Perhaps so…

"I'm going to help the king. He's right, though—breaking the dam could bring down the fortress." Philip's eyes were grim. "In case I don't get through this, know that I do think of myself as your brother. And I think you're just about the bloody best sister a fellow could ask for."

A strong impulse to kiss him rose in her chest. She didn't. Instead, she responded, "Thank you. Now go—go to my father."

He turned on the heel of his boots and left, dashing towards where the king was also running to Thane's mountainous throne.

"Arliss, we need you, now!" Brallaghan's voice was insistent. "I care about you, and I care about winning this fight. Come quickly!"

Still facing the dais, she shook her head. Brallaghan had always been her friend, but now she knew that was all he could ever be. She didn't want to break his heart. But he could never give her what Philip had already given her.

She faced him. "I'm sorry, Brallaghan. Do what you can about breaking the dam. I have to help Philip."

She strode away from the wall and towards the embellished room. Thane's army had aligned together. The snakes moved like a second unit of troops.

And facing them—only she, Philip, Kenton, and Nathanael.

Wood splintered behind her. Swords chopped through the doors on either side of the waterway entrance. Erik and his troops burst through the doors as they whooped and called out "For Reinhold!"

Arliss's attempt at a last stand became an exultant charge of the army.

Chapter Thirty-Three: Sorcery and Magic

The left wing of the fortress lay emptied of guards, so Arliss entered the opulent room and its exotic furnishings. A flash of white light met her eyes. Her hand dropped from the door handle.

An enormous plant, its vines and streamers spreading out across the floor in every direction, stood in the place of the tiny sprout which Arliss had planted only a few days before. White flowers clustered upon the chest, crept up the bedpost, and blanketed the floor with a gleaming white as of snow. Lasairbláth had to be a magical plant, in one way or another. Never before in her life had she seen something grow this quickly and this beautifully.

Ivory petals so filled the slender vines that some flower clusters had already fallen off, drying upon the hard dirt floor. She stuffed as many as would fit into the pockets of her dress.

With the lamps unlit, the room was dark, but one thing was strangely missing: the violin she had played just a few days ago. Thane said it had belonged to one of his men. Why had he removed it?

It didn't matter. There was a battle to fight. She exited the room and flew back into the bailey of the fortress.

She had an arrow nocked and ready.

Ilayda glanced back and forth between the snakes and the troops that rushed to meet Erik's company. Cupping her hands around her mouth, she shouted, "Erik! Over here!"

He turned about, his long legs pumping as he dashed over to her and Brallaghan. Lord Adam took his place at the head of the Reinholdian soldiers even as they joined the fray with Thane's warriors.

Ilayda gave him no time to recover his breath. "You have to help us."

"Help you in what way?"

Brallaghan stood from his crouch by the wall. "We're going to break down the wall. Arliss ordered it."

"Well, she *approved* of it," Ilayda said. "Which isn't exactly the same thing."

Erik gripped his longbow. "How on earth do you expect to bring down this wall? It's massive, and it's thick."

"We don't have to bring down the wall," Brallaghan said. "We can let the river do it. Release enough of the river, and it'll crumble the wall bit by bit."

"Are you sure?"

"Yes. We just need to dig ditches where the two doors are on either side of the river entrance. If we can get water flooding in through that way, it'll undermine the foundation."

"That won't do anything fast. You do realize that, I hope?" Erik fisted around the grip of his longbow, obviously anxious to return to battle.

"We know," Ilayda said. "But there is still a chance. A hope." As she finished speaking, a drop of water splashed onto her eyelashes. She blinked upwards. The clouds had started to release their contents directly over Thane's stronghold. She murmured again, "A hope."

"Of course there is a hope." Arliss strode toward them holding her bow and arrow in one hand, and a fistful of Lasairbláth in the other.

Arliss handed out the shining petals as quickly as she could, emptying her pockets.

"There are many more flowers—more than you could possibly need—in the left gallery, first room on the right. Get all you need from there, but be careful. I will cover for you when I can, but I may be busy. You have to pile as much Lasairbláth as you can against the walls." She gave a worried glance at the sky. "And pray it doesn't rain too much."

Across the fortress, the torches flamed halfway up the stony mound at the back of the clearing. They sat in iron sconces lodged into the sides of the platform at points well higher than a man's head. She snatched up a fistful of Lasairbláth for use against the snakes and turned.

Philip was fighting Cahal, not far from the right-hand staircase up the dais. Snakes surrounded the clash of swords which had spread throughout the bailey. The devilishly cunning creatures darted in and out, hissing and biting at the Reinholdians wherever they could.

It was clear: Thane commanded these creatures through some form of sorcery, training them and bending them to his will. She shuddered to think of a mind that was that powerful—and that corrupted.

"Very well," she whispered to herself. "You have sorcery. I will fight you with magic."

She pierced a cluster of petals with an arrowhead and killed a serpent which was gliding towards Lord Adam. She poisoned three more snakes in the same way, but at least eight or so still crawled in and out of the frenzy. She had just two arrows left. She couldn't risk to use them both on snakes.

An arrow whizzed past her head, sending her adrenaline spiking as she glanced about to see who shot at her.

Erik had crowned his arrow with white petals. The snakes gave up on attacking the main fray of arms and came slithering, hissing towards Arliss and Erik.

She dashed towards the left colonnade, jumped and rebounded off of the wall—both for momentum and to avoid the serpents. One turned about, coiled, and sprang at her, but she stuck it with an arrow before it could reach her. Behind her, Erik shot snake after snake. She didn't turn around again, but kept running, darting around the fighting in an effort to reach Philip—and her uncle—and her father.

She arrived just in time to see Philip ending his fight, not by killing Cahal as he could have, but by slamming his head into the side of the stony platform. Cahal crumpled to the ground, unconscious. Philip's eyes met hers and she nodded, silently applauding his chivalry in ending the fight so.

Her father's burning yell drew her attention to the top of the dais.

Thane and her father had been fighting relentlessly atop the immense heap of rock. Kenton held his own, but Thane was in his home, and far too clever at his own tricks. He played the offensive and forced Kenton to take step after step backwards.

Kenton swung wide.

Thane ducked. Then he sliced his sword up into Kenton's, forcing his arm backwards and throwing off his balance.

Arliss watched in horror as her father fell from the dais—grappling with the air—and slammed into the ground below.

Chapter Thirty-Four: Promise

Nathanael, his sword bared and ready, dashed away from the main fight and leapt up the left stone staircase to challenge Thane.

Arliss hurried to her father and knelt beside him. "Are you all right?"

Kenton gasped for the air which had been blasted out of his lungs. "Does it look…like it?"

"I have to go. Thane must be stopped." Arliss licked her dry lips.

"No!" He gripped her hand. "No, do not go up those stairs!"

"I *must*."

"I know you are willing to die—even for me. I see that now. And I am sorry for whatever I did to cause you to leave and produce all this mess in the first place. But his fight is not with you."

"It's not with you, either. At least, not you alone. Thane has enemies everywhere he turns. Still, it is my duty to protect my people."

"But you are a young woman."

"I know—it is not within any man's honor to kill a woman. Father, it will not come to that. I will try to reason with him. You must trust me."

Kenton grimaced as he gasped for air. Perhaps he had broken a rib or more, but he still managed to utter a few more words. "I trust you now, Arliss. It is Thane I do not trust."

She nodded, then shouted towards the ongoing clash of swordsmen, many in utter deadlocks. "Lord Adam!"

Ilayda's father turned his head.

"Get someone to help my father—now! Make sure he gets out of here alive!"

She gave one last, wistful look at her father. Then she turned and leapt across the river which bisected the entire fortress, heading for where Philip stood by the right side of the mound.

Philip ached. His wrists ached from hanging in those rope bonds, from struggling against them, and from tearing free. His shoulders ached from slamming against the wooden door of his cell to bash it open. His arms ached from wielding the long sword. His eyes ached and wanted to shut from sheer lack of sleep.

It was time to end this. Arliss wouldn't have the stomach to kill Thane. But if it came to it, he would.

Arliss strode towards him and gripped his left shoulder. He grimaced, but apparently she didn't notice. "I have to get to the torches."

She pointed upwards at the stone mound. A blazing torch perched in an iron rack embedded in the stone. An identical one stuck in the opposite side of the mound as well.

"You don't ask for much," Philip huffed.

She was already wrapping a handkerchief round her last arrow. "You must trust me."

"I do trust you—even though at this point, I've got a bloody long list of reasons not to." He smirked, his sword still upraised.

She tilted her head in almost-mock frustration. "You're starting to talk like me again. But here is my reason: I need another fiery arrow, and to make one of those, you rather need some fire. The only fire in this fortress is in those torches, and it's starting to rain."

As if to amplify her words, several drops dotted their shoulders.

"All right. Why, exactly?"

"We're going to make the wall explode."

He raised his brows, but he knelt and offered his hands.

She stepped onto them, pressing against the stone mound to keep her balance. "All right, lift."

He hoisted her up the wall. As he did, the falling rain thickened, dousing the already-struggling flame. She covered the wrapped arrowhead to make sure it stayed dry before she leapt back to the ground.

Rain wasn't going to make this battle any easier. And it certainly wasn't going to help them blow up the wall.

Philip rubbed his sore palms together. "What now?"

Arliss returned the way she had come, pleading that God would relent with the rain shower. She leapt back across the river, and Philip surged after her. They found Adam struggling to drag Kenton's body farther from the fighting.

"Any grand ideas now, princess?" Adam gritted his teeth.

"I'm working on it." She planted a foot on the bottom step of the left stairwell and turned to Philip. "Cover for me. I'm going to climb halfway up and see if I can reach the torch from there. The length of my arm plus the length of the arrow ought to be enough."

"Go." Philip tilted his sword back and forth in a standard guard position.

She had almost reached the middle of the stone stairs when the grunts and shouts at the top of the mound became too loud and erratic for her to ignore. Looking up, she saw Thane mercilessly beating down on Nathanael as their fight raged on. Nathanael was faltering. Even she could notice flaws in his form.

She felt for that last arrow to place on the bow. Perhaps, if she aimed just perfectly, she could injure Thane without killing him—and without piercing Nathanael on the way to him. She drew back the arrow and searched for the most propitious target.

She had no time to find a mark. Even if she had, her arrow could not have reached in time. Every moment seemed as a thousand. She helplessly watched Thane's cruel smile as he penetrated Nathanael's defenses. His sword pierced the center of her uncle's torso.

Nathanael staggered back towards the staircase. He tripped and tumbled down towards her. Bracing herself against the stone, she brought his fall to a halt. Her eyes had already flooded when she looked into his—eyes which held the strong resolve of a dying man.

"No." She gripped his hand. "I have done this to you. I have done all of this."

He clamped down on her hand with surprising strength. "Arliss, none of this is your fault. Thane would have attacked us no matter what you had done. If not for you, we could all be dead."

Grunting down the pain, he leaned up and kissed her forehead gently, even as she had kissed his at that knighting just one week earlier. She felt like that had been someone else, another person's body she had inhabited. It all seemed so distant now.

Nathanael still held on, both to life and to her hand. "Never stop fighting. Thane will not stop until he sees Reinhold destroyed, or until he himself is destroyed. Promise me, Arliss, that you will not let him prevail! He comes from a more ancient evil than you know."

"I promise. I promise." She trembled.

He laid his head back, his eyes almost closed. "Tell your mother I love her." A quiet breath escaped his lungs, and his hand lost its grip on hers.

She bent over him, kissing his sweaty forehead as he had kissed hers. Then, she glanced up towards Thane as she slowly pushed herself to her feet. There was a reason Thane had not disturbed Nathanael's last words.

Philip's and Thane's swords collided in a flash of shimmering metal.

Chapter Thirty-Five: One Final Arrow

As she hurried to and from the wall with armfuls of Lasairbláth, Ilayda had seen most everything that had happened. Now, dropping the last of the snowy petals against the wall, she stood on her toes in order to see through the throng of soldiers and swords.

Arliss stood halfway up the left staircase, just above Lord Nathanael's body, and she seemed to be motioning for Ilayda. Ilayda gestured to herself. Arliss nodded, but also pointed behind Ilayda to Erik and Brallaghan.

Ilayda understood. "Arliss needs us. Hurry!" She dashed toward the far left, forcing her way to the stone mound.

Brallaghan dragged behind. "But the wall—"

"Oh, come on." Erik took the lead as they reached the base of the stone staircase.

Rain pattered on Ilayda's face as she shouted up to Arliss. "What now?"

Arliss's voice seemed deeper, darker—hoarse and dry, Ilayda thought. "Erik, Brallaghan—get my father out of here. He is wounded and cannot walk. You must also get my uncle's body out. Lord Adam will help you. Do it quickly, and get everyone away from the wall as soon as you can!"

"But what about the dam?" Brallaghan was incredulous.

"You handled the flowers, didn't you? Let me handle the rest. Now go!"

Ilayda held Arliss's gaze for a moment. She didn't want to leave her friend to her death. But Arliss knew what she was doing.

She turned to leave.

Reaching as far out from the stairs as she could, Arliss held the bound tip of her last arrow in the flame. It caught easily enough. How easily would it be extinguished?

Atop the platform, Thane and Philip parried back and forth, their swords flying like a hurricane. Careful not to blow out the flame with her movements, Arliss tested every step up the mound. The higher she got, the more she could feel and smell the chilly mountain air. Up above, the clouds had all but blotted out the sinking sun.

As she reached the top, the duel swung in Thane's favor. Philip cut down from his shoulder at Thane, who sidestepped the cut and brought his curved blade down sharply on Philip's. Philip tried to spin his way out of the deadlock, but Thane thrust his sword over and around Philip's neck halfway through the spin. Both blades pressed against Philip's neck.

Arliss found the flat stone at the pinnacle of the platform and readied her arrow. She glared at Thane. "Release him, or I destroy this fortress."

Thane laughed. "You cannot destroy this fortress, Arliss. It is impregnable, and you know it."

"No human fortress is impregnable. All strongholds can be demolished."

Below them, Erik and Brallaghan bore away Kenton's wounded form, and Lord Adam carefully hoisted away Nathanael's slender body. Reinholdian guards cleared a path for them even as Erik called for the retreat.

Tilting his head towards the scene beneath them, Thane scoffed at Arliss. "Your forces are retreating. Your uncle is dead. Your father is wounded. And here, I hold the life of your friend in my very hands."

She lifted her drawn bow. "And I hold your life—the life of your fortress—in mine." Rain began to fall lightly again. "Please, Thane. Neither of us have to do this. You don't have to keep killing and destroying. You are one of us—a man of Reinhold, my cousin. You said so yourself!"

"I was never a man of Reinhold. I could never be such. No matter what, you would all drive me away as you did twelve years ago."

"You drove yourself away with your greed and pride."

"What choice did I have? To be a slave to Kenton or a slave to myself?"

"There are other choices a man can make. Submission is not always bondage. You could have been a noble citizen of this realm."

"I had no other choice. Now you—you have a choice to make." He pressed his sword, and thus Philip's own sword, against Philip's neck. "Will you have my life, or his?"

Her heart pounded, her chest heaving with tension. Philip caught her eye for a moment, a determined glint still sparkling in his eyes' many colors. With a glance, he signaled below them, down to the river, and Arliss understood his thoughts.

"I would choose both your lives, if only because I do not desire the blood of my own kin to be on my hands. But I cannot allow this evil to keep eating away at the heart of my land. Thus, I do not ask forgiveness for what I must do, nor do I pity the rage it will cause you. But I do pity you, Thane."

"Spare me that, Arliss," he hissed. "I don't need your pity. You will die once I'm done with the son of Carraig."

She raised her bow and found a good aim, near the center of the front wall, where an immense pile of white flowers clustered even higher than the rest of the piles which spread the length of the fortified dam. "All men die. But we shall not die this day."

Her fingers relaxed, and she released the second fiery arrow of that long day. Philip slipped down out of Thane's grasp. Thane's sword sliced back on thin air where Philip's neck had been.

A sound like a thousand crackling fires erupted behind them, and Thane turned to look just as the wall exploded. The flame from the arrow trailed through the flowers, creating dozens of brilliant white flares. Countless stones collapsed to the ground in a heap of flaming rubble. Then, rushing slowly at first as if it had to regain its strength after so long an imprisonment, the river came running and leaping over the wall's destruction. Water drenched the warriors in the bailey as they pursued the Reinholdian forces.

Thane's head snapped back towards Arliss and Philip, his eyes livid with rage. They gave him no more chance to soliloquize or to attack them. They joined together and thrust him from the top of the dais.

With a great splash, Thane landed in the middle of the overflowing river which cut through the base of the mound. He stabbed his sword into the riverbed to slow the flow of water which carried him on towards the dark opening. The water was too strong for him to hold on.

"You have destroyed my fortress," he shouted, "but you have not destroyed me! Know that I will have revenge upon the land of Reinhold! I shall fulfill my oath, and I shall break your line!"

And he was gone.

Chapter Thirty-Six: The End of the Beginning

Some stories end rather suddenly, leaving hardly a trace of having ever happened at all. Others lumber on, casting loose threads and unanswered questions even as they resolve others. Arliss soon saw that her story fell into the second group: her tale still had many threads to tie up and many questions to be answered.

Thane had fled. Where, no one knew. The important thing was that he had been purged from the realm. Arliss and Philip entered the hole Thane had disappeared through, but they found no sign of him. Instead, they found something remarkably different from what they expected: a lush oasis, nestled within the corners of four mountains. The river which ran beneath the stone mound exited the other side as a majestic waterfall which tumbled down into a vast pool surrounded with greenery. And thus Arliss discovered the true heart of the land of Reinhold.

A few stragglers from Thane's army had escaped the destruction of the fortress and still roamed abroad in the darker parts of the forest. Arliss knew she and her company could do cleanup later.

First they had to deal with their own problems, their own sorrows. Nathanael was borne back to the city with a great procession of mourning. Seeing the bier, Elowyn cast herself down beside her fallen brother and wept until the deep wells of her eyes had dried up. Yet afterwards many said she became even more kind and wise than before.

Arliss kept her promise and saw to it that Philip and Erik obtained official knighthood. Brallaghan, too, was knighted, though not before Philip—much to the chagrin of Lord Brédan.

But he had little reason for shame, because Arliss insisted that the new Sir Brallaghan be made head of the city guard in Nathanael's stead.

As for Ilayda, she managed to escape the battle with little more than the usual crick in her neck. And, no matter what happened, she continued to insist on calling Arliss "silly princess!"

Just three days after Thane's defeat, Arliss sat in an immense chair in the castle library, loose ends and questions filling her mind.

Chief in her mind stood the mysterious visitor in the burgundy cloak, who had vanished without even a hint of his paths or intentions. From where had he come? He had disappeared in the direction of the sea. Did he dwell on the isle? And what connection did he have with Thane?

Her father's thick Bible lay wide open on the arm of her chair. On her lap, the ancient leatherbound book, which seemed to hold so many secrets, lay open across her legs. She had reread the entire volume from the beginning, and now had only one page left. She was about to turn the final page of the book when the door opened and the sound of heavy boots clamped into the library.

She looked up at her father, a true smile spreading across her face—feeling truer than it had felt in a long time.

Kenton picked up his Bible, gently closing it as he stroked the creased spine. "It seems I was wrong."

"About what?" Arliss ventured.

"About stories. You know, I told you stories couldn't save a man's life. Well, you and your fiery arrow leapt from the pages of legend and saved our city." He gazed at the faded volume of Scriptures. "And I realize that this book—this life-saving book—is one great story, the story of blindness becoming sight and death becoming life. What makes it so great is that, beyond any other story, it is true."

"It is *truth*." Arliss stood. "Father, I—I am sorry. I ought not have run away. I ought not have defied your orders."

Kenton reached for her face, stroking her golden hair behind her ear. "I ought not have pushed you away. I was too blind to see that, despite your rashness, you were in the right. Peasant and princess are not so different at heart."

At his words, her heart quavered with a hopeful thrill. "You mean…"

"Philip is a fine fellow. Or *Sir* Philip, as I suppose I ought to say."

She laughed. "I think he'd rather leave the title off. But you are right: we are not so very different, after all."

Nodding, Kenton took her hand and led her to the window of the library. She set the old book on the reading stand beside the window and looked out. The last page of the book slid and turned itself.

Far below, in the queen's garden, a colorful mix of people and plants streamed throughout the lush grove. Her mother sat upon a bench not far from where Nathanael had been buried. Philip sidestepped a sprawling burst of newly-planted Lasairbláth, his cousins Erik and Keelin following behind him.

Whether Philip saw her out of the corner of his eye, or whether some impulse in his heart urged him to look up, she did not know, but he gazed up at the high library window at that moment. Even up on the second story, she could see his eyes, still as curiously filled with colors as the first day she had seen him. A smile spread across his lips as he looked up at her, and she allowed the smile on her face to spread into a laugh.

Despite the last words of the book beside her, which proclaimed "The End" to all its readers, she knew it was not the end.

It was only the end of the beginning.

Bo Burnette

Acknowledgements

It would be impossible to thank all the people who have inspired the nearly five-year journey that became this book. This story and its characters have been so much a part of me that—if our paths have crossed—you can be sure you have inspired me. I hope that, perhaps, I have inspired you as well.

But for those specific people, the really legendary ones…

My mom and dad—biggest cheerleaders and supporters. Thanks for pestering me to write even when I sometimes didn't feel like it. And thanks for putting up with me when I wrote even when I had other things to do.

My older sisters, Kendall and Courtney—for criticizing me when I needed it, and for understanding me when no one else did.

My youngest sister, Susanna—for waiting patiently. This story is for people like you.

And my other sister, Kelley—you read this book before anyone else. You understand it better than anyone. Even eating cheese.

Abigail—you know who you are.

Connor—the very first person I bounced these ideas off of. They've come a long way, but I owe the foundations to you.

Linda Yezak, my incomparable editor—you're a gem. I couldn't have asked for someone more honest or hilarious to make this story worth reading.

Chrissy and all the folks at Damonza—for the splendid cover.

Kelsey—creator of the stunning map of Reinhold. You're more talented than you know. And thank you to Dylan, who knows why.

And finally my Creator, my Savior, who inspires me to create tales that remind us that life itself is a legend.

Bo Burnette / 250

If you enjoyed the story, would you consider writing a review on Amazon or Goodreads? Thanks!

Bo Burnette lives and breathes stories, finds adventures everywhere, and survives mainly on coffee and tea. He has several books with his name on their covers, most notably World War II biography *Denver and the Doolittle Raid*, middle-grade mystery *The Lighthouse Thief*, and *The Reinhold Chronicles* trilogy.

Bo Burnette / 252

Continue the adventure with Arliss and company!

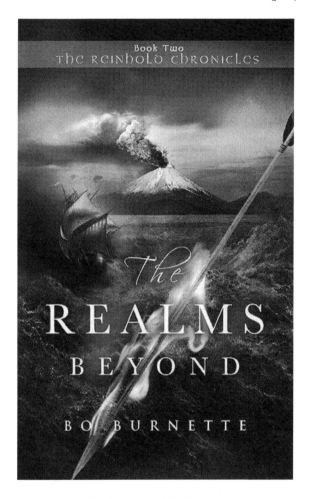

The middle chapter of *The Reinhold Chronicles* trilogy

The clan of Reinhold fled from the Isle of Light thirteen years ago. Now—armed with her bow and determined to reclaim lost treasures—Princess Arliss wants to go back.

"I could hear the music again, and somehow it seemed louder than before."

Every day, Miss Erikson hears mysterious music coming from behind a locked door at the Lang School of Fine Arts. When the strict Mrs. Borg demands she leave the door alone, Miss Erikson's curiosity propels her to uncover the secrets of the ever-closed door. As she pursues the source of the inexplicable music, she must finally face the grief of the past she has long tried to ignore. (A 3,000-word short story by Bo Burnette)

A historic lighthouse. A suspect thief. An intolerable cousin.

The Fourth of July is always a big holiday on Saint Simons Island. But this year, while coping with a visit from his contrary cousin, 14-year-old Ethan discovers strange happenings at the historic lighthouse. Soon he is caught up in an unexpected adventure and a quest to save his beloved lighthouse.

A story of bravery, cunning, and sacrifice during World War II.

The 1942 Doolittle Raid on Japan—America's first strike after the Pearl Harbor attack—is now accessible to all ages in this lavishly photo-illustrated book.

Made in the USA
Columbia, SC
19 February 2020